A NEST EGG TO DIE FOR

BRIAN DAFFERN

BHD
Publishing

To Penny

Thank you for being the only cryptid to support me with warm hugs and unconditional love.

CHAPTER 1

The emergency phone's shrill ring pierced through my dreams at 6:17 AM. I fumbled in the dark, knocking over both my water glass and lamp, before my fingers found the vibrating menace.

"Doctor Sterling," I said, still half-asleep.

"Doc, we've got a situation." The voice belonged to Todd, one of our night handlers at Heritage Crest Cryptid Reservation. "Baby dragon with hiccups."

I sat up straighter, sleep falling away. "Hiccups? That doesn't sound too—"

"Flaming hiccups," Todd said. "She's setting things on fire with each one. We've got her contained in the emergency intake area behind your clinic, but..." There was a *whoosh* sound, followed by muffled cursing. "Yeah, we need you. Now."

"On my way." I was already pulling on my clothes, hopping on one foot as I wrestled with my sock. "Keep her away from anything flammable. And Todd? Try humming. Sometimes that calms them down."

I heard him start to hum what sounded suspiciously like "Smoke on the Water" before I hung up. Appropriate, if a bit on the nose.

Thirteen minutes later, I pulled into Heritage Crest's Veterinarian Clinic entrance, the technology generated fog that surrounded our town parting just enough to let me see the road. The "Veil," as locals called it, was thick this morning, wrapping around the Victorian-style clinic building like a cozy blanket. To outsiders driving nearby, the fog made our little town nearly invisible – which was exactly the point. After all, you couldn't have people accidentally stumbling upon a town full of cryptids and supernatural creatures.

I heard the hiccups before I even got out of my car – each one followed by a distinctive *FWOOSH* and what sounded like increasingly creative swearing from our night staff. I grabbed my medical bag from the passenger seat, double-checking that I had my fireproof gloves. Mom had drilled that particular lesson into my head after my first dragon case. The scar on my left forearm was a permanent reminder of the memory.

The emergency intake area was as chaotic as I'd expected. Three handlers in flame-resistant gear were trying to maintain a safe perimeter around a baby storm dragon close to the size of a large dog. Her scales were a beautiful swirling pattern of steel gray and electric blue, puffed out in distress. Her mother, ten times larger, was curled protectively around her, looking both concerned and embarrassed – an impressive feat for a dragon.

"HIC!"

A small fireball erupted from the baby's mouth, sailing past my head and singeing the shoulder of my favorite clinic coat. I patted out the smoldering fabric with a sigh. That was the third coat this month.

"Good morning to you too," I said, approaching carefully. The mother dragon's eyes tracked my movement, but I could sense no hostility in her posture – just worry and a hint of exasperation that I suspected most parents could relate to.

I reached out with my gift – that peculiar ability that let me communicate with cryptid creatures. It had manifested when I was a kid, much to my mother's delight and my older sister Penny's initial jealousy. It now formed a crucial part of my duties as Heritage Crest's veterinarian.

"Hello," I projected to the mother dragon, keeping my mental voice calm and professional. "I'm Doctor Sterling. Can you tell me what happened?"

The mother's response came as a mix of images and emotions, the way most lizard-based cryptids communicated. I saw the baby, whose name translated roughly to Jasper, sneaking out to the sanctuary's north pond last night. Glowing dots flickered around the water—fireflies. Despite her mother's warnings, Jasper had decided they looked tasty.

"Ah," I said, dodging another hiccup-induced fireball. "Fireflies. That explains it. Their bioluminescence can react with dragon fire glands and cause... well, this."

"Can you fix it?" Todd asked, still humming between sentences. "Your containment room's looking like a toasted marshmallow."

I kneeled to get a better look at Jasper, staying just outside flame range. "The good news is this is fairly common. The bad news is —" FWOOSH " — we're going to need to wait while the fireflies work their way through her system. But we can help with the symptoms."

I opened my medical bag and started pulling out supplies. "First, a cooling mist to help reduce the fire gland inflammation." I mixed a solution of crystallized moon water and mint leaves – the rare variety, not the regular garden type. Regular mint just makes dragons sneeze, and sneezing dragons are even worse than hiccupping ones.

"Mrs. Dragon," I addressed the mother, "I'm going to need your help keeping your child still while I administer this. It won't hurt, but it might feel a little strange."

The dragon nodded, adjusting her position to better hold her squirming offspring. As I approached with the misting bottle, Jasper let out another hiccup, this one accompanied by both flames and a small puff of smoke that formed itself into a grumpy face before dissipating.

"I know, I know," I said soothingly, both out loud and mentally. "Nobody enjoys having the hiccups. But this will help." I managed to get three quick sprays of the cooling mist down the throat and around her chest before she could hiccup again.

The effect was almost immediate, and the next hiccup produced only a small spark instead of a full fireball. Palpable relief washed over the mother.

"There we go," I said, continuing to mist at regular intervals. "The mint helps counteract the fireflies, while the moon water cools the fire glands. She should be back to normal in an hour or so, though I'd recommend keeping her away from the pond for a while."

The mother dragon sent me an image of Jasper grounded in their cave for a week, accompanied by a feeling that translated to *"Oh, trust me, she's not going ANYWHERE for a long time."*

I couldn't help but smile. Some parenting experiences were universal, regardless of species.

"Now," I said, addressing the handlers while keeping an eye on Jasper, "dragon hiccups can be tricky. They're not like regular hiccups where you can just hold your breath or drink water upside down – though please don't try that with a dragon anyway. The key is to—" I ducked another reduced spark "—treat both the condition and symptoms simultaneously."

Todd nodded, still humming his fire-themed playlist. I heard him switch to 'Great Balls of Fire' and had to admire his commitment to the theme.

"The cooling mist addresses the physical inflammation," I said, demonstrating the proper spraying technique. "But you also need to account for the fire resonance. That's what the mint does. It helps ground and neutralize excess reverberating energy."

I spent the next few minutes explaining the finer points of treating dragon hiccups while playing a game of dodge-the-spark with Jasper's smaller flame bursts. By the time my receptionist, Alice, arrived, the baby dragon was down to just producing small smoke rings with each hiccup.

"Doctor Sterling," Alice said from the doorway, keeping a safe distance from the lingering smoke, "Jerry McKinnon is here with Ziggy for their checkup. I put them in the reflective examination room."

"Already?" I checked my watch, surprised to find it was almost 8 AM. "Right, thank you. I'll be there as soon as—"

"Hic." A tiny smoke heart floated up from Jasper.

"Well, looks like someone's feeling better," I said, giving the baby dragon a gentle pat. To the mother, I added, "Keep her quiet today, plenty of cool water, and bring her back if the hiccups return or if she develops any unusual smoke shapes. Though the hearts are pretty cute."

The mother dragon's gratitude washed over me in a warm wave. I gathered my slightly singed supplies and headed inside, leaving Todd to handle the discharge paperwork with Alice. As I walked to the examination room, I could hear him starting on 'Ring of Fire.' At least someone was enjoying themselves.

The reflective examination room was what it sounded like, a room lined with specially treated mirrors designed to prevent accidental petrification during basilisk examinations. Among the clinic's many specialized rooms, each catered to unique cryptid needs. For instance, we had to cleanse the unicorn suite of excess magical energy regularly to prevent spontaneous rainbow generation, while we used the fireproof phoenix examination room, a very fancy one, just for flaming cryptids.

I found Jerry McKinnon sitting on one of our examination chairs, Ziggy the basilisk wrapped around his arm. Jerry was a tall, thin man in his fifties who ran the local Starlight Cinema. He'd adopted Ziggy about a year ago, after the basilisk had been rescued from an illegal exotic pet ring.

"Morning, Doc!" Jerry's cheerful voice echoed in the mirrored room. "How's tricks?"

"Oh, you know, just getting fired up for the day," I said, gesturing at my singed coat. "Baby dragon with hiccups."

"Ouch." Jerry winced. "Is that what all the singing was about? I could hear it from the waiting room."

"Todd's developed a very themed approach to dragon care." I pulled on a fresh pair of examination gloves. "How's our favorite basilisk doing?"

Ziggy lifted his head at the mention of himself, his feathered crest rising in pride. Unlike his larger cousins, Ziggy was a rare miniature basilisk, the size of a corn snake. His scales were an unusual shade of cobalt blue that seemed to shimmer in the room's carefully adjusted lighting. It was beautiful.

"He's been great," Jerry said, beaming as a proud parent. "Those spicy mice you recommended for his diet have worked wonders. He typically eats them in one bite. Haven't had a single issue with his venom glands acting up."

I nodded while beginning my examination. "That's excellent. The capsaicin helps regulate venom production in smaller basilisk species. Plus, it gives them a bit of a kick, which they enjoy. Don't you, Ziggy?"

The basilisk preened, sending me a mental image of himself triumphantly catching and eating his favorite snack. Then, unexpectedly, his thoughts turned to something else – concern about Jerry, images of loud noises late at night near the theater. It was times like these that I wished the reptile-based species communicated as easily as the fairies or other mammal species. Certainly, would help in these scenarios. They could speak to me in words if they wanted, but preferred emotions. They only used words mentally with those they were very close with.

"Hold still a moment," I said to Ziggy and Jerry as I checked the basilisk's venom glands. They were indeed in perfect condition, but I was more interested in what Ziggy was trying to tell me. "Jerry, has anything unusual been happening at the theater lately?"

"Funny you should ask," Jerry said, his normally cheerful expression clouding. "I've been hearing some strange noises, especially around the back alley near Doctor Green's research facility. Probably just the usual weird science stuff, but..." He trailed off as Ziggy wrapped himself more tightly around his arm, refusing to let go for the next part of the examination.

"Hey now," I said, draping my hand down Ziggy's back. "What's got you so worried?"

Ziggy's response was a jumble of protective feelings toward Jerry and unclear images of shadows moving in the darkness. It was not unusual for a basilisk to be protective of their bonded human, but this felt different – more urgent somehow.

"It's probably nothing," Jerry said, though his tone suggested otherwise. "Just some late-night activity over at the research facility. Doctor Green's been doing some kind of late-night study or something. He blares phoenix mating calls late at night. You can hear it even when a movie is playing. Lots of coming and going at odd hours. I yelled at him the other day and he got real upset and denied even being in his lab that night. Nothing to worry about, just an argument."

Phoenixes were notoriously particular about their breeding habits, and unauthorized observation could cause serious problems. They mostly did it during the darkest part of the night for the quiet and lack of prying eyes. Green needn't have been at his lab at night. But before I could ask more questions, the clinic's warning chimes sounded. The musical tone indicated new arrivals at the main entrance. I'd been expecting them. Two new sasquatches.

"Perfect timing," I said, finishing up Ziggy's examination. "Everything looks great. Keep up with the spicy mice diet, and I want to see you both back in three months, unless any issues come up before then."

"Good to hear."

"Sorry to cut this short." I made quick notes in Ziggy's file. "But sasquatch intake requires immediate attention, or they leave poop everywhere in protest. Alice will help you."

Alice appeared, as if summoned. "Ready to escort Mr. McKinnon and Ziggy," she said professionally, though I caught her subtle eye roll at the musical chimes. She'd be the one cleaning up any protest crap, after all.

Jerry stood, Ziggy still around his arm. "Thanks, Doc. Oh, about what I was saying with Doctor Green's research—"

"I won't say a word," I said, already heading for the door. "And Ziggy?" I said to the basilisk, "Keep watching out for him, but let me know if you see anything specific, okay?"

Ziggy's agreement came with a feeling of fierce loyalty that warmed my heart. As Jerry and Ziggy left through their special corridor (designed with mirrors angled to prevent any chance of accidental eye contact with the basilisk), I caught Alice's knowing look.

"Sparkles is on the afternoon schedule." She reminded me with just a hint of mischief in her voice. "Her owner called this morning, insisting that her horn is showing blemishes."

I groaned. Sparkles was essentially a very large, very dramatic unicorn with some Gemsbok ancestry. She was also a hypochondriac who developed a new "life-threatening" condition at least once a week.

"Let me guess – the horn looks fine?"

"Got it in one." Alice grinned. "But first, those bigfeet or bigfoots, whatever the plural is, are about to start their protest any second. I'm sure of it."

"Right, right, I'm going. And they prefer Sasquatch. The other name makes them feel body shamed." I straightened my singed coat and headed for the main entrance. Just another morning at Heritage Crest's only cryptid veterinary clinic. Between flaming hiccups, protective basilisks, and hypochondriac unicorns, who had time to worry about strange noises near the theater?

I really should have worried though. In mornings like this, you can never predict how a routine checkup or a simple comment might unexpectedly thrust you into a murder investigation.

CHAPTER 2

The lunch rush at Rosie's Diner was in full swing as I slid into our usual corner booth, my veterinary coat still slightly smelling of smoke from my morning rounds. The familiar scent of coffee and fresh-baked pie mingled with the distinct aroma of Koko Loco roses from the window planter boxes. My sister Penny and our mother Clara were already deep in a heated discussion. I had successfully processed the sasquatch with no poop incident, and I was ready to eat.

"All I'm saying is that she's perfect for him," Penny said, jabbing her fork in my direction as I sat down. "She runs the pet supply store, already knows about the supernatural creatures, and she's single!"

"I see you've started without me," I said dryly, flagging down Rosie for my usual coffee. "And by 'started,' I mean trying to manage my love life again."

Mom shared a knowing look with a tiny fairy perched on her teacup, both shaking their heads in synchronized disapproval. The fairy, no bigger than my thumb, had made herself quite comfortable among the sugar packets, occasionally dipping her diminutive wings into Mom's chamomile tea.

"Dear," Mom said, offering her teaspoon to the fairy as a diving board. "Your sister means well. Though her methods are about as subtle as a mapinguary in a China shop."

"Hey!" Penny protested. Her eyes sparkled with mischief. "I'll have you know my matchmaking success rate is a solid sixty percent."

"Only if you count that skunk ape falling in love with his reflection in the mirrored glass of the grocery store," I said. Rosie as she placed a

9

steaming mug of coffee in front of me. "Which, as I understand from Doctor Foster, took three weeks of therapy to sort out."

The little cryptid giggled in unison with mom, a sound like tiny wind chimes, before diving gracefully back into her tea. A small splash sent droplets arcing through the air, each one catching the light like miniature rainbows.

"Speaking of lovesick creatures." Penny leaned forward, her sheriff's badge catching the sunlight. "How's that griffin doing? The one that kept writing bad poetry?"

I groaned, running a hand through my hair. "Don't remind me. Do you know how hard it is to explain to a griffin that rhyming 'wings' with 'wings' fourteen times isn't actually poetry? Just bad Dr. Seuss imitations."

"At least he's trying." Mom chuckled, her green eyes twinkling. "Remember when you first discovered your gift? You spent three whole days trying to convince the garden snails to form a synchronized swimming team."

"I was eight!" I protested, feeling my cheeks heat. "And they were very enthusiastic about it. Their timing was just... off."

Penny snorted. "Oh please, tell me more about little Mark's snail adventures. I don't remember this story. It sounds like it could be prime blackmail material."

Mom's expression softened as she stirred her tea, the fairy now doing lazy backstrokes through the ripples. "If you insist. It was quite something, watching him discover his gift. I'll never forget that spring morning in the garden."

There was no stopping mom when she had that look. She launched into the narrative; I succumbed to a wave of vivid memories, as fresh as yesterday. I'd been helping her in the herb garden or at least trying to. Most of my "helping" consisted of making mud pies and asking endless questions about the various plants she used in her veterinary practice. A sense of enchantment hung in the air, surrounding each unique and extraordinary item. They were things I would never learn in regular school.

"Mom, why does this one have so many lines and dots?" I asked, pointing to a silvery-leafed plant.

"That's sage, dear. It's essential for treating unicorn colds," she explained. "Their sneezes tend to create rather spectacular rainbow explosions without it."

I'd been about to ask another question when I heard it - a tiny voice, somewhere between a whisper and a song. Initially, I believed I hallucinated. However, additional voices emerged, forming a chorus of tiny discussions.

"Excuse me, but could someone help me? My wing is rather crumpled," came a delicate voice from behind a foxglove.

I peered around the purple flowers to find a small fairy, sitting dejectedly on a leaf. The heavy morning dew had crumpled her iridescent wings.

"Oh!" I said. "Don't worry, I can help. Mom uses her hair dryer to fix crumpled papers all the time! It can't be that different."

The fairy had looked up at me in surprise. *"You can understand me?"*

"Of course I can... wait, should I not be able to?"

That's when I noticed my mother watching me with an expression of wonder and pride. "Mark," she said, "you have a unique gift."

Back in the present, Penny was shaking her head. "Meanwhile, I spent the next three months talking to every animal I could find, convinced my gift was just 'running late.' And I got nothing."

"The neighbor's cat certainly appreciated your daily sessions," Mom said with an obvious tease.

"That cat was working through some serious issues!" Penny defended. "And gift or no gift, Mr. Whiskers and I made genuine progress."

"Is that why he still runs away whenever you come over?" I asked innocently.

Penny threw a sugar packet at my head. "At least I didn't start a snail synchronized swimming team."

"No, you just tried to convince a squirrel to become an accountant. Do you know he kept trying to tell you he wanted to be a fiction writer and counting was boring?"

"He was very good with nuts! It seemed like a natural career progression!"

Our laughter was interrupted by Rosie arriving with our usual orders - a club sandwich for Penny, garden salad for Mom, and my standard grilled cheese with a side of Rosie's famous curly fries. The fairy in Mom's tea had graduated to doing elaborate diving routines off the spoon, drawing appreciative looks from the other diners.

"Oh, before I forget," Mom said, reaching into her bag, "I finished the last of the retirement paperwork this morning. It's official now - the clinic is all yours, Mark."

The weight of those words settled over me like a heavy weighted blanket. I'd been working alongside Mom for years, learning everything I could about supernatural and cryptid veterinary medicine, but somehow having it official made it feel more real.

"You're ready," Mom said, reading my expression. "More than ready."

"It's just a lot."

"Don't worry, I'm down to the final interviews with two candidates for another doctor. Once I pick, I will have them come out and they can help you in the clinic. Are you sure you don't want to talk to them first?"

"I trust you. That's not what I meant, though."

"I know." She smiled.

"But what about the sanctuary's rare creatures?" I poked at my grilled cheese. "The phoenix breeding program, the unicorn rehabilitation center... those are your projects. You've spent decades building relationships with these beings."

"And now they trust you just as much, if not more," she said. "Just last week, Aurora let you check her tail feathers without setting your hair on fire. Do you know how long it took me to earn that level of trust from a phoenix?"

"Three years and sixteen singed eyebrows," Penny supplied. "I kept count."

Before I could respond, the diner's bell chimed, and a familiar voice called out, "Uncle Mark! Uncle Mark!"

Harry, Penny's husband, had arrived with Jake and Emma in tow. At eight and six respectively, my niece and nephew were bundles of endless energy and curiosity, especially when it came to my work.

"Uncle Mark!" Emma bounced over to our booth, her braids flying. "Did the baby dragon stop having hiccups? Did you fix it? Can I see it? Please, please, please?"

"Slow down, sweetie." Harry laughed, sliding into the booth next to Penny. "Let your uncle at least finish his lunch before the interrogation."

"But Daddy," Emma protested, pulling out a folded piece of paper from her pocket. "I drew what I think she looked like! See? I think I got her scales just right!"

I examined the crayon masterpiece, which showed a green chicken headed snake with legs wearing what might have been a top hat. "This is amazing, Emma! Though I don't remember Jasper wearing such fancy headwear."

"That's her theater hat," Emma explained, seriously. "Every dragon needs a theater hat."

"Can't argue with that logic," I conceded, as Jake squeezed in next to me.

"Mom said you got your coat singed again," Jake said, eyeing the darkened fabric with admiration. "Was it the hiccupping dragon? Did it breathe fire? How big was the explosion?"

"No explosions today, thankfully," I assured him, though I noticed both kids looked disappointed by this news. "Just a minor incident, but all is well."

Penny's phone buzzed, and she frowned at the screen. "Speaking of check-ups, got another complaint about screeching noises near Dr.

Green's research facility. He plays those research videos so loud. Probably just the phoenix research he is doing or the usual weird science stuff, but..."

"Jerry mentioned something about that."

I caught the subtle shift in Penny's tone, the way her eyes flickered to Mom. After years of working in Heritage Crest, we'd all developed a sense of knowing when something wasn't quite right.

Mom met my gaze, and I recognized the look in her eyes - the same one she'd get when she knew a sickness was more complicated than it appeared. "Trust your instincts," she said. "That's one gift all Sterling's share, whether or not we can talk to creatures."

Jake broke the moment by accidentally knocking over his chocolate milkshake he brought in from outside. The small colony of fairies that had been resting under the table relocated to the window planters, their tiny voices raising in protest as drops of milkshake rained down.

"Sorry!" Jake called out to the retreating fairies, who were now huddled among the petunias, shooting him disapproving glances. Rosie rushed over with a few towels and helped Penny clean it up.

"Here," Mom said, ignoring the clean-up and reaching into her bag, again. "Speaking of instincts, I want you to have this."

She pulled out a worn leather notebook, its pages yellowed with age and obviously well used. I recognized it immediately - her clinic notebook, filled with decades of observations, treatments, and insights about cryptid creature care.

"Mom, I can't take this," I said. "This is your life's work."

"Exactly," she said, pressing it into my hands. "And now it's yours to build upon. Besides, I made a copy of the important pages."

I held the notebook and felt the weight of its pages and the knowledge that seemed to hum within its leather binding. The magnitude of what it represented struck me. Not just the information contained within, but the trust my mother had in me to carry on her work. She would still be around, but somehow this felt final.

"Thank you," I said, tucking the notebook into my coat pocket.

"Just promise me one thing," she said, her expression serious despite the fairy now attempting to surf on her teaspoon.

"What's that?"

"Try not to let any more snails form synchronized swimming teams. The garden has never quite recovered from their training sessions."

Our laughter filled the booth, and I felt a deep sense of gratitude for my family - this wonderfully weird, magical, supportive group of people who understood what it meant to be part of Heritage Crest's supernatural and cryptid community. Sure, my sister might never stop trying to set me up with every eligible person in town, and my mother might never stop telling embarrassing stories about my childhood mishaps, but I wouldn't have it any other way. Besides, those snails had shown real potential. Their timing was... ahead of its time.

The comfortable family moment was interrupted by a commotion at the diner's entrance. Sparkles, my hypochondriac unicorn patient, had somehow squeezed her pearlescent bulk through the door and was now standing in the middle of Rosie's, her horn casting rainbow reflections across the walls.

"Doctor Sterling!" she whinnied dramatically, sounding both pitiful and accusatory simultaneously. It was lucky the rest of the patrons, except mom, couldn't understand her. *"My horn is definitely dulling! Look! It's practically transparent!"*

I sighed, setting down my half-eaten grilled cheese. "Sparkles, we talked about this yesterday. And the day before. And twice last week. Your horn is fine."

"What is she saying?" Penny asked. She was holding back her children from rushing to hug the cryptid. "Is there a problem?"

I shook my head to the negative.

"But it's lost at least two degrees of sparkle!" Sparkles tossed her flowing mane, nearly knocking over a stack of menus. *"I measured it with my personal glitter-meter!"*

"You don't have a glitter-meter," I pointed out.

"Well, I should! Then you'd believe me!"

Penny was trying hard not to laugh at my expression, while Mom just shook her head fondly. She'd dealt with Sparkles' imaginary ailments for years before passing the torch to me. She shared the same gift as me, which is another reason Penny tried so hard to talk to cryptids.

"Uncle Mark," Emma said. "Why is the unicorn wearing a tin foil hat?"

I hadn't seen it at first, but sure enough, Sparkles had fashioned what appeared to be an elaborate helmet out of aluminum foil, complete with holes for her ears and a special compartment for her horn.

"It's a horn-healing helmet!" Sparkles announced proudly. *"I read about it on UniBook."*

"Sparkles," I said as patiently as I could, "we've talked about getting medical advice from social media."

"But it has five stars! And three rainbow emojis!"

The fairy on Mom's tea was now doubled over laughing, creating tiny ripples that threatened to splash over the cup's rim. Even the usually stoic Rosie was fighting back a smile as she navigated around Sparkles with a pot of coffee. She didn't understand the conversation, but a giggle escaped her lips at the ridiculousness of it all. Some people found it chaotic, but the majority stayed in this community for the work and cryptid creatures that roamed freely across the roughly one hundred square mile preserve.

"Look," I said, standing up. "How about we continue this during our appointment later today. We can conduct a proper check-up at the clinic. With actual medical equipment, not kitchen supplies."

Sparkles considered this, her shiny hat catching the light. *"Will you use the sparkle-o-scope?"*

"What now?"

"The sparkle-o-scope! It's the latest in horn diagnostic technology. I saw it on-"

"Let me guess, UniBook?"

She nodded enthusiastically, causing several pieces of tin foil to flutter to the floor.

"Right," I said, making a mental note to have a serious talk with whoever was running these unicorn medical advice groups. "We will talk. But right now, you're blocking the pie display, and I think Mr. Johnson really wants his slice of cherry."

Indeed, the elderly successful auk scientist was eyeing both the pies and Sparkles with increasing impatience. Being stuck between a hungry old man and his dessert was never a good place to be.

"Oh, alright." Sparkles sighed dramatically. *"But if my horn falls off before this afternoon, I'm leaving a strongly worded review on RateMyVet."*

As Harry helped me guide the bedazzled hypochondriac back outside, I could hear Jake asking Penny, "Mom, can I get a tin foil hat, too?"

"Only if you promise not to get medical advice from UniBook," Penny said dryly.

After making me swear to check her horn's 'sparkle quotient,' Sparkles was on her way. I returned to find Mom looking thoughtful.

"You know," she said, "Sparkles might be onto something with that tin foil hat. Not medically, of course, but it gave me an idea about the griffin's poetry problem."

"Mom, no," I said with a groan, already seeing where this was going.

"Just hear me out! If we could redirect his energy into interpretive dance instead..."

"The last time we tried that, he ended up choreographing a flash mob in the town square," Penny said, reminding her. "It took three weeks for the anal sac secretion marks to fade from the pavement."

"But you have to admit, his dance skills were impeccable," Mom defended.

"Until he tried to add the Riverdance finale," I said. "The mayor still flinches whenever someone mentions performance art."

Emma tugged on my sleeve. "Uncle Mark, can I come see Sparkles later? I want to draw her with her hat!"

"Please don't encourage her," I said. "The last thing we need is a trend of unicorns wearing kitchen accessories."

"Too late." Harry smiled and showed us his phone. "It's already trending on UniBook. #TinFoilHornChallenge is going viral."

I dropped my head onto the table with a *thunk*. "I don't suppose anyone wants to trade jobs? Penny? Want to be a vet for a week? I'll handle law enforcement."

"Not a chance." She grinned. "Besides, you'd hate it. There's a strict 'no snail synchronized swimming' policy in the sheriff's department."

"That was twenty years ago!"

"And yet, somehow, still relevant," Mom said, sharing another knowing look with the fairy in her tea.

The fairy, who had been doing the backstroke, suddenly sat up straight, her tiny wings spraying droplets across the table. She zipped over to the window, pressing her diminutive face against the glass.

"What's wrong?" I asked, recognizing the signs of distress. They were excellent early warning systems for cryptid disturbances.

"Something feels... off," the fairy said. *"Near the edge of town, by the research facility. The air tastes wrong."*

I caught Penny's eye, seeing my concern reflected there. The earlier call about strange noises felt more significant. Her phone buzzed again. "It looks like there's a disturbance at the phoenix habitat. The recent mother is agitated."

"Aurora? Do you need me to come with?"

"Nah, there is no indication it's medical," Penny said.

Mom reached into her bag and pulled out a small velvet pouch. "Here," she said, handing it to Penny. "Phoenix feather powder for calming. For emergencies only. Though knowing you, you'll need it sooner rather than later."

"Mom, this is your emergency stash," she protested.

"I'm retired, remember? Besides," she said. "I've got three more pouches at home. Did you think I'd give you my last one?"

As if on cue, Penny's phone buzzed again. She frowned, again. "Another call about the phoenix habitat. Looks like I need to get out there."

I looked down at my half-eaten lunch, then at the concerned fairy by the window, and finally, at Mom's expression. Sometimes being part of a family of supernatural cryptid professionals meant trading warm grilled cheese for cryptid care.

"Right," I said, standing up. "I should get back to the practice just in case. Call me if you need me."

Penny and I stepped out into the sunshine and gave each other a hug before she rushed off. I patted the notebook in my pocket. Sometimes the best preparation for the future was a healthy respect for the past and maybe a tin foil hat, just in case Sparkles was onto something after all.

Jake's voice followed us out: "But Grandma, if Uncle Mark started a snail swimming team, can I start a slug soccer league?"

The last thing I heard was Mom's laughter and Emma's excited planning for uniforms. Some things in Heritage Crest never changed.

I turned the corner towards my clinic and saw a pretty woman with auburn hair walking towards me. She was staring down at her phone, mumbling something in a staccato and contorting her face in a frown. Whatever had her upset was taking all her attention. I stepped to the side to let her pass, but at the last second, she turned and ran into me.

I caught her before she fell, but her phone wasn't so lucky. It faced me from the ground, displaying a bank's name and red negative numbers on it.

"Watch where the hell," the woman screamed, but stopped herself. She took a deep breath and a meek voice, continued, "Sorry, I wasn't watching."

"No harm," I said. "Are you okay?"

"Sure. Thank you." The woman picked up her phone and scurried away.

I watched her turn the corner and disappear. That was the most female interaction, family excluded, that I had in over a year. Maybe my sister and mom were right. I needed to meet someone.

CHAPTER 3

I heard Sparkles before I saw her. The clip-clop of hooves against the clinic's tile floor, accompanied by dramatic sighs, only meant one thing - my most hypochondriac patient had arrived.

"Doctor Sterling!" Alice, my receptionist, called out as I finished updating a chart. "Sparkles is here. She's wearing..." Alice paused, squinting through the glass partition. "Is that gauze wrapped around her horn?"

I grabbed my stethoscope and poked my head around the corner. Sure enough, the pristine white unicorn had wrapped her spiral horn in what appeared to be an entire roll of medical gauze, complete with a sad little bow on top. Her owner, Mrs. Pembroke, stood beside her with an apologetic smile.

"Fifth visit this month," I muttered, checking the calendar. "And it's only the fifteenth."

"She believes her horn is dulling," Mrs. Pembroke said, patting Sparkles' neck. "She's been absolutely beside herself all morning."

The unicorn tossed her flowing silver mane and let out another theatrical sigh. *"It's true, Doctor Mark,"* she said. *"Just look at it! Even mommy knows and she can't understand me. The spiral is clearly losing its luster. I'll be the laughingstock of the entire herd!"*

I approached, trying to keep my face neutral. After years of treating supernatural creatures, I'd learned that the bedside manner was just as important with cryptids as with humans. Maybe more so, given how many of them could read emotions.

"Let's have a look at that horn, shall we?" I reached for the gauze. "Though I have to admire your wrapping technique. Very thorough."

"I used the whole thing," the unicorn said proudly. *"Mrs. Pembroke keeps some in the stable for emergencies. Though she refused to let me use the pink sparkly bandages."*

"What is she saying?" Mrs. Pembroke asked.

I sighed. "She is upset you didn't let her use the pretty gauze."

"Because those are for my granddaughter's craft projects. They were streamers anyway," she said. Sometimes I forgot she couldn't hear Sparkles' side of our conversations.

As I carefully unwound the gauze, Alice documented the visit in our records. "Should I file this under 'Actual Emergency' or 'Sparkles Being Sparkles'?" she asked, paying no mind to Sparkles or Mrs. Pembrook being there.

"Let's wait for the official diagnosis," I said diplomatically, although the answer was clear to us both. The last layer of gauze fell away, revealing Sparkles' horn in all its perfectly spiraled, shimmeringly magical glory. Not a scratch, dull spot, or imperfection in sight.

"See?" Sparkles whimpered. *"It's practically OPAQUE!"*

I bent closer, making a show of examining the horn from every angle. "Hmmm. Well, the crystalline structure appears intact. Magical resonance is strong. No signs of oxidation or mineral depletion." I straightened up. I wanted to ask how she managed to wrap it with hooves, but decided that was a rabbit hole I should stay out of. "Sparkles, your horn is in perfect condition."

The unicorn stamped a delicate hoof. *"But what about the rainbow reflections? They seem at least 2.3% less vibrant than usual!"*

"Actually." I pulled out a small rock from my pocket that I gathered on my walk back to the office. It was nothing special, but Sparkles didn't know that. I ran the ordinary rock up and down her horn, stopping occasionally for impact. "Your horn's rainbow index is reading at 98.7%. That's well above average."

"Oh." Sparkles' ears perked up. *"Above average, you say?"*

Mrs. Pembroke recognized the shift in her pet's demeanor. "Is everything alright, Doctor?"

"Perfectly fine. In fact, Sparkles here has one of the most brilliantly luminescent horns I've seen this month." I knew I was laying it on thick, but sometimes that's what it took.

"*Well.*" Sparkles preened, "*I take excellent care of it. Did you know I spend three hours every morning polishing it in the grass dew?*"

"That explains the exceptional shine," I said, feigning having to shield my eyes. "Though you might want to ease up on the emergency visits. Too much handling, even with gauze, could actually dull the finish."

Sparkles' eyes widened in horror. "*It could? Why didn't you say so sooner? Mommy!*" She nudged her owner toward the door. "*We need to leave immediately! My horn requires its afternoon rest!*"

I bit back a smile as Mrs. Pembroke allowed herself to be herded out of the exam room. "Thank you, Doctor Sterling," she called over her shoulder. "Sorry about the false alarm!"

"All part of the job," I assured her, watching Sparkles prance past the waiting area, head held high to show off her superior horn to the other patients.

Alice appeared at my elbow with the next chart. "That's one way to handle it," she said, pushing her long purple hair out of her face. "You will probably regret mentioning that bit about handling causing dullness. Now she'll probably wrap the horn in silk when she's not showing it off."

"Better than having her in here every other day convinced it's turning green or developing spots or who knows what else. Has my sister called at all?"

"No, were you expecting her?"

"Not really. Just thought she might need me. No worries."

A shadow fell across the lobby doorway. A young griffin stood there, right wing slightly dragging, trying hard to look tough despite the pain clear in his posture.

"*Um, excuse me,*" he said, voice cracking slightly. Most cryptids could speak if they chose and I would hear English, though many preferred telepathic communications. "*I had a bit of an accident.*"

I recognized him immediately - Griff, one of our teenage residents who'd recently started hanging around with an older crowd of griffins. "Come on in," I said, gesturing to the larger exam room we used for our bigger patients. "What happened?"

"Nothing!" he said and switched to mental communication as he limped past. *"I just... maybe tried a new flying move. That's all."*

"Would this new move happen to involve the triple backward spiral dive that the adult griffins were practicing yesterday?" I asked, gently extending his wing to check for damage. "The one I specifically remember telling the younger griffins not to attempt without proper training?"

Griff had the grace to look embarrassed, feathers ruffling slightly. *"It looked easier when they did it,"* he admitted. *"And Skye was watching, and I thought..."*

"Ah." I maneuvered the wing joint, noting where he flinched. "Trying to impress someone special?"

The griffin's eagle eyes widened. *"How did you- I mean, no! I just wanted to prove I could do it!"*

"Uh, huh." I pressed lightly along the primary flight muscles. "Well, the good news is nothing's broken. You've got some strained tendons and what's going to be impressive bruising, but with proper rest and rehabilitation, you should make a full recovery."

"How long?" Griff asked. *"The spring flying competition is in three weeks!"*

"That depends entirely on how well you follow my instructions." I grabbed a bottle of healing liniment - a special blend my mother had perfected for wing injuries. "Two weeks minimum of no aerial acrobatics. Light gliding only, staying under twenty feet. Daily stretches and exercises that I'll show you. And I fixed him with a stern look, no more attempting advanced maneuvers without proper supervision."

"But-"

"Unless you'd prefer, I visit your mother and inform her on how this happened?"

Griff deflated, tail drooping. *"No sir. Two weeks of rest. Got it."*

I worked the liniment into the wing muscles, paying attention as the herbal paste took effect. "You know, if you want to impress Skye, there are better ways than risking a flight-ending injury."

"Like what?" he asked, trying not to sound too eager.

"Well, I happen to know she volunteers at the sanctuary intake for new residents. They're always looking for help with the younger avian species." I wrapped his wing with a supportive bandage. "Just something to think about."

A hopeful gleam appeared in Griff's eyes, but before he responded, Alice stuck her head in. "Doctor Sterling? The phoenix chick is here for its regeneration monitoring. And," she lowered her voice, "Doctor Green is with them."

I finished securing Griff's bandage. "Right on schedule. Griff, you're all set. Remember - no stunts, daily exercises, and check back with me in three days."

"Thank you, sir." He headed for the door, then paused. *"Um, about the sanctuary volunteering..."*

"I'll put in a word with the coordinator," I said. "Now go rest that wing!"

Following his exit, I proceeded to the hallway's end, the last room on the left. The door was open, and I saw a softly glowing phoenix chick, its worried parent, and the tall, distinguished figure of Doctor Victor Green. He looked like a college professor with his sweater, but stood at attention like a drill instructor. The chick, Ashtok, was already showing the telltale signs of an impending regeneration. Its golden coat had taken on a slight reddish tinge, and tiny sparks occasionally drifted from its feathers. The phoenix completed three rebirths in their youth. This would be Ashtok's first.

"Ah, Doctor Sterling." Green stepped forward, hand extended. "I hope you don't mind my observing. First regenerations are fascinating from a research perspective."

"As long as it's alright with Aurora." I nodded to the adult phoenix, who was watching Green with unusual intensity. Phoenixes were generally friendly creatures, but something about the researcher seemed to put them on edge.

Aurora ruffled her magnificent feathers. *"I would prefer as few observers as possible,"* she communicated. *"This is a delicate time, but I have learned he is persistent. If he just observes, I am okay with it."*

I translated her concerns diplomatically. "Perhaps we should keep things quiet and calm for now. First, regenerations can be quite stressful."

Green's smile tightened, and he moved to the far side of the room. "Of course, of course. I'll take a few notes from over here, if that's acceptable?"

Before I responded, Ashtok had a tiny burp, producing a shower of sparks. *"It feels funny,"* the chick complained. *"All hot and tight, like I ate too many peppers."*

"That's normal," I assured both chick and parent, pulling up the sanctuary's records on my tablet. "Your temperature is rising according to the schedule. How long has the sparking been happening?"

"Since this morning," Aurora answered. *"The glow started about an hour ago."*

I nodded, making notes while surreptitiously watching Green do the same. His interest in our phoenix population had seemed academic enough when he first arrived, but lately, it seemed more intense.

"Fascinating," he said, peering up from his notes. "And how many successful first regenerations has the facility recorded this year?"

Aurora's feathers bristled. *"Why does he want that information?"* she asked. *"What does that have to do with Ashtok's health?"*

"Doctor Green," I said. "Would you mind giving us some privacy?"

He withdrew with obvious reluctance. "Is something wrong with the chick?"

"No, nothing like that. Medical confidentiality and all that."

"Of course. Though I'd love to discuss your phoenix population statistics later. For my research."

He left and Aurora relaxed. *"There's something off with that man,"* she said. *"He asks too many questions about our numbers, our habits, our regeneration cycles."*

"All the scientists are supposed to be respectful and non-intrusive. I could ask him to cut his field research time. Has he been bothering you?" I asked, concerned.

"Not exactly. But he watches. He's always watching." She curved a protective wing around Ashtok. *"I don't trust him."*

"I will mention it to the sheriff." I made a mental note to discuss this with Penny later. Maybe we could limit his time in the habitat. For now, though, I had a nervous phoenix chick to focus on. "Alright, Ashtok, let's check your temperature and progression. Then we'll talk about what to expect when the real fireworks start."

The rest of the day passed in a blur of routine cases and minor emergencies. A pixie swarm with sneezing fits (caused by someone planting non-native flowers in their territory). A young chupacabra with a toothache. Through it all, I kept thinking about Aurora's concerns regarding Doctor Green. Had he crossed a line?

During a brief break in the schedule, I tackled my mother's old office. She'd retired last month, but I'd been putting off organizing the space. It felt strange, claiming it as my own after seeing her work here for so many years. However, the paperwork was finalized, and I had to move on.

Sorting through a filing cabinet, I felt something out of place - a cool blue button instead of just metal and paper. I pushed it and after a soft click of a latch, discovered a hidden compartment containing an assortment of specialized cryptid treatment tools I'd never seen before.

"Mom, you crafty old woman," I said, examining each item. Some I recognized from her stories. The crystal tuning fork used to diagnose frequency imbalances in bloops, the sun silver eye dropper for the drying eyes of a mapinguary, and even sliver pliers for who knew what. Others were new to me. Many of these looked like field instruments from her younger days as a retriever.

A knock interrupted my exploration. "Doctor Sterling?" Alice called. "Doctor Foster is on line three and wants to compare notes on a recent patient she saw with an anxiety disorder. And Doctor Green is still in the lobby asking if you would give him a note about extra sanctuary access for evening observations."

I sighed, replacing the tools. "I'll take Doctor Foster on the phone in here. As for Doctor Green." I hesitated. "Tell him all access requests have to go through proper channels. I can't do anything to change that."

I picked up the phone and pushed the lighted button. "Doctor Foster," I said. "How is the town's only cryptid therapist?"

And thus, my day continued in running from phone call to phone call, room to room, and even one field visit. By evening rounds, I was ready for this day to be over. The early wake-up call seemed days ago. I made my final checks, noting with satisfaction the peaceful atmosphere in the creature zones. Driving through the sanctuary was always a peaceful experience, especially when there were no emergencies. The pixies' sneezing had subsided, the new sasquatch was settling in, and Griff was resting his wing instead of showing off.

I arrived back at the clinic as Alice was leaving. She dropped off the day's reports just as I sat down. "Oh, and Doctor Sterling? I told Doctor Green how to get more access. He has made seven different requests for sanctuary access in the past week alone."

I frowned. "Seven? He has plenty of opportunity to go there. What is he looking for, that takes that much time?"

"He says he only went there a few times." She shrugged. "Thought you should know."

"Thanks, Alice. Not sure if he's a liar or loses track of time. Either way, I will deal with it if the tries to bug us again. Go home, it's been a long day. Have a great night."

She left, and I climbed up to my favorite thinking spot - the clinic's roof. The sunset splashed spectacular colors across the sky, and the evening air buzzed with supernatural creatures settling down and nocturnal ones waking up.

The sun sunk below the horizon. Something wasn't quite right. Green's excessive interest in the phoenixes, Aurora's unease, the repeated requests for records. Ut all added up to something. But what?

I smiled, pushing my concerns aside for now. What could go wrong in a small town dedicated to protecting these wondrous creatures? I was so naïve.

CHAPTER 4

The shrill ring of my phone pierced through what had been a peaceful sleep. Would I ever get a full night's sleep now that mom had retired? The struggle was real.

I groaned, fumbling in the darkness for the source of the noise. The display showed Penny's face, her sheriff's badge prominently displayed in the profile picture. Nothing good ever came from late-night calls from law enforcement, even if that law enforcement happened to be your older sister.

"It's three in the morning. Someone better be dead," I said into the phone, then immediately regretted my choice of words when I heard Penny's sharp intake of breath.

"Mark, I need you at the Starlight Cinema. Now." Her voice carried that tone she reserved for serious situations - the one that meant she was wearing her sheriff hat rather than her big sister hat.

I sat up, alert. "What's wrong? Is it Ziggy?"

"Just get here. Fast." The line went dead.

So much for my first decent night's sleep in weeks. Ever since Mom's retirement, the workload at the clinic had doubled. Apparently, word had gotten around that I could speak with supernatural creatures like her, and now everyone in Heritage Crest wanted me to check if their cryptid pet was just being dramatic or if there was a problem. Spoiler alert: it typically involved drama. Especially with Sparkles.

I threw on the first clean clothes I could find, a worn pair of jeans and my favorite flannel shirt. Grabbing my medical bag, I headed out into the night. Heritage Crest was different after dark. The ever-present fog that kept our town hidden from the outside world seemed thicker, more alive somehow. Streetlights cast halos through the mist, creating an otherworldly atmosphere that reminded me why some of our more poetic residents called it the Veil. The cryptids that were nocturnal roamed in their reserve sections. It was utterly enchanting.

The Starlight Cinema's vintage neon sign cut through the fog like a beacon. Even from a distance, I could see the police cars parked outside, their red and blue lights painting the mist in alternating colors. Yellow crime scene tape blocked off the theater's entrance, and my stomach dropped. This was not good.

I approached and spotted Officer Rivera questioning Tommy Chen, one of our town's local night security guards. Tommy's usually pristine uniform was rumpled, and his face was ashen. Rivera, on the other hand, looked as immaculate as ever in his pressed uniform, immune to the late hour. Sometimes I wondered if he slept in that outfit. I subconsciously tried to smooth out the wrinkles in my shirt, but it was no use.

"Doctor Sterling." Rivera nodded as I passed. "Your sister's upstairs."

"Thanks. You okay, Tommy?" I asked, noting how the guard's hands trembled as he clutched his thermos.

"I... I found him, Doc," Tommy said, his voice barely above a whisper. "I was doing my rounds and..."

Rivera cut him off with a raised hand. "We'll continue this later, Mr. Chen. Doctor Sterling, the sheriff is waiting."

I made my way through the theater's art déco lobby, my footsteps echoing off the marble floors. The place usually had the aroma of popcorn and excitement. Tonight, it smelled like fear and something else - something close to death.

Penny met me at the top of the stairs, her face grim. "Thanks for coming." She was in full sheriff mode, her long dark hair pulled back in a severe braid, her green eyes sharp and focused.

"Want to tell me what's going on?"

She gestured for me to follow her down the hallway toward the offices. "It's Jerry McKinnon."

My heart sank. I'd just seen Jerry yesterday for Ziggy's check-up. The little basilisk had been in perfect health, if a bit spoiled by too many spicy mice treats. "What happened?"

"See for yourself," Penny said, pushing open the door to Jerry's office.

The first thing I noticed was the body. Jerry lay sprawled behind his desk, his reading glasses askew on his face. The second thing I noticed was the strange blue substance around a wound on his neck. It looked almost like venom.

"Is that basilisk venom?" I asked, moving closer to examine the residue. The area had two puncture marks and the skin around the wound looked like a third-degree burn.

"That's what we need you to tell us," Penny replied, her voice tight. "And there's something else."

A soft keening sound drew my attention to the corner of the room. There, huddled beneath Jerry's coat rack, was Ziggy. The miniature basilisk's brilliant blue scales had dulled to a sickly gray, a sure sign of extreme emotional distress.

"Oh, buddy," I said, approaching. When dealing with a traumatized cryptid, especially one involved in their owner's death, you can never be too cautious.

"Hello, friend-healer," Ziggy's voice echoed in my mind, trembling and weak. He used words with me instead of emotions. This was bad. *"The nice-warm-Jerry won't wake up. I tried singing to him like he likes, but he won't wake up."*

My heart broke a little. Despite their fearsome reputation, basilisks were incredibly loyal creatures, and Ziggy devoted himself to Jerry. He would die to protect his owner. "I know, buddy. I'm sorry."

"I didn't hurt him!" The thought hit me so hard I stumbled. *"I would never hurt the nice-warm-Jerry! I love him. He gives the best spicy mice and scratches the perfect spot under my crest, and he keeps me warm."*

"Shh, it's okay," I soothed, sending waves of calm through our mental connection. "Can you tell me what happened?"

Ziggy's memories came in fragmented bursts: *"Sleeping in my special basket... Strange sounds... Jerry-friend talking loudly... Bright flash... Cold feeling... Want to help but can't move... Sleepy... Strange smell like burning ice... Then I sleep, then I wake up and Jerry-friend not moving."*

"What's he saying?" Penny asked, watching our interaction.

"He's innocent," I said, standing up. "And this isn't normal basilisk behavior. I know what it looks like, but they don't attack their owners. They are fiercely loyal."

Officer Rivera chose that moment to enter the room. "With all due respect, Doctor Sterling, we have a dead body with what appears to be basilisk venom around the bite, and a basilisk at the scene. Occam's Razor suggests-"

"Occam obviously never dealt with supernatural creatures." I interrupted him. "Look at the pattern of the residue. Basilisk venom is more concentrated at the point of entry, creating a starburst pattern as it spreads. We need to test it before jumping to conclusions. This is too uniform, too deliberate. Plus, the way Ziggy describes what happened, I think someone tranquilized him."

I moved closer to Jerry's desk, noticing details I'd missed in my initial shock. His calendar was open, showing a note about a late-night interaction with Doctor Victor Green. Why does this guy continue to show up in my life? Several papers about phoenix research, some marked with Jerry's distinctive red pen annotations, lay scattered across his desk. He was researching something.

"Tommy mentioned seeing Doctor Green enter through the back entrance last night," Penny said, following my gaze to the papers. "But Green told a deputy he was conducting night observations at the sanctuary."

"The security cameras might tell us more," Rivera suggested.

I shook my head, pointing across the room to a camera system smashed on the desk. "They won't. Someone disabled them. Whoever did it made sure there was no evidence."

Penny picked up Jerry's phone with her gloved hands from where it had fallen under his chair. She used his face to bypass the security screen. "There's a partial text here about 'suspicious activities at Green's lab across the alley.' It's unsent."

"Jerry mentioned to me he had an argument with Green about something, but that it was all worked out. Maybe it's the same one."

In the corner, Ziggy shook uncontrollably, his body wracked with fear. *"Friend-healer, my scales feel wrong. The air tastes like danger."*

"I understand. You just rest." I turned to Ziggy. "I want to check something. So, please stay still."

I narrowed my eyes and scratched his head. Every supernatural creature had a unique tooth configuration, like a fingerprint. Basilisks all had fangs, but the spacing, size, and shape were different. I eyeballed the space between the extended teeth and what I found confirmed my earlier suspicion - Ziggy's bite didn't match the dimensions around Jerry's wound. It was obvious if you knew what to look for.

"The basilisk is innocent," I announced. "His teeth configuration doesn't match the evidence. Plus, I am positive that whatever the blue liquid is, it's not basilisk venom. It's too watery. Someone went to a lot of trouble to make this look like a basilisk attack."

Rivera frowned. "Sheriff, we need to contain the creature until we can verify-"

"I'm verifying. I'll take full responsibility for him." I really didn't like Rivera. He gave off bad vibes. "He needs medical attention anyway. This level of emotional trauma can be dangerous for basilisks."

Penny studied me for a moment, then nodded. "Okay. But keep him at the clinic where we can find him if we need to."

"Doctor Sterling," Rivera said as I began preparing Ziggy for transport. "Remember that your gift, while useful, doesn't make you a detective. Leave the investigation to the professionals."

I was about to reply when Penny's phone buzzed. Her expression darkened as she read the message. "We've got another problem. There was a security breach at the phoenix sanctuary."

"Didn't you go there yesterday?"

"I did. The mother, Aurora, I think you said her name was. She was agitated about humans watching her from the bushes. It could have been anything. We took a report, and that was the end of it. They may be related, though."

I looked down at Jerry's scattered research papers, then at the traumatized basilisk in my arms, and finally, at my sister. This situation was more complex than just a murder, especially when supernatural beings were involved.

"Get Ziggy settled," Penny said, reading my expression. "Then we'll talk."

I nodded, cradling the distressed basilisk closer as I headed for the door. Whatever was going on, whoever had killed Jerry, they had gone to elaborate lengths to frame an innocent creature. In my experience, people who hurt animals - supernatural or otherwise - rarely stopped at just one crime.

Looking down at Ziggy's dulled scales, I made a silent promise to both him and Jerry. I would find out who did this, no matter where the investigation led. After all, I had a unique advantage - creatures never lied to those who could truly hear them, and I felt the mother phoenix would have quite a story to tell.

But first, I had a traumatized basilisk to care for. One crisis at a time - that's what Mom always said. I carried Ziggy out of the theater and into the foggy night. I couldn't help but wonder what other secrets were hiding in the Veil tonight, waiting to be uncovered.

The misty streets of Heritage Crest seemed to hold their breath as I made my way to my truck, the basilisk curled in my arms. Somewhere in the distance, a silkie sang its soothing night song, the sound carrying like a reminder that in our little hidden town, nothing was ever quite what it seemed.

This felt like only the start.

CHAPTER 5

I woke up on the couch and made my way to the clinic's special care unit. After the wake up call a few hours ago, I'd barely slept, my mind racing with fragments of Ziggy's distressed memories and the lingering image of that strange blue substance around Jerry's wound. I didn't want to leave him, so I elected to sleep on the couch in the breakroom.

The basilisk was where I'd laid him - curled tightly in one of our heated recovery enclosures, his normally vibrant scales still dulled to a sickly gray. A half-eaten spicy mouse lay untouched nearby, which was concerning, given Ziggy's usual enthusiasm for his favorite treats.

"Morning, buddy," I said, both aloud and mentally. "Ready to talk some more?"

Ziggy uncurled slightly, his feathered crest drooping. *"Friend-healer didn't leave me,"* he projected weakly. *"Promised you wouldn't. You say truth."*

"Of course I told you the truth. I won't lie to you." I settled cross-legged in front of his enclosure, deliberately keeping my posture relaxed and non-threatening. "Think you can tell me more about what happened last night? Anything you remember might help."

The basilisk's memories came in clearer fragments this time, less clouded by initial shock and grief: *"Was sleeping in a special basket under Jerry-friend's desk. Nice-warm basket Jerry-friend got special for me. Then voices - Jerry-friend and other-voice. Loud voices. Angry mean woman. I move to the corner."*

"Can you remember what they were saying?"

35

"Jerry-friend said, 'not right' and 'must report.' Other-voice angry. Angry lady said she give ten thousand something. Then a bright flash, cold feeling. Wanted to help but couldn't move. Then sleep." Ziggy's mental voice trembled. *"Strange smell like burning ice. Not normal."*

I made careful notes, both physical and mental. I did a blood test before laying down last night. They indeed had knocked him out. The paralysis and then sleep were interesting – why would someone tranquilize him. How did they know he was there? Another piece that didn't fit.

"You said there was a strange smell," I said. "Like burning ice? That's an unusual combination. Had you smelt it before?"

"Yes! Like when nice-warm-Jerry puts ice in hot coffee. But stronger. Bad stronger." Ziggy's crest lifted slightly with excitement at being understood, then drooped again. *"Should have protected Jerry-friend better. Bad basilisk."*

"Hey, none of that," I said. "This wasn't your fault. Someone went to a lot of trouble to make it look like basilisk venom on the wound, but they got the details wrong. They came prepared to put you to sleep."

"Not... my fault?" Hope flickered through our mental connection.

"Definitely not. In fact-" I broke off as footsteps approached, accompanied by voices. One I recognized as Penny's. The other was Doctor Green. Great.

"...assure you, Sheriff, my research is entirely above board. I have all the proper permits and clearances."

"I'm sure you do, Doctor Green. We just need to verify your whereabouts during certain time periods."

They rounded the corner - Penny in her sheriff's uniform, looking like she'd gotten about as much sleep as I had, and a tall, distinguished-looking man in his fifties. Everything about him screamed 'respected scientist,' from his stylish glasses to his pressed khakis. He appeared equally arrogant, mirroring his demeanor from yesterday's arrival with the mother phoenix.

"Ah, Doctor Sterling." Green smiled. "It's great to see you again. I forgot to mention previously, your mother's research on phoenix regeneration cycles was groundbreaking. I cited her work in my last paper."

I stood, brushing off my jeans. "Nice to see you again." I lied. "Though I wish it were under better circumstances."

"Yes, terrible business with Jerry. I hardly knew him, of course, but any death is tragic. Especially when it involves one of our community." He glanced at Ziggy's enclosure with what looked like genuine concern.

"Don't like him," Ziggy projected. *"Smells like secrets. Bad."*

Interesting. Basilisks were excellent judges of character - it was part of what made them such loyal companions. I kept my expression neutral as I asked, "You mentioned hardly knowing Jerry, but I understand you had an interaction with him the other night? Is that correct?"

A flicker of something - surprise? concern? - crossed Green's face before his polite smile returned. "Ah, no, I'm afraid there must be some mistake. I conduct night observations at the phoenix sanctuary every night within the allotted times only, of course. Critical research period, you understand. The pre-breeding behavior patterns are fascinating. I wouldn't be anywhere near his theater."

"Funny," Penny said. "Because Tommy Chen remembers seeing you enter the theater through the back entrance that night."

"Your security guard must be mistaken. As I said, I was at the sanctuary all night. My research logs will confirm it."

"Not voice I heard. He lies though," Ziggy projected. *"Smells like Jerry-friend's office. Old smell, not new, but there at some time."*

I filed that information away while maintaining eye contact with Green. "What exactly does your research involve? Is it just observation? I understand you're interested in our phoenix population."

"Oh yes! Remarkable specimens you have here. I'm studying their breeding patterns, particularly the environmental factors that influence egg development. Which is why I was so thankful you let me observe the examination you conducted. Did you know that temperature variations as small as half a degree can affect the thickness of the egg's shell? It could even cause them to hatch early. Fascinating stuff."

He launched into a detailed explanation of phoenix reproductive cycles, complete with technical terminology and academic references. The information was flawlessly accurate - almost textbook perfect.

Penny caught my eye, giving a subtle nod toward the hall. "Doctor Green, if you'll excuse us for a moment. I need to consult with my brother about Ziggy's care and the homicide."

"Of course, of course. I was coming here to see if you have received my request for extended observation."

Here it was. Even amid a murder close to home, his research still held his focus. "I'm sorry, we are in the middle of a death as the sheriff said. My assistant should have shared with you the proper channel for such an endeavor."

"She did, yes. However, I thought from professional to professional you might help me. Your employee has no idea what's at stake. She is nice, but after all, she is just a secretary."

"She is much more than just a secretary. I'll have you know that she is quite intelligent and very professional. Please follow her instructions." I had to take a deep breath.

"Of course. I had to ask." He looked around nervously. "I should check my monitoring equipment anyway. Please let me know if you need me for anything. Those temperature readings won't record themselves!" He chuckled at his own joke, then headed out the clinic exit with just a hint of too much haste.

As soon as he was out of earshot, Penny turned to me. "Sorry about that. He was walking by when I came in and followed."

"I figured as much. What an ass."

"Well? Anything new?"

"Ziggy says Green is lying about not ever being at the theater. Says he can smell traces of him in Jerry's office from before last night. So, maybe he wasn't there last night, but he was in that office recently."

"That tracks with what Harry found. He's been analyzing the security footage, or I should say, trying to. Someone did a half ass job of smashing the hardware, but specific time periods had been backed up to the cloud. We are downloading those now and hoping for something."

I frowned. "Green's only been here a few months. Does he show up at all?"

"That's what we need to find out. Harry says the timestamps of some of the missing footage matches up with Green's reported observation periods. He may be telling the truth, but it will be difficult to say for sure without the complete footage."

I ran a hand through my hair, a habit Mom was always telling me would make me go bald early. "Regarding the substance around Jerry's wound - have you obtained the results?"

"Not yet. I am expecting them later today."

"I already know it's fake, but the confirmation will be reassuring. Plus, thinking more about the burn. It doesn't spider out like veins which is typical in a bite. Another thing, Ziggy described the room as smelling like 'burning ice.' I did some research before bed last night."

"Meaning?"

"I think someone was trying hard to make this look like a basilisk attack while using a different kind of substance. The characteristic 'burning ice' smell signifies water decomposition from intense heat, resulting in a pungent, acidic odor resembling a blend of burned plastic and ozone. The burn marks on the wound matches up to this. Basilisk venom causes petrification, not burns. Anyone with actual experience with basilisks would know that."

"And Green's supposed to be an expert on phoenixes, not basilisks," Penny mused. "So, either he's branching out..."

"Or someone wants us looking in his direction. He could just be an idiot, but as much as he annoys me, I don't think that's true." I glanced back at Ziggy's enclosure. The basilisk had started nibbling at his spicy mouse, which was a good sign.

"I did a blood test on Ziggy, and he was shot with a tranquilizer. I found the puncture mark on his back as well. Also, I'm betting the blue substance is ordinary rattlesnake venom, maybe with some blue food coloring."

"I will make sure we take Ziggy off the list and try to shelter him from any part of this investigation."

"What do we know about Green's background?"

"On paper? Impressive. Multiple degrees, published research, grants from all the right institutions. But Harry's digging deeper, looking for anything unusual in his financial records or communication patterns."

"I never asked, what is that like having your husband report to you?" Harry worked for Penny in the sheriff's office. He handled all the cyber related items and office administration.

"Not now. You can bust my chops later. Focus."

"Fine. And what about his research? The phoenix breeding study?"

"That's where it gets interesting. The sanctuary board approved his project six months ago, but some of his reports seem... off. Details that don't quite add up. I asked mom to look through them since she knows more about phoenix research protocols than anyone."

I was about to respond when my phone buzzed - a text from Alice: "Emergency at phoenix sanctuary. Aurora agitated, refusing to let anyone near the nesting area."

"Speaking of phoenixes," I showed Penny the message. "Want to come see what has our resident mother phoenix so upset?"

"I have been working leads throughout the night and need to get out there anyway."

"You going to be able to stay awake."

"Just lead the way, little brother."

CHAPTER 6

We found the phoenix sanctuary in chaos. Aurora, our largest and oldest phoenix, sat perched atop her favorite roosting spot, her magnificent golden-red plumage blazing with agitation. She seemed a different animal than the one I saw the previous day. Every few seconds, she would release a burst of warning flames at anyone who tried to approach.

"What happened?" I asked a deputy, who was trying to coordinate the sanctuary staff's response from a safe distance.

"Routine morning check. Everything was fine until Doctor Green's assistant tried to take the daily egg temperature readings. The phoenix flared up and lost it. Started flaming at everyone."

"Where's the assistant now?"

"In the bungalow, getting treated for minor burns. Said her name's Violet Newsome. She's been working with Green for a few weeks."

I approached the nesting area carefully, reaching out with my gift. "Aurora? It's Doctor Green. Can you tell me what's wrong?"

The phoenix's response was a jumble of angry images and emotions: *"Wrong-cold-touch on eggs. Not-right-presence. Danger-threat-protect!"*

"Anything?" Penny asked.

"She's not making much sense. I think something feels wrong about her eggs. She keeps projecting images of cold and danger."

"Doctor Sterling?" An unfamiliar voice joined us - smooth, with a hint of anxiety. I turned to find a woman in her late twenties wearing a blackened lab coat over dark black jeans, sweatshirt, and shoes. Her dark hair was escaping from what had been a neat bun. Despite the burns on her sleeves, she looked more put-together than I usually did on my best days. It took a moment before it hit me. I recognized her. She was the lady that ran into me on the street the day before.

"You must be Ms. Newsome. Are you alright?"

"Please, call me Violet. And yes, a few minor burns. Entirely my fault - I should have approached more carefully." She smiled apologetically as I strained to hear her soft-spoken low voice. "I'm usually much better with the phoenixes, but I suppose they need time to get used to fresh faces."

"You're having a rough couple of days." I was trying to be cute.

"What do you mean?" she asked. I could detect a slight tinge of paranoia. "I'm fine. Everything's fine."

I smiled. "I meant since you ran into me yesterday on the street and dropped your phone."

"Not sure what you're talking about." She smiled. "I didn't run into anyone yesterday."

I nodded, both confused and slightly concerned. Something about her smile didn't quite reach her eyes, but before I could analyze it further, Aurora let out another warning screech. This one came with a blast of images so strong I stumbled: *Wrong numbers! Missing warmth! Protect-defend-attack! Gone! Gone! Gone!*

"Mark?" Penny steadied me. "What is it?"

"She keeps insisting something's wrong with the numbers. I will try to find out more."

"Aurora, can you lift up so I can count your eggs?"

"I trust. You only do for moment to find gone! Gone! Not woman." The phoenix lifted and stepped back, giving me just enough time to count six eggs. She sat back down on them.

"Ms. Newsome."

"Violet, please."

"Sorry, Violet. Can you please pull up the egg monitoring logs you have and tell me how many there should be?"

Violet tapped rapidly on her tablet. "According to Doctor Green's latest report, Aurora's clutch has six eggs, all within normal temperature range for this stage of development."

I squinted through the heat distortion at Aurora's nest. "I count six eggs as well."

"So, then, why is she upset?" Penny asked.

"Wrong," Aurora screamed.

It didn't make sense. Aurora always knew how many eggs she possessed. "May I see that?" I asked.

Violet handed her tablet over to me and, sure enough, the latest report showed six eggs. I scrolled back a week on the sheet, saw what I was looking for, and pinched to enlarge the field. I handed it to Penny with a sigh. "That's the issue."

Penny's eyes darted to Violet and showed her the screen. "What do you make of this?"

"That's impossible," Violet said. "I checked the count last night during my observations. There were definitely six."

"Then how come a week ago the log shows seven? And why wasn't it caught?" I asked.

"It must have been a typo on my part," Violet said. "Eggs just don't disappear."

"Wrong!" Aurora's mental voice boomed in my head. *"Cold-touch took warm-life! Protect others to the death!"*

"Mark?" Penny's voice had taken on that particular tone that meant she was shifting from sister mode to sheriff mode. "What is she saying?"

"She's saying." I frowned, trying to sort through the phoenix's emotional projections. "She's saying someone took one of her eggs. Someone with a cold touch. There have always been seven."

Violet's perfectly shaped eyebrows drew together in concern. "But that's not possible. The sanctuary has state-of-the-art security. The only people with access to the nesting area are Doctor Green and me, and we would never take an egg without permission."

"When did Aurora last see seven eggs?" Penny interrupted.

I asked, and the phoenix spread its wings and yelled, *"Last night, friend-Mark."*

"Last night she says."

"Are you sure you are hearing her correctly? That's not possible. During my observations last night. Around 2 AM. There was six."

"Lies!" Aurora's mental voice was deafening. *"No can count-night-observer! Cold touch in darkness took! Face covered."*

I must have winced at Aurora's volume, because Penny stepped closer. "What now?"

"Aurora says Violet here can't count or didn't count last night. Someone with a cold touch in the darkness took it. They were wearing a mask or something."

"Ms. Newsome." Penny's voice was neutral. "Is there any chance you didn't count the eggs last night and might just not be remembering?"

"I'm sure I did. It's a habit. Is it possible? I guess, but very unlikely."

"Would you mind showing me your observation logs? And the security footage from your shift?"

"Of course! Though I should probably check with Doctor Green first. Protocol, you understand. He gets furious if I don't follow his standards."

"Of course," Penny said, faking a smile. "I understand completely. In fact, why don't you go find him right now? I need to interview him. I'm sure he'll want to know about this situation. And let him know that this is not a request."

Violet hurried off, her lab coat fluttering behind her. As soon as she was gone, Penny turned to me. "Well?"

"Aurora's definitely missing an egg. This isn't normal protective behavior." I studied the angry phoenix, noting how she seemed to shield her nest. "And that bit about the cold touch. Remember what Ziggy said about the smell in Jerry's office? Like burning ice? And the cold."

"You think there's a connection?"

"I think we need to look at those security logs. Both incidents have Doctor Green associated with them. That can't be a coincidence."

Penny's fingers flew over her phone. "And I'm having Deputy Martinez ask perimeter security to monitor all the exits and get my permission before anyone is allowed to leave Heritage Crest. If anyone tries to bolt with a phoenix egg, we'll catch them."

She trailed off as Julie Niman rushed up, her face pale. Julie was a sanctuary technician and in charge of the overall environmental readings of this half of the preserve. We dated once in high school. "Mark? Sorry, Doctor Sterling."

"Mark's fine."

"Mark, you need to see this. We were doing a routine check of the environmental controls, and we found something... unusual." She led us to a maintenance panel hidden behind a decorative rock formation. "These temperature readings? There's a pattern of micro-adjustments over the past week. Someone's been gradually lowering the ambient temperature in small enough increments that it wouldn't trigger any alarms."

I examined the readout. "How low are we talking?"

"About three degrees total. Not enough to harm adult phoenixes."

"But enough to impact egg development," I said. "Or maybe enough to cause and egg to go dormant in preparation for transport?"

Penny's eyes narrowed. "Transport?"

"Phoenix eggs are incredibly temperature sensitive," Julie said. "They must be maintained at exact levels, or they won't be viable and hatch. But if you wanted to move one, hypothetically., you'd need to gradually lower its temperature first. Get it into a dormant state."

"Like putting it in suspended animation," Penny mused.

"Exactly," I said. "Also, if you put an egg in cold storage and suddenly took it out and into room temperature, it would probably hatch within moments, regardless of if it was ready."

"And how much would a viable phoenix egg be worth on the black market?"

"More than either of us will make in our lifetimes."

Aurora's angry screeching had subsided into a low, mournful keening. *"Protect-warn-failed. One-warm-life gone. Must save others. Kill to survive. Need chick back. No hatch. Not time."*

"We'll find it," I promised her. "Just hold on."

Penny was already calling in backup and organizing a sanctuary-wide search. But something told me we wouldn't find the missing egg near here. Someone had gone to a lot of trouble to set this up - the security system tampering at the theater, the gradual temperature adjustments in the sanctuary, the elaborate framing of Ziggy.

This wasn't just an opportunistic theft. This was a carefully planned operation. And somehow, maybe Jerry had stumbled onto it.

Another text from Harry dinging Penny's phone interrupted my thought. She read what it said. "You need to see this. Found deleted security footage from the theater back alley. Timestamp matches Jerry's time of death. Shows someone entering from the direction of the lab campus, but it's too grainy to get an identity. But there is something you should see. Video corrupted but might be recoverable."

"These are connected. I'm sure."

Penny started toward the sanctuary exit and paused. "I need to go look at this. Mark?

"Yeah."

"Be careful. If we're right about this..."

"I know." I glanced back at Aurora, still maintaining her protective vigil. "If these are connected, someone could be willing to kill to keep this quiet."

As if to emphasize the point, Penny's phone buzzed again. Another text from Harry: "BTW - checked Green's background. His credentials look solid because they're copied by a real researcher. The real Doctor Victor Green died six months ago."

"Think it's time to have that chat with Green. Maybe I can go get more out of his research assistant while I'm at it?" Penny said.

I followed Penny. "I'm going to go with you."

"Not this time, little brother. I need you to join the search for the egg. I will track Green down and find out what he has to say."

Somewhere in our little hidden town, someone was sitting on a fortune with a stolen phoenix egg, probably planning their next move. The question was: would we figure it out before anyone else got hurt?

Looking at Penny's determined expression, I felt we were about to find out. After all, as Mom always said, no one messes with Heritage Crest's creatures and gets away with it.

Everything seemed to cast blame on Doctor Green. He might be the thief, perhaps the murderer, or possibly both. Now we had to prove it.

CHAPTER 7

The sanctuary itself was a marvel of engineering - a massive glass dome reinforced with protective transparent steel and temperature regulation controls for each cryptid covered just over 100 square miles. Different sections maintained distinct microclimates, from volcanic-inspired nesting areas to temperate perches where the phoenixes could observe the sanctuary's daily operations.

I spent most of the day searching for the missing egg. You would think with all the advancements it would be easier, but we found nothing. After a few hours of sleep, I dragged myself off the clinic couch with the weight of Aurora's loss sitting heavy on my shoulders and put my shoes on. The mental image of her mournful keening haunting me. I'd promised her we'd find her egg. I just wasn't sure how to deliver on that promise.

"Any updates?" I asked, poking my head into the reception area where Alice was updating the day's schedule. Nine o'clock approached on the analog clock on the wall behind her desk. I was perpetually exhausted, but the sanctuary residents were too important for me to sleep. Especially, when they were in pain.

"Nothing yet," she said, not looking up from her computer. "Sheriff's team called about ten minutes ago. They're expanding the search radius in the habitat near the north perimeter."

"Anything more on the town search?" Penny was getting permission to start a building-to-building search in the town, but the politics of overly sensitive scientists and their research were delaying an extended search.

"Not that she said."

"At this rate, they won't be searching the entire town until tomorrow," I said.

Alice looked up, her expression softening. "You look terrible."

"Thanks. I feel terrible." I ran a hand through my hair, which I'd forgotten to comb. "Keep thinking about Aurora. If we don't find that egg soon it will be devastating."

"You'll find it," Alice said with more confidence than I felt. "If anyone can, it's you. I'm sure of it."

I appreciated her faith, even if it seemed misplaced. "Hope you're right. I'm heading out to join the search, again. Call if any emergencies come in."

"Will do and Mark," she said as I turned to leave. "Your gift won't help anyone if you pass out while you're searching. It won't hurt to eat and catch up on some sleep."

I nodded. That was sound advice. My ability to speak with cryptids would aid the search, although I doubted its usefulness before the egg hatched. There was no awareness to talk with.

I started my search back at the phoenix sanctuary. Not because I thought the egg would be there. The sanctuary had been searched multiple times already, but I needed to center myself and reconnect with the case at its core.

The drive took only a few minutes, but it gave me time to organize my thoughts. We had a timeline for the egg theft, thanks to Aurora's keen memory. It disappeared on the same night Jerry was killed. We knew someone had gradually adjusted the temperature controls to acclimate the egg to colder temperatures, suggesting premeditation.

What we didn't know was who had taken it. Doctor Green was the obvious suspect, with his obsessive research into phoenix breeding cycles. But something about that didn't sit right with me. Green, arrogant and single-minded, seemed genuinely passionate about studying phoenixes, not exploiting them.

Then there was his assistant, Violet. She'd been at the right places at the right time, but was that suspicious or simply part of her job?

The sanctuary was already bustling with activity when I arrived. Teams of security personnel were methodically checking and rechecking areas, while others examined the surveillance systems for any missed evidence. I spotted Deputy Rivera directing a team near the main phoenix habitat.

"Doctor Sterling," he said as I approached. "No luck so far."

"I didn't expect any," I admitted. "This area's been searched multiple times already."

"True, but your sister insists we be thorough." He gestured toward a cluster of buildings to the east. "We're moving to check the feeding facilities next. Doctor Green's lab is my primary focus until we can get permission to access the rest of the town buildings. I was heading over there now."

"He gave us the permission?" I asked.

"Yeah. He offered it up right away. Almost eager."

"Odd. Mind if I tag along?" I asked.

Rivera shrugged. "Sheriff said to give you full access. Just don't touch anything without gloves."

I followed Rivera's team to the research complex, a collection of modern buildings that stood in stark contrast to the Victorian architecture of the rest of Heritage Crest. Doctor Green's lab occupied the largest building, its steel exterior gleaming in the morning light.

Inside, the lab was immaculate - too immaculate. The antiseptic smell of cleaning products hung in the air, as if someone had recently done a thorough scrubbing. Rivera's team spread out, examining every cabinet, drawer, and storage container.

I wandered over to Green's desk, my eyes drawn to a framed photograph. It showed a much younger Green standing beside a female phoenix, his expression one of wonder and pride. The photo was old and yellowed with age.

"Doctor Sterling," one deputy called, drawing my attention. "You might want to see this."

"What did you find?"

He was standing by a bookshelf, holding what appeared to be a journal. "Found it hidden behind some textbooks."

I took the journal, careful to handle it by the edges and flipped through the pages, I found detailed notes on phoenix breeding cycles, temperature regulation experiments, and egg development theories. Nothing damning, until I reached the last pages.

"Subject 7. The egg shows promising resistance to temperature fluctuations," I read aloud. "Gradual acclimation protocol proceeding as expected. Transfer to cold storage scheduled for Tuesday night, after staff departure."

Tuesday night - the night Jerry died. The night the egg disappeared.

"Looks like we have our smoking gun," Rivera said over my shoulder.

"Maybe," I replied, but something still felt off. The writing was similar to the babble I had heard out of Green. I recognized the cramped, precise script from requisition forms he'd submitted to the clinic. But while most of the journal contained the dry, clinical observations of a scientist, these final entries felt different. More calculated, less passionate. He was smarter than this.

I was about to mention this to Rivera when my phone buzzed. It was a text from Penny: "Need you at the north perimeter ASAP. Potential lead."

"I've got to go," I told Rivera, handing him the journal. "My sister needs me at the north perimeter."

"We'll bag this for evidence," he said. "Looks like your Doctor Green has some explaining to do."

I didn't correct his assumption. Better to let the evidence lead us where it may.

CHAPTER 8

The north perimeter of the sanctuary was the least developed area of Heritage Crest. It was a mixed landscape of dense forest and open meadows that served as a buffer between the cryptid habitats and the outside world. As I pulled up to the ranger station that marked the boundary, I spotted Penny's jeep parked haphazardly across two spaces - a sure sign she'd arrived in a hurry.

I found her standing near a maintenance shed, deep in conversation with Tommy Chen, the security guard who'd discovered Jerry's body. Tommy looked even more rumpled than the previous night, his uniform creased and his hair sticking up at odd angles, as if he'd been pulling at it.

"There he is," Penny said as I approached. "Tommy was just telling me about some unusual activity he observed two nights ago."

"Mark," Tommy nodded, looking uncomfortable. "Sheriff asked me to walk you through what I saw."

"Two nights ago?" I frowned. "That's after the egg count changed, but before Jerry was murdered?"

"It might still be relevant," Penny insisted. "Tommy, tell him."

Tommy cleared his throat. "I was doing my usual rounds, checking the perimeter fences. Around 2 AM, I spotted someone moving through the trees with a flashlight. Thought it might be kids sneaking around. It happens sometimes, so I followed."

"And?" I prompted when he hesitated.

"And it was your mother," Tommy said, looking even more uncomfortable. "She was carrying some kind of container and heading toward the old maintenance tunnels."

I blinked in surprise. "My mother? Are you sure?"

"Positive," Tommy nodded. "I've known Doctor Clara my whole life. She was moving fast, keeping to the shadows. I called out to her, but she acted like she didn't hear me."

"Where did she go?"

"She disappeared into one of the tunnel access points before I could catch up. I figured it was nothing until I heard the egg had gone missing."

I looked at Penny, who was observing me. "That doesn't make any sense. Mom's retired. She has no reason to be out here at 2 AM."

"That's what I thought," Tommy said. "It was odd enough that I made a note in my log. I was going to follow up on it yesterday, but with everything that happened with Jerry." He trailed off, his expression clouding.

"The maintenance tunnels run underneath most of the sanctuary," Penny explained. "They were built decades ago for utility access, but many sections have been abandoned as the sanctuary expanded."

"I know what they are," I said, perhaps more sharply than intended. I was always overly defensive of Mom. "But why would Mom be using them? And what was she carrying?"

"That's what we need to find out," Penny said, her sheriff voice firmly in place. "You should be there when I question her, given the personal connection."

I didn't like what she was implying, but I couldn't deny the facts. If Tommy saw Mom with a container, heading into hidden tunnels in the middle of the night, two days after a phoenix egg went missing. There had to be an explanation.

"Let me talk to her, first" I said. "Before we tear apart the tunnels."

Penny hesitated. "Mark, I know she's our mother, but if she's involved—"

"She's not," I said. "I'm sure there's a logical explanation. Just let me talk to her first. Please."

After a moment, Penny nodded. "Fine. But I'm coming with you."

"No," I said. "If both of us show up, she'll know something's wrong. Let me handle this. I'll call you as soon as I know anything."

Penny clearly didn't like it, but she relented. "Two hours."

"Two hours," I said. "That's all I need."

As I drove to Mom's cottage on the edge of town, my mind raced with possibilities. There had to be a logical explanation for what Tommy saw. Mom had devoted her entire life to protecting the creatures of Heritage Crest. The idea that she could be involved in stealing Aurora's egg was absurd.

Unless. A memory surfaced. Mom, years ago, rushing into the house late at night, her clothes covered in ash and her expression grim. "Sometimes," she'd told us. "We have to make difficult choices to protect those who can't protect themselves."

She'd never explained what happened that night, and Penny and I had known better than to ask.

Mom's cottage stood in a small clearing surrounded by ancient oak trees. Unlike most homes in Heritage Crest, hers had no fence - unnecessary, given her gift with cryptids. Various creatures wandered freely through her garden, from ordinary squirrels and rabbits to more exotic visitors: a small delegation of pixies tending to her flower beds, a young sasquatch helping to stack firewood near the porch.

I parked my truck and took a moment to steady myself. I didn't want to seem accusatory. Mom could read me like a book on the best of days.

"Mark!" she said from the porch before I'd even closed the car door. "What a lovely surprise! I was just making tea."

She looked normal. Not sure what I expected. Her silver-streaked hair pulled back in its usual braid, her green eyes bright with welcome, her clothes practical as always: jeans, a flannel shirt, sturdy boots. Nothing about her suggested secret midnight activities or stolen phoenix eggs.

"Hey, Mom," I said, climbing the porch steps to accept her hug. "Sorry to drop by unannounced."

"Nonsense." She waved off my apology. "You know you're always welcome. Come inside. You look like you could use a proper breakfast. Have you been sleeping at all?"

Before I could answer, she was guiding me into the cottage, its interior as familiar and comforting as always: walls lined with books on cryptid care, the scent of herbs drying in the kitchen, the gentle hum of chime music in the background.

"Sit," she instructed, pointing to the kitchen table. "I'll fix you something to eat while we talk."

I sat obediently, watching as she moved around the kitchen, pulling eggs and bread from the refrigerator. For a woman in her sixties, Mom moved with the energy of someone half her age.

"So," she said, cracking eggs into a bowl. "How's the search for Aurora's egg going? Any leads?"

Direct, as always. I should have anticipated it.

"Actually, that's why I'm here," I said, deciding to take the same approach. "Tommy Chen thinks he saw you two nights ago, around 2 AM. Near the north perimeter carrying some kind of container."

Mom's hands paused for just a fraction of a second before continuing to whisk the eggs. "Did he, now?"

Not a denial. My stomach tightened.

"He said you went into the old maintenance tunnels," I continued, watching her carefully. "Didn't respond when he called out to you."

Mom added salt and pepper to the eggs, her movements deliberate. "And what do you think about that, Mark?"

"There must be some explanation," I said. "Tommy might have been mistaken. Or there's a reason you were there that has nothing to do with the missing egg."

She poured the eggs into a heated pan, the sizzle filling the silence between us. When she spoke, she measured her words.

"Tommy wasn't mistaken."

My heart sank. "Then you want to tell me what you were doing out there in the middle of the night?"

Mom turned to face me, her expression unreadable. "No, I don't."

"Mom?"

"Mark." She cut me off gently but firmly. "I need you to trust me. Can you do that? Without explanations, without evidence. Just... trust me."

I stared at her, surprised by the directness of her request. Throughout my life, Mom never sought blind faith. She'd always encouraged questions, insisted on evidence, taught us to think critically.

"Aurora is missing an egg. Someone stole it."

"I heard. I spent the night searching. It's horrible."

"Does this have something to do with the egg?" I asked, unable to let it go.

Mom turned back to the stove, flipping the eggs with practiced ease. "You should be asking a different question."

"Which is?"

"Who stands to benefit from stealing a phoenix egg? And why now, specifically?"

I frowned, considering. "The black market for cryptid trafficking is huge. A phoenix egg could be worth millions to the right buyer."

"Yes." Mom nodded. "But timing matters. Why take an egg from this clutch at this time? Phoenix eggs are laid in cycles. This isn't the first opportunity someone would have had."

"If you go that route, it makes you look guilty. Someone could say you did it to get a retirement nest egg. No pun intended."

"Hmmm." She appeared to not have considered that. "I suppose it does. What else?"

She slid the eggs onto a plate, added toast, and placed it in front of me before sitting down across the table.

"I don't know," I admitted. "Maybe because security was looser with the new research team? Doctor Green's presence created disruptions in the usual routines. Who cares?"

"Perhaps," Mom said, though she didn't sound convinced. "Or perhaps someone knew something about this clutch that made it valuable beyond the usual market price. Something unique?"

I looked up. "Stop with always trying to get me to think through things. Just tell me what you mean?"

Instead of answering directly, Mom reached into her pocket and pulled out a small, iridescent scale - unmistakably from a phoenix, but unlike any I'd seen before. Instead of the usual gold-to-red gradation, this scale shifted through colors like an aurora borealis, blues, and greens dancing across its surface.

"Where did you get that?" I asked.

"From Aurora's mother, many years ago, before you were born," Mom said, placing the scale carefully on the table between us. "It was a gift, freely given, in exchange for helping her through a difficult hatching. I carry it for good luck."

I stared at the scale, my breakfast forgotten. "I've never seen coloration like that before."

"Few have," Mom agreed. "It's a rare genetic variant. Most phoenix experts believe it died out centuries ago."

Understanding dawned slowly. "Are you saying Aurora's eggs might carry this gene? That they could hatch into phoenixes with this coloration?"

"Not all of them," Mom said. "But one, perhaps. The one that's gone missing, specifically."

"How would anyone know which egg carried the gene? They all look the same."

Mom's smile was tight. "Not to someone with specialized equipment. The kind of equipment Doctor Green brought with him. Equipment designed to detect subtle genetic markers through the shell."

My mind raced through the implications. "If Green discovered one egg carried this rare gene..."

"It would be worth far more than the others," Mom finished for me. "Not just to collectors, but to researchers. People would pay exurbanite amounts for a phoenix egg in general. However, scientists who special-ize in cryptid genetics would pay twice anything for the chance to study such a specimen."

"You believe Green stole the egg?" I asked, though it still didn't make sense. If Green wanted to study the genetics, why not do it openly, as part of his research?

"It seems to me," she said, carefully, "that we shouldn't jump to con-clusions. I don't think Green is involved. But I also believe that the egg needs to be found, and quickly. Aurora deserves to have her child re-turned, whatever its genetic makeup."

She stood up, taking her teacup to the sink. "I have some errands to run this morning. Why don't you finish your breakfast, and we can talk more later?"

Her abrupt change of subject wasn't lost on me. "Stop trying to dis-tract me. Are you involved in this somehow?"

She turned, her expression softening. "Mark, have I ever done any-thing that wasn't in the best interest of the creatures under our care?"

"No," I said. "But that doesn't answer my question."

"It's the only answer I can give you right now," she said. "Please, trust me. And perhaps don't mention our conversation to your sister just yet. Penny sees things in black and white. My situation has nuances and speaking of distractions, I don't want to hinder her."

"She is waiting for my call. She had plans of putting her entire team in the tunnels." Before I could press further, a noise from the back of the cottage caught my attention - a soft thud, like something being dropped.

"What was that?" I asked, alert.

"Probably just the wind," Mom said. "Those old oak branches some-times hit the roof when it's gusty."

But today lacked wind. The fog had lifted to reveal a still morning.

"Mom," I said, rising from the table. "Is there someone else here?"

"Mark, leave it," she said. I was already moving toward the hallway that led to the bedrooms and her study.

The sound had come from behind her study door, which was uncharacteristically closed. Mom kept it open most times, since the room had the best view of the garden and the visiting cryptids.

"Mark, please," she said.

I turned it slowly, half-expecting it to be locked, but it opened. Inside, the study looked normal at first glance: bookshelves lining the walls, her desk positioned by the window, various cryptid-care tools and specimens neatly arranged on shelves.

Then I saw the cooling unit tucked under her desk, looking out of place among the antique furniture and handwritten journals. High-tech and new, with digital controls and a biometric lock.

"What is this?" I asked, turning to face Mom, who had followed me into the room.

She sighed, shoulders slumping. "It's not what you think."

"Then what is it? Because it looks an awful lot like the kind of equipment, you'd use to transport a phoenix egg."

Mom closed the door behind her, leaning against it as if suddenly tired. "It could also transport a Lensivity Plant."

"A what?"

"Lensivity. It is a rare plant that is only found a few places in the world, and I found it in the sanctuary."

"You need to start over," I said.

"Continuing my hobby of cataloging the plant life of the sanctuary and how the cryptids might contribute to the extinct flora in the world, I discovered this plant. I have collected samples to have it tested. This might give us the ability to revitalize it."

"I'm not buying it. Why would you be out in the middle of the night?"

"The law say we can't remove vegetation from the reserve. If I was caught, I would get in trouble. So, I snuck out a small sample. But please, don't tell your sister."

"She will keep asking. I might leave out the detail of you stealing a small plant, but she won't let it go. Plus, what was that sound if it's just a plant."

Mom reached down and picket up a few pictures on the floor. "The unit vibrates a lot and must have knocked these to the floor.

She crossed to her desk, unlocking a drawer with a small key she kept on a chain around her neck. She pulled out a file folder and handed it to me. "If you don't trust me, here is my work on it so far."

I opened the folder to find meticulous notes and photographs. All about this plant. I looked up from the file. "And the egg? How does that fit in?"

Mom hesitated. "I never said it did."

"The container Tommy saw you carrying," I said. I wanted to believe her. "It was this one here?"

Mom's expression shifted, and for a moment, she looked every bit her age. "Yes. I know it is normally used for cryptids, but it was all I had."

"Did it work?"

"Not as well as I'd hoped," she admitted. "But, I was able to get the genetic make-up out of the sample. So, I guess that's a win.

I closed the folder, my mind racing. "Mom, you need to tell Penny all of this. Now. Before more people think you took the egg. There were deputies and others around when Tommy told us."

"I will," she said. "After the investigation, though. She doesn't need this as well."

Before I could respond, my phone buzzed in my pocket. Penny. Of course.

"It's Penny," I said. "My two hours are almost up."

Mom nodded, decision made. "Then we should go to her. Together. It's time she knew what I was doing, I guess."

We headed for my truck. I couldn't shake the feeling that Mom still wasn't telling me everything. She'd answered my questions, explained her presence in the tunnels, but something about her demeanor suggested she was holding back. But she was my mother. If I couldn't trust her, who could I trust? Would she lie to me?

"Hopefully, she's in a good mood," I said, sliding into the driver's seat. "And listens before she arrests us both."

Mom smiled as she buckled her seat belt. "Your sister has always had a flair for the dramatic. Must be from your father's side."

CHAPTER 9

I dropped mom off to Penny, but didn't stay. I wanted no part in that discussion. Instead, I made my way to the phoenix sanctuary to check on Aurora.

"Good afternoon, Aurora," I said as gently as possible. Usually, she'd respond with a gentle mental greeting, but she just ruffled her feathers and turned away.

"Wrong... wrong... wrong... more wrong." Her agitated thoughts were chaotic.

I approached, noting her unusual posture. Phoenix body language was subtle. A cocked head could mean anything from mild curiosity to impending combustion. "Did something else happen?"

"Humans. Watching. Always watching. Still no egg." She mantled her wings protectively over her perch. *"Numbers wrong."*

"I understand. We are doing everything we can to find your child."

Instead of answering, she launched herself from her perch in a burst of flame, circling the sanctuary's upper dome before returning to her nesting area. I followed her with my eyes, trying to parse her unusual behavior while imagining what she must be going through. In all my years working with cryptids, I'd never seen any of them this disturbed. She had good reason. However, with any animal that could kill you in an instant, it's best to watch unusual behavior carefully.

The nesting area was a specially designed section, with individual alcoves for each phoenix family. I noticed something odd about Aurora's nest. She had built up branches and leaves to fill the void of the missing egg.

"I know this is a tough time. I assure you that everyone is looking for your egg."

"Where?" she asked.

"Where are they looking?"

"No... Where they are?"

"Well." I let out a breath. "There was a murder in town as well. So, two crises going on."

"What is this murd-der?"

"One human killed another and not for food."

Aurora's eyes widened. *"To take life for no reason. Sad. But my child still lives. If we are all important here. Find living, then find death maker."*

Her logic wasn't wrong. Had the egg been human, it would have received priority. I struggled for an answer or some type of defense, but she was right. "They are both important."

The phoenix shook her head. *"You think true, but not. What going on now?"*

I muttered, pulling up the video footage on my phone. "We know that your baby is still in the sanctuary, and we will find the egg. I'm going to review all the files and video again. You can watch with me if you like." I switched to the sanctuary's security logs, scanning for any unauthorized access during night hours. Several entries had been marked as 'routine maintenance' during times when we didn't perform maintenance. I'm sure my sister and her team already looked at this, but they would not be as familiar with the schedule I was. I had to mention it to Penny.

"Doctor Sterling!"

I turned to find Violet Newsome hurrying toward me. In contrast to the dark clothes, she wore the last time I saw her, she was now wearing what you'd expect a scientist's assistant to look like - a sharp blazer, practical shoes, glasses that somehow looked both professional and stylish. Her dark hair was pulled back in a neat bun, though a few strands had escaped, giving her a windswept appearance.

"I didn't expect anyone else here," she said, breathless. "Doctor Green asked me to check the temperature readings before he arrives."

Aurora's feathers bristled, small sparks dancing along their edges. *"False-speaking human. Watches too much. Asks wrong questions."*

" Why aren't you out there searching?" I asked, keeping my phone screen angled away from her. "Aurora is still very agitated."

"Oh? Doctor Green is very demanding and can be mean." Violet adjusted her glasses, peering at the phoenix with what seemed like genuine concern. Her cheeks were wet, and she looked scared. "Should I reschedule the observations?"

"What do you think?" It came out more angry than sarcastic. The scientists in this town, although smart, had no sense of etiquette or empathy.

"Given the circumstance, I guess we should." She looked conflicted.

"Might be best." I made a show of checking Aurora's vital signs. "Phoenixes can be sensitive to stress. Too much attention can affect their regeneration cycles."

"I understand. I'll leave her be and just grab a few numbers off the unit." Violet pulled out her tablet, making notes. "Though it's fascinating how their stress responses manifest physically. The color variations in their flame patterns, the changes in their..." She trailed off.

Her knowledge seemed impressive - almost too impressive for someone who'd only been working here a few weeks. She moved to check one of the environmental control panels, her fingers flying over the interface with practiced ease.

"How long did you say you've been studying phoenixes?" I asked, trying to sound curious.

"Oh, I wrote my thesis on their breeding patterns," she replied without looking up. "Specifically, the effects of temperature variation on egg development. It's crucial to maintain precise conditions. This is my first time in the field. After hearing the temperatures had been tampered with, I'm just going to make sure the readings on the climate controls are normal and then I will be out of your hair."

Aurora's mental voice was sizzling. *"Some human Cold-bringer. Egg-stealer. LIES."*

I fought to keep my expression neutral as Violet finished her work. "Well, I should finish checking in with the search party."

"Of course." She smiled. "Oh, and Doctor Sterling? I heard about what happened to Jerry McKinnon. Such a tragedy. How's his little basilisk doing?"

Something in her tone made me smile. "As well as can be expected," I said. "Ziggy is grieving deeply."

"I can imagine."

I let out a sign. "Listen, I know you are in a tough position with Green. If he gives you any trouble about not having your work done, you can send him to me or the sheriff. We'll explain it to him."

"Thank you." Giving a nervous smile, she gathered her things and headed away. "Best to keep them secure during such difficult times. We wouldn't want any more incidents."

As soon as she was gone, I turned back to Aurora. "Tell me everything you remember about the last night before and after your egg disappeared. Every detail."

The next hour was a crash course in phoenix perception. Their understanding of time and space differed from ours. They experienced events as layered moments, like looking at all the pages of a book simultaneously. Certain details stood out: the mention of seeing more people than normal, visits during the do not disturb time, and the precise timing of the extra people to avoid the guard rotation. She described the two times she left her nest, which helped to narrow down when the egg might have been taken. I needed to pass that on to Penny.

I cross-referenced the sanctuary's access logs with Green's published research schedule on my tablet. The discrepancies were subtle but significant. Small time gaps with check-ins and minor inconsistencies in the environmental data. Someone had been careful to make everything appear routine. I needed to check in with Penny on how her talk with

Doctor Green went and to share these inconsistencies her team may not know enough to catch.

Then, it hit me. Violet asked about Ziggy earlier. How did she know about the basilisk when most of the long-term residents had no idea he was in the community. Was I getting paranoid or was there something there?

"Protect the eggs," Aurora's thoughts pressed against my mind and disrupted my paranoid thoughts. *"The cold hurts them. Makes them sleep too deep. I know egg cold. Help."*

"I promise," I said, reaching out to stroke her crest. "We'll figure this out."

My phone buzzed. I read the text, "Let's meet for dinner at Rosie's and catch up. I have some more information, and I hope you do as well."

My stomach grumbled and the mention of dinner. It neared seven at night. I guess I needed to eat and catch up.

CHAPTER 10

Rosie's Diner was empty save for a few tables in the back. Penny was sitting alone in a booth on the opposite side of the room. I slid in on the leather and let out a breath. "What a day?"

"You're telling me," Penny said. "We have a lot to cover."

"How did your talk with Green go?" I asked.

"As you can imagine, it was frustrating with that man, but I was able to verify a few things. He is the real Doctor Green, and his credentials do check out. Apparently, a lot of his accounts and information online were hacked. It's easy to see why someone would go to the trouble to make him look fake online. Harry made a few phone calls and verified he was on the up and up. Green is an ass still the same. When he talks about phoenix care and research, he sort of sounds like Mom. It's an obsession. I can't imagine him doing anything to hurt an egg."

"Unless that's all an act."

"What do you mean?"

"I don't know. Maybe it's because I just don't like him. Who knows?"

Rosie walked up to the table, put a couple glasses of water down, and asked, "Are you ready to order?"

"Give us a few," Penny said, and Rosie scooted off.

"How did it go with mom?" I asked.

Penny sighed and dragged her hand down her face. "What in the literal hell? Did you actually see this plant she claims to be collecting?"

"Well, no but- "

She slammed her fist on the table. "I can't just take her at her word. It's a disturbance I don't need. What in the literal hell is she thinking?"

"She says that's why she didn't say anything."

"I don't buy it."

"You want me to make her show me?"

"No. I'll do it. But thanks."

"I had another conversation with his assistant," I said, hoping to change the subject.

"Violet?"

"Right. She paints a picture of Green as a strict by-the-book kind of guy with no tolerance for interruptions or lack of results. She teared up when I brought him up. I had the impression she was terrified of him."

Penny shook her head. "Great. Another young woman abused by an over inflated male ego."

"Hey, I'm sitting right here."

"Comment still stands. Besides, I don't consider you male."

"That's not much better."

"You're more like sort of male."

"Cute," I said. "I talked more with Aurora as well. According to her story, someone had to have grabbed the egg when she flew to gather food or use the bathroom. It was two brief windows, so someone had to be watching and waiting."

"Damn," Penny said. "I wish we could have cameras in the habitats."

"You know we can't. The cryptids let us observe when they want us to, but we can't spy on them."

"I know, I know. Just frustrating. Anything else?"

"Aurora also mentioned that more people were observing her. She thinks we all look alike, so it could be the same person, just watching longer."

"That tracks. Maybe they were tracking her patterns to determine when to steal the egg."

"Yeah, that's my guess. What about you?"

"Beyond what I told you about Green, we have been gathering evidence and coming up with a suspect list."

"Anything?"

"Well, the analysis of the venom came back, and you won't believe this. It was blue slushy."

"Slushy? As in the drink?"

"Yeah. From the concession stand of the theater." Penny narrowed her eyes. "Tell me, little brother, what does that tell you?"

I thought for a moment, and then it hit me. "This was not a planned murder. Something happened and Jerry was killed. They panicked and tried to frame Ziggy. That also explains why it was not a good imitation."

"Exactly," she said, smiling. "I'll make an investigator out of you yet. Further, the doctor says the neck wounds were made postmortem."

"Wait, how did he die, then?"

"It looks like a heart attack."

"The tranquilizer I bet. If they had a dose for Ziggy and shot Jerry with the same dose, it could have slowed his heart too much."

"That is the working solution. There was a small puncture in the chest where it appears he was shot with the dart."

"So, maybe his death was accidental."

"Possibly. Or they were aware what the dose would do and shot to kill on purpose. My guess is it could be someone familiar with the dosages."

"That will not help. Just about every scientist, guard, and person who works in the sanctuary has access to tranquillizer guns and know how to use them. Hell, even I do. Anything else?"

"Jerry's office was clean from prints, not even Jerry's, or any other evidence. It was obviously wiped down."

"What about the rest of the theater?"

"It's a public location. There would be tons of fingerprints and such."

"Other suspects?"

Rosie walked up at that moment. "Are you all ready to order?"

I looked at the menu quick and ordered a burger and my sister ordered a salad. Rosie lingered near the table.

"Everything okay?" I asked.

"Sorry," she said with an embarrassed smile. "I heard you talking when I walked up about suspects. Jerry came in here a lot. I don't want to talk out of turn, but you should talk to his ex-girlfriend. She's crazy."

"I wasn't aware he had one," Penny said, making a note. "Any idea of her name?"

"Crystal," Rosie said. "Crystal Lockhead, I believe. She lives in the bungalows near the town entrance."

"Thank you," I said, and Rosie left the table. "That is something. Ziggy said it was a woman. And beyond Violet, we don't have any other female candidates."

"We have mom."

"Come on. No way she's involved."

"We shall see. I'm sure Ziggy is certain, but we have to find more evidence beyond his smelling senses."

"Any other leads?"

Penny smiled. "There is a former employee that he fired. Some of the neighboring stores said it was bad. And guess what? The former employee is also a woman."

"I'm still stuck on the woman thing," I said. "Tommy was sure that he saw Green on his rounds."

"Green still denies that," Penny added.

"We should talk to Tommy again. Is it possible he saw someone dressed like Green or coming from a certain place and he assumed it was him? Distance might make a difference."

"Good point. Let's talk to him in the morning. I can swing by and get you at eight."

"That would be great. My first appointment isn't until ten."

"Sounds good."

"So, in summary, what do we have here?"

"We have a reputable witness, Tommy, who says he saw Green enter the building before the murder. Green denies it and Ziggy says he wasn't there. Ziggy says it was a woman, and we have his assistant, ex-girlfriend, and former employee with a possible motive. Plus, Mom. I am keeping her on the list."

"Whatever."

"It doesn't hurt that they are all female. And let's not forget the missing egg, with no leads except it must be stored somewhere cold. We will hopefully find it when I get the go ahead to search the labs. Video is useless so far, but hopefully more can be recovered. The video at the gates to the sanctuary is a lot to go through. It will take Harry days to review every camera. We are hoping he gets lucky sooner than later. Beyond that, nothing else. We believe the two are connected, but no evidence to really support it other than the notes found on Jerry's desk."

"According to TV, we need to answer means, opportunity, and motive."

"You watch too much TV, but you aren't wrong."

Rosie delivered our food, refilled the water, and started to leave. I stopped her. "Can I ask you a question?"

"Sure, dear."

"You don't happen to know the lady that used to work for Jerry that he recently fired?"

Rosie nodded. "Her first name is Bob. But I think that's a nick-name."

"So, girlfriend Crystal, female employee, Bob?"

"Sorry I don't have more."

"That helps, thank you," Penny said.

Before either of us could ask another question, Harry rushed into the restaurant and sat down with us. He was twitching with excitement. "I found something."

"Take a breath, honey," Penny said.

"Do you call all your employees, honey?" I asked.

"Don't be an ass." She turned back to Harry. "What did you find?"

Harry opened his laptop, and we gathered around his screen as he pulled up footage from the sanctuary's surveillance system. "As you know. The habitat lacks cameras, but several entry points exist between the town and the fence line and those do. Watch the timestamp here," he pointed. "See how it jumps?"

"Someone tampered with the records?" Penny leaned closer.

"Not just tampered. They wrote over them. But they missed something." Harry's fingers flew across the keyboard, pulling up lines of code. "There's a backup system that logs card swipes, separate from the main video network. Guess what it picked up on the night Jerry died?"

The data showed a card key swipe, followed by what looked like the door never closing.

"Someone propped the hatch open," I said. "Whose card was it?"

"It is an unregistered card. It shouldn't be able to open a door."

"Who has access to create a card like that? It had to be someone in the sheriff's office or a perimeter guard."

"So, it had to be law enforcement that did it and now covering their tracks?"

"And doing a pretty good job of it," Harry said. "If I hadn't been specifically looking for irregularities in the video patterns, I never would have found it."

"None of our suspects work then," I said.

"Not necessarily," Penny said. "There could be partners or a group. We just don't know much without more details."

"Speaking of details." Harry pulled up another screen, "Your mom came by today. We found something interesting in Doctor Green's research logs. Or rather, what's missing from them."

The logs showed gaps - subtle ones, but once you're aware what to look for, they were obvious. Times when equipment was signed out, but no results recorded. Temperature variations in the habitat units with no corresponding experiments logged. That happened around when the video stopped recording.

"Could be sloppy record-keeping," I said, though I didn't believe it. Doctor Green was many things, but sloppy wasn't one of them.

"Or it could be someone deliberately created gaps to hide some unauthorized activities?" Penny said. "Harry, can you cross-reference these times with the sanctuary access logs?"

"Already did. Check this out."

"There's a gap in Green's logs that aligned with the missing time on the footage," Penny said, reading the screen.

"Exactly," Harry said.

"We need more proof." She voiced what we were all thinking. "Circumstantial evidence won't be enough."

We spent the next hour reviewing the same evidence and suspects. We looked for some other way to view this. Penny had to keep reminding me to take in the complete picture, not just how I felt about Green.

Exhausted, we said our goodbyes after nothing new revealed itself. I headed out.

It was almost eleven when I got back to the clinic. Ziggy was asleep and resting. His scales looked a little better. Instead of disturbing him, I snuck out and headed home. I needed a shower and a good night's sleep.

CHAPTER 11

"Good morning," I said, climbing into Penny's jeep. I may have the 'talking to cryptids' gene, but she had the 'prompt' gene. Her punctuality was absolute. At 7:59, I stepped into the crisp morning air, and she was waiting. There were days where I would love to have the 'prompt' gene, but no matter how hard I tried, it was just never going to happen.

"Morning," she said, pulling away from the house. "Were you able to sleep any?"

"I did. Crashed without a choice. You?"

"A little bit. I'm fine."

"You look like crap," I said. Honesty between siblings, there's nothing like it. "I can do this on my own."

"You aren't even on the force. Nah, it will be fine."

"If you say so." We rode in silence for about ten minutes before I spoke up. "What's the plan with Tommy's interview. Good cop, bad cop. Are you going to lean on him? Maybe threaten?"

"You seriously need to stop watching so many cop shows. You went to high school with Tommy. We're just going to talk to him."

Heritage Crest was a transient town with so many scientists coming and going. Tommy was one of the handful of people like Penny and me that grew up in Heritage Crest. He was a good guy and even though we didn't hang out much, I still considered him a friend. Despite that, this was my first interrogation. "Got it. So, I'm good cop."

"You're no cop," she snapped. "Just a friend helping the community with a tragedy."

"You're no fun," I said.

She turned to me, and I saw in her face. I was talking to the sheriff, not my sister. "Listen and listen good. This is not fun. Someone is dead and there is a large theft of a living creature. Many are distraught and still in danger until we find this killer. We are not on an adventure, in a tv show, or anything else. You will follow my lead and do whatever I tell you. Understand?"

"Buzz kill." Humor was my defense mechanism, and it was hard to turn off the jokes when I was nervous. It took a moment to realize what I was doing and to notice the stress, worry, and concern on Penny's face. "Sorry. I will try to wrangle it in."

"Another thing," Penny said. "Based on the report from the medical examiner and the footage Harry was working, we can narrow it down to a two-hour window for Jerry's murder. Midnight to two in the morning. But for the love of God, say nothing. Let me give out the details where appropriate."

We rode in silence for the next five minutes and I felt instant relief when we pulled in front of Tommy's apartment complex. I was trying to stay quiet and reserved, but it was painful. We climbed the stairs to the second floor and knocked on the door. Penny turned to me and gave me the look. The one she perfected when we were kids that said, don't speak.

Tommy opened the door, and his eyes stretched wide. "Uh. Good morning. What's up?"

"Can we come in and talk?" Penny asked.

"Sure. I just got off, so I'm a bit of a mess."

We entered the small apartment and were ushered to the couch. Passing the open bedroom door, I saw a woman lying on her stomach with the blanket pulled up over her. It clung to her curves and slight frame, but I couldn't see any facial details. At first, I wondered if it was a dead body, but then she moved.

"What can I do for you?" Tommy asked, taking a chair opposite us.

Penny gave a half smile. "Now that some time has passed and your adrenaline has calmed, I just wanted to check in with you on what you saw and if you remember anything else."

Tommy's hand twitched on his bouncing left knee. I passed a glance to Penny. She saw it, too.

"Nothing more comes to mind," he said, giving it thought before speaking. "Doctor Green was at the door earlier that night. Then, on my next round through the area, I noticed all the lights still on in the theater and the door was ajar. I stuck my head in and called out and when there was no response, I thought I would make sure the building was secure."

"And that's when you found him?" I asked. Penny shot me a glare to shut up.

"Yeah. I came across him in his office with Ziggy a few feet away. His basilisk had turned on him and killed him."

"Actually, it turns out…" Penny kicked my leg, and I shut up.

"Anything else you can remember?" Penny asked. "Any minor detail might help?"

"Nothing comes to mind."

"And you are sure it was Doctor Green? Could you be mistaken?"

Tommy nodded. "I'm sure it was him."

"Ok. Thank you. Sorry to have bugged you," Penny said, standing.

"No biggie. Just headed to bed," Tommy said, leading us to the front door.

Penny exited first, and I turned to Tommy. "You have to tell me how you keep getting women. I'm struggling."

Tommy smiled. "We've only been seeing each other for a little over a week. I'll let you know how it works out."

Once I was back in the jeep, Penny turned on me and I was expecting a tongue lashing, but her face looked soft. "I know you're new to this, and I probably should have emphasized it more before going in. We don't feed the witnesses or suspects any information on what we know unless we must. That way they have a choice of messing up and giving us a detail they couldn't have known unless they were the killer."

My only response was simple. "I'm sorry."

"No, I'm sorry. I need you on this and I am being too harsh. Apparently, I need to get a little more sleep."

I put my hand on hers. "Hey, I understand, and no harm done."

She started the car up, and we pulled away. We hadn't driven too far when Penny said, "He seemed nervous. Not shaken, but like he was lying about something. I can't put my finger on it. I wonder if had something to do with the woman in his bed."

"You saw that," I said. "I asked him, and he said they've been dating a week. Maybe he didn't want to wake her."

"It seemed a little odd."

"You're telling me. I haven't had a date in forever."

Penny laughed, and I saw some tension leave her shoulders. "That's because you never listen to me."

My phone buzzed in my pocket. I retrieved it and read the message. "Looks like I had a cancellation. I don't need to be back until noon."

"After I dropped you off, I was going to go talk to Crystal," Penny said. "You want to go."

"The crazy ex-girlfriend? Hell, yeah. I would love to see a walking cliché."

CHAPTER 12

Penny drummed her fingers on the scratched metal table, studying the woman across from us. Crystal Lockhead - or 'Crazy Crys' as Jerry's neighbors had dubbed her when interviewed, was what you'd expect from someone who'd earned that nickname. Crystal had feathers stuck to her clothes and what appeared to be a homemade headdress fashioned from colorful materials and tiny bells. She wore an age-yellowed wedding dress with cat faces printed on dozens of small sticky notes haphazardly sewn across the bodice. Her hot pink hair twisted into dozens of tiny buns, each secured with a different colored rubber band. Her mouth only had lipstick on the top lip and the mascara had seen better days, possibly last week. She remained stunning, regardless. I had never met anyone so beautiful.

"Miss Lockhead," Penny said. "Thank you for seeing us."

"I figured you would come by soon." Tears slowly trickled down her cheek. "Jerry doesn't have any biological family left, and we were going to be married."

Penny and I exchanged looks. I cleared my throat and asked, "We understood that you two were not together anymore."

"Just a minor hiccup." She waved her hand as if brushing the statement away. "We were just taking a break."

"Can you tell us where you were two nights ago, between midnight and two in the morning?" Penny asked.

"Is that when he died?" Crystal asked. "How did he go? Was it a heart attack? I was always telling him to stay away from red meat."

"It's an ongoing investigation and I can't comment," Penny said. "Please, just answer the question."

"I just knew something terrible would happen to him!" Crystal's bright blue contact lenses made her eyes seem unnaturally large as she leaned forward. "I warned him about that pet. Did you know it's a basilisk?"

"We are aware," Penny said.

"The only one in town," Crystal continued. "They aren't really pets, but they aren't illegal either. It was a monster."

"Please. Stay focused. Your whereabouts two nights ago, please."

"I was here. Yes, it was the middle of the night, so I would've been here. And before you ask, I live alone. I only have eyes for my Jerry."

It was hard to put my finger on it, but the tears had dried up and she was talking like he may still be alive. I felt about as comfortable in the cramped living room as a Great Dane in a dog carrier. The vibes radiating off her made me jittery, but I still found her gorgeous. I spoke up and gained another look from Penny. "According to your social media posts, you and Jerry broke up eight months ago?"

"Eight months, two weeks, and four days." Crystal's smile was dreamy. What the hell was wrong with me? I needed a date. "Not that I'm counting. Jerry and I were soulmates, you know. Past lives and everything. I did a past life regression. We were star-crossed lovers in ancient Egypt. I was a high priestess, and he was-"

"Miss Lockhead." Penny interrupted. "Back to where you were. You said you were here alone. Can you remember what you were doing?"

"Oh, that's easy. I was conducting a ritual to remotely cleanse Jerry's aura of negative influences." She rifled through an enormous purple handbag covered in glitter and one enormous cat, producing a phone. "I livestreamed the whole thing online. Four hundred viewers! Well, mostly bots, but still."

We exchanged glances. Penny pulled out her notebook. "And this ritual involved what exactly?"

"Standard stuff. Candles, sage, my special crystal grid. I arranged his photos in a pentagram and burned some of his old t-shirts."

"His shirts?" My eyebrows shot up. "How did you get those?"

Crystal waved a hand dismissively again, her jewelry jingling. "Oh, he left them at my place. I kept them safe, of course. In my Jerry Box."

"Your Jerry Box?" Penny asked.

"For memorabilia! You know - movie ticket stubs, some hair from his brush, the tooth he got removed last year. Collectables." She must have noticed our expressions shift because she added, "The dentist was going to throw it away! What kind of person throws away a perfectly good tooth?"

Penny cleared her throat again. "Miss Lockhead, did you have any contact with Jerry in the weeks before his death?"

"Define contact." Crystal began playing with one of her pink hair buns. "I mean, I didn't talk to him directly. Not after that silly restraining order incident, blown out of proportion by the way. I respected his boundaries. Mostly. I just shopped at his grocery store. And joined his gym. And I signed up for the same pottery class, but that was pure coincidence. Occasionally, I would stop by his trash and collect dental floss, but never when he was around."

"Dental floss?" I asked and gained a glare from Penny to stay muted.

"Yes. I have his entire collection of dental floss over the past year. It is all cataloged by date and flavor!"

She dumped her purple purse onto the table. Among the cascade of objects were dozens of used dental floss pieces, each carefully labeled and stored in individual tiny Ziploc bags. She held one out to me. "See? This one's from last Christmas. You can still smell the turkey!"

"Miss Lockhead." Penny tried to ignore the conversation. She looked like she was developing a migraine. "Did Jerry mention having any enemies?"

"Only the shadow people who live in his walls. I tried to warn him about them. That's why I installed sixteen security cameras around his house. I don't have access anymore. He shut the whole thing down and threw it away. If he still had those, he might not had gone through this nasty business. It is a shame. I had an excellent view of his bathroom. Do you know he sings show tunes in the shower? I've composed a symphony based on his water usage patterns!"

Penny leaned forward. "What about Monday night? Did you see him then?"

"No! I was home the whole time, doing the cleansing ritual. I can prove it! That was why I needed my phone." Crystal started scrolling through her phone frantically. "Here's my livestream. It started at 9:45 PM - see the timestamp? And it went until about three because proper aura cleansing takes time, especially when you're dealing with negative influences like that beast he was harboring."

We watched as she turned the phone towards us, showing a dimly lit video of herself surrounded by candles, waving sage smoke over photographs while chanting. The timestamp in the corner matched her story. Penny shook her head. "And you didn't leave your apartment at all during this time?"

"Of course not! Breaking a ritual circle is seriously bad juju. Besides, my cats were helping, and they get very cranky if you interrupt their spiritual work." She clutched her phone to her chest. "Is that why you're here? You think I hurt Jerry? I would never! We're destined to be together in every lifetime. I even got a tattoo of him!"

She pulled up her sleeve and revealed an intricate tattoo of Jerry's face, surrounded by what appeared to be a pentagram made of tiny hearts. "And look!" She yanked up her dress to show her knee, where another tattoo declared 'JERRY + CRYSTAL 4EVER' in Comic Sans font. "There are seventeen of these. Would you like to see the one on my-"

"NO!" We both shouted in unison and Crystal dropped the dress she was pulling way too high.

Penny raised a hand. "That won't be necessary, Miss Lockhead. Just one more question. Did Jerry ever mention having problems with anyone? Any threats or concerns? Maybe an enemy?"

Crystal's expression darkened. "Besides that, dumb witch? He had to fire her, you know. She started acting crazy."

"Do you know her name?" I asked.

"Uh... Rob or knob. Something like that."

"Bob?"

"Yes, that's it. Bob."

"Do you know a last name?"

"No, sorry."

Penny closed her notebook. "I'm curious. You were under a restraining order and have been separated for over eight months. How did you know about the employee? We were led to believe that firing was fairly recent."

"Jerry told me about it when I ran into him at pottery class."

"Told you what?" Penny prompted.

"That he had to let her go. She was a creepy lady."

"Creepy lady?" Penny asked.

"Yeah. She kept leaving origami birds on his desk. Black ones with threatening messages on them. Jerry said it was probably her idea of a joke, but..." She leaned in conspiratorially. "I'm very sensitive to negative energy, and when he mentioned those birds, my crown chakra started tingling like crazy. That's always a bad sign."

"Did he mention anything else?"

"No, but he said the birds started showing up right after he asked her to straighten up. She was some ex-con who'd learned origami in prison." Crystal's eyes went wide. "Oh! And the birds were made from pages of death poetry! Jerry showed me one. It was filled with all that stuff about ravens and darkness. Super negative vibes."

We exchanged another glance. This was the first we'd heard about any origami birds. The search in his office had produced none. That was strange enough that it would stand out. Of course, he could have thrown them away.

"Thank you, Miss Lockhead. You've been very helpful." Penny stood, signaling the end of the interview. "We may need to contact you again if there are more questions."

"Of course! Anything to help find Jerry's killer." Crystal walked us to the door. "Oh, and if you talk to the origami lady. Tell her those paper birds she makes are throwing off her spiritual alignment. She should invest in some proper Madagascan leach cleansing. I can recommend a vendor."

"We will let you know if we need anything else in Jerry's death," Penny said.

"JERRY ISN'T REALLY DEAD!" Crystal shrieked, causing both of us to jump. "He's simply transitioning to his next incarnation. I've already prepared for the resurrection ritual. All I need is his body and three drops of unicorn tears."

She pointed to a Mason jar on a nearby shelf filled with what looked suspiciously like tap water and glitter. "See? Their tears are extra potent during the full moon."

"I can assure you..." I touched Penny's arm to stop her and shook my head no.

"Great." It was all I could manage as we slipped away from Crystal with courteous nods and smiles.

Leaving, we returned to the jeep.

"Interesting," I said. "Fascinating and all those other kinds of adjectives while I'm pretty sure Jerry's ex-girlfriend is more focused on their continuing relationship than homicide."

"Those origami birds are worth checking out." Penny was already pulling away. "The thing about the employee with a prison record and a thing for death poetry is a lead I wasn't expecting. That will help us narrow down who this Bob is, since everyone in town must go through a background check. I should find a name pretty quick."

"Awesome."

"Sometimes the best information comes from unexpected sources. Even if those sources keep their ex-boyfriend's pulled tooth in a memorabilia box."

"Don't remind me. I'm going to have nightmares about that." I shuddered. "Was it me or did she seem like super model beauty?"

"She was pretty. Why?"

"I love Jerry, but she was way out of his league. Do you think that could be something?"

"Maybe, but I doubt it. I think her personality skewed the looks."

"Yeah, I guess."

"Are you in love, little brother?"

"No. She's pretty but..."

"It has been a while. If you would just take me up on the women I try to send your way. You might find love."

I pointed at her. "No. I'm fine. You need to stop."

Penny laughed and I could see more tension leave her shoulders. She pointed back towards the door we just left. "Don't worry, I'm not stupid enough to connect you with someone with that many challenges. I sort of want you to be happy."

"Uh, huh." I gave her a playful look of skepticism.

As we drove back to my clinic, I couldn't help but wonder if Crystal's livestreamed ritual was the airtight alibi, it seemed. After all, I had seen enough cop shows to understand the line between eccentric and dangerous could be remarkably thin. But my gut told me Crystal Lockhead, despite her peculiarities, was what she appeared to be - a woman whose love had twisted into obsession, but not murder. She was too pretty to kill someone. I just hoped it was my gut talking and not something else.

The origami birds, though. That was another story entirely. I had learned long ago that the smallest details often held the biggest secrets. And something about those black paper ravens, folded from pages of threats, sent a chill down my spine that had nothing to do with crown chakras or spiritual alignment.

CHAPTER 13

Penny stopped her jeep in front of my clinic. The parking lot was alive with some kind of pixie protest outside the front doors. Dozens of tiny, glowing beings hovered near the entrance, wielding miniature picket signs that read "No Basilisks!" and "Keep Our Clinic Safe!" in glitter writing.

"Really?" I muttered. "It's only been a few days."

"Want me to disperse them?" Penny asked.

"No." I dragged my hand down my face. "It will only make things worse."

"You sure?"

"Yeah, you got more important things to do. Talk to you later." I got out and heard her chuckling as I shut the door. Glad she could still laugh.

Alice met me at the door with a steaming cup of coffee and an apologetic expression. "They started gathering around dawn. Mrs. Pembroke brought them coffee and tiny donuts, which... probably wasn't helpful."

"She started this?" I asked.

"Not sure, but she is definitely supporting them."

I watched as one energetic pixie did loop-de-loops with a sign that appeared to be written in glow in the dark tissue paper barely glued to the poster board.

"Don't they realize Ziggy's just staying here since his owner was murdered? He's in protective custody, so to speak."

"I tried telling them that." Alice dodged a pixie who'd had clearly too much caffeine. "But they're insisting that all basilisks should be banned from the clinic. They started a hashtag campaign: #NoMoreSnakes."

"Basilisks aren't even technically snakes." I sighed, taking a much-needed sip of coffee. "They're a unique subspecies of-"

My phone buzzed - Penny calling. "Please tell me you're not calling about the pixie protest."

"Nah, that is your problem." My sister sounded distracted. " I forgot to ask when you were done for the day so we can catch up again."

Alice and I walked inside, and I glanced at my schedule for the day, already knowing I'd need to rearrange it. "How about four?"

"Perfect. Have a good day?"

"It will be. First, I need to deal with some politically motivated pixies."

"Do I want to know why they are out there?"

"Probably not. See you soon."

I turned to Alice. "I'm assuming our first appointment is here."

"They are," Alice said. "Room three. You need anything else?"

"Try to explain to our tiny protesters that species discrimination isn't exactly aligned with the clinic's values? And I would hate for them to be banned."

"On it." She nodded. "But you know I can't understand them. Also, you might want to make sure the window is closed in the examination room. They've started chanting nonsense."

Sure enough, the air was filled with high-pitched voices singing. *"Hey hey, ho ho, basilisks got to go!"* It would've been more intimidating if they weren't each the size of my thumb. People would hear squeaks, but I could make out the words.

The day was a blur of one appointment over the other. I barely had time to use the bathroom twice and thank goodness for crackers in the breakroom or I might have starved. However, the day wasn't all bad. Sparkles didn't come in and there were no emergencies. It was close to four when I finally made my way up front. I had almost forgotten about the protest, but those little bigots were still out there.

"They're still at it," I said.

"This is a new shift. I think the others got tired," Alice said, a slight smile.

"Are they causing any problems?"

"Nope. They've been perfect little protestors."

"That's something, I guess. If you don't need anything from me, I think I will head out."

"There was one thing." Alice looked down, took a deep breath, and met my eyes.

"What it is?"

"I would like to adopt Ziggy. I know how to handle a basilisk, and the poor guy is all alone. He has been through enough to be forced to deal with those fear mongering pixies. I want to give him a home."

I smiled. "Are you sure?"

"Certain."

"Then, sure. Let me ask him. I think that will be nice."

I walked to the back and before I could say anything, Ziggy looked up, and said, "Yes, oh yes please. She is not warm-scary. So nice."

Ziggy was overjoyed to live in a new home. His fear of abandonment was palpable until the mention of Alice brought a glimmer of hope. He and Alice would be great together. I shared it with Alice, and she started to cry. I patted her arm awkwardly. I did not deal with women crying very well.

Twenty minutes and one sneaky exit later out the back door, I walked into the Heritage Crest Sheriff's Station. The place always felt like a strange mix of modern law enforcement and a real estate office. Nothing like the shows.

Penny was in her office, surrounded by files and what appeared to be surveillance footage playing on multiple screens. She sat at her computer, typing rapidly. The cramped office had a standard issue filing cabinet marked "Cryptid Evidence - Do Not Open Without Gloves."

"Good, you're here," Penny said without looking up. "Harry cleaned up the footage from the night of the murder."

"Do we have a face?" I asked.

"Unfortunately, no. I've been watching it over and over."

"Is there any way to clean it up more?"

"This is the best we're going to get."

I leaned closer to the screen. A small, hooded figure entered the theater. "Those timestamps." I pointed to the corner of the screen. "They match the time window of the murder."

"Exactly." Penny sighed. "But here's where it gets weird. There is no footage of Green and the figure on the screen was petite and has their face hidden. Which means..."

"Tommy lied to us." I frowned. "There is no way that figure could be Green. They're too small. He could not have mistaken this figure."

Before we could discuss this further, Deputy Rivera stuck his head in. "Sheriff? There's a situation at the monthly Cryptid Protection League meeting. Someone's calling for all basilisks to be registered as dangerous animals."

Penny groaned. "Let me guess. The pixies got organized?"

"They were just walking around with signs. I didn't take them seriously," I said. "I had no idea they would visit the CPL."

"It's worse." Rivera grimaced. "They've got a petition. With glitter."

Penny rubbed her temples. "Right. Mark, you're coming with me. We need to stop this before it gets out of hand."

CHAPTER 14

The Cryptid Protection League met in the town hall, a Victorian building that somehow looked both imposing and whimsical with its cute cherub statues and frosted windows. Today, concerned citizens, cryptid owners, and what appeared to be the entire pixie population packed the meeting room.

Mrs. Pembroke stood at the podium, reading from a scroll that sparkled. "And furthermore, given the recent tragic events, we propose that all basilisks be required to have their eyes removed and be registered with the sheriff's department as Class 3 Dangerous Creatures. He killed his owner. We can't allow him in our community. He is a menace."

"Oh no," I yelled. "Not the Class 3 designation."

Penny squeezed my arm in warning as several heads turned our way. They usually reserved the Class 3 designation for creatures posing significant risks to public safety. Like dragons with anger management issues or chupacabras going through rebellious phases. Putting basilisks in that category would make them impossible to keep as pets.

"Mrs. Pembroke," I spoke up from the back of the room, trying to keep my voice steady. "May I address the council?"

The room went quiet, except for the soft tinkling of pixie wings. I made my way to the podium, very aware of all the eyes, human and otherwise, following my movement.

"I understand everyone's concerned about safety," I said. "But let's look at the facts. In the past five years, there has been exactly zero incidents of basilisk-related petrification in Heritage Crest. Zero! You know what we have had, though? Seventeen cases of unicorn-induced rainbow damage to public property, twenty-three instances of griffin aerial showboating requiring roof repairs, and let's not forget last summer's Great Pixie Stardust Bomb Incident."

Several pixies had the grace to look embarrassed. The town hall's east wall still glowed when the sun hit it from a certain direction.

"The point is," I said. "We can't start discriminating against entire species based on fear and misconception. Ziggy isn't just Jerry's pet. He's a member of our community. He is going through a mourning right now. He has been here for years, and no one had a problem.

"We didn't know he was here," a random pixie yelled out.

"Exactly. Because he isn't a threat to anyone. And the evidence increasingly suggests he's innocent."

"What evidence?" someone called from the back.

I exchanged a look with Penny, who gave a slight nod. "Jerry was killed by reaction from being shot with a tranquilizer gun, not basilisk venom or Ziggy's stare. He was killed by another human."

A murmur floated through the crowd. The pixies stopped sparkling quite so aggressively.

"I've known Ziggy since he was rescued," I added. "Treated him, talked with him, and watched his bond with Jerry grow. If you could hear him, you would know his nature. The basilisk I know wouldn't hurt anyone, let alone the person he loved most in this world. You should all be ashamed of yourselves."

The room was silent for a moment. Then, from near the ceiling, a tiny voice said, *"But what about the glitter?"*

"What about the what?" I blinked. It took everything for me to push down my urge to rage. I kept telling myself they didn't have a grasp on human concepts. "All that glitters is not gold."

There was a collective gasp from the flying cryptids. A pixie fluttered down to eye level. *"But sir, if we can't protest basilisks, what are we supposed to do with all this activist glitter?"*

I pinched the bridge of my nose and took a deep breath. "Maybe redirect it toward actual problems? Like the pterodactyl who keeps drawing inappropriate pictures in the sky with his cloud manipulation above the elementary school?"

"Ooh!" The pixie's wings perked up. *"Anti-aerial graffiti campaign! With glitter!"*

Immediately, the room felt less tense. The pixies began discussing new protest possibilities, their previous anti-basilisk fervor forgotten in the face of a more interesting target.

Not a single human objected or said anything else on the subject of basilisks. The room dispersed, and another idea occurred to me. I turned to Penny. "What if we got it wrong and this has nothing to do with the phoenix? What if someone found out about Ziggy and killed Jerry or had an argument about it?"

"You mean two unrelated incidents. That's a thought. We need to think through all possibilities."

As the meeting devolved into smaller discussions of the few remaining people, Penny's phone buzzed. Her expression darkened as she read the message.

"What is it?" I asked.

"We have the name and address of the fired employee." Penny glanced around to make sure no one was listening. "And guess what else? Tommy Chen filed a maintenance request for the phoenix climate control system yesterday. The report said he heard strange noises coming from inside the control box."

Tommy Chen, the security guard who'd found Jerry's body. The same Tommy Chen who'd mentioned seeing Dr. Green entering the theater that night. The liar. "I looked at it yesterday. It was fine."

"We need to..." I stopped as another buzz from Penny's phone interrupted me.

Her face was pale. "Change of plans. Tommy just missed his start of shift check-in. This can't be a coincidence."

"That doesn't sound good."

"Odd to the say the least. We should check it out."

"He has to know that someone would have noticed."

"For sure. And according to Harry, no one has left the facility." Penny looked across the room and found Mrs. Pembrook. "Give me just a minute. I need to ask Mrs. Pembrook a favor."

"Sure, I'll wait out by the jeep," I said.

CHAPTER 15

The exit to the town hall was in the back of the room. I made it through the crowd with little to no interaction with the concerned citizens. Hopefully, this was the last we would hear about basilisk fears. But part of me knew it wouldn't be.

I paused at the exit as movement caught my eye in the second to last pew. A familiar silhouette stood – Violet Newsome, her newly lightened auburn hair unmistakable even in the fluorescent light. My hand instinctively moved to my phone, debating whether to text Penny, but curiosity won out. What was Doctor Green's assistant doing at an anti-basilisk meeting?

She noticed me and her eyes lit up in genuine surprise. "Doctor Sterling. What are you doing here?"

"Same as you, it seems." I gestured vaguely with my hand. "To see what this craziness is about."

"Guilty. Curiosity got the better of me. Now I have a headache." She smiled, looked away shyly, and then, back at me. Was she flirting? If so, she was not good at it. Of course, I was no expert myself. "Though I imagine talking to cryptids all day probably gives you a worse one."

Something in her tone made me pause. It wasn't quite mocking, but there was an undercurrent I couldn't place. Professional curiosity? Envy? Skepticism?

"Depends on the creature," I said, keeping my voice light. "Sparkles, the hypochondriac unicorn is definitely migraine-inducing. The quieter ones, not so much."

Violet nodded with a smile. "Sparkles was in the apothecary store earlier with Mrs. Pembroke. Something about her horn developing a British accent."

Despite my exhaustion, I laughed. "Of course she was."

Violet's expression remained fixed in polite interest, though her fingers tapped an irregular rhythm against her purse strap. "I've never actually seen a unicorn up close. They really are quite stunning. Doctor Green's research focus doesn't intersect with them much."

"Just phoenixes, right?" I asked, trying to sound casual. "How's the research coming? I don't know if the observation reports are yours or his."

A flicker of something happened in her eyes. Annoyance? Or maybe alarm crossed her face before her professional mask slipped back into place. "Mostly me. We're in a critical observation phase. Doctor Green prefers to keep initial findings private until we have conclusive data and then, I write them up."

"Makes sense. I'd love to read them some time."

Violet shifted her weight towards the door. Her hand tightened almost imperceptibly on her purse. That caught my attention.

"It's unpublished research," she said, a slight flush creeping up her neck. She walked towards me. "Preliminary findings only."

"Understood. Well, maybe someday I can take a look at them." I stepped aside to let Violet exit the row, noticing how she automatically checked her watch, an expensive piece that seemed out of place on a research assistant's salary. "Are you heading back to the lab?"

"Yes," she said, a touch too quickly. "Doctor Green asked me to check on some experiment readings."

"Do you ever get a break?"

She gave a tight smile. "Are you asking me out?"

"No," I said, loudly. The word caught in my throat. My words surprised her, and I realized how I must have sounded. "Sorry. I didn't want you to think I was being inappropriate. I didn't mean to shout."

"I was kidding," she said. "I do work a lot. Science doesn't keep regular hours, Doctor Sterling."

"Mark." I corrected. "And tell me about it. Just last week I had to deliver a baby newton at three in the morning. Proud parents, but the father kept trying to challenge me to a duel with his six horns for touching his mate inappropriately."

Violet laughed, and for a moment she seemed relaxed. "That must be interesting, hearing their actual thoughts."

"Mostly. it's complaints about the food and requests for belly rubs," I said. It earned another laugh.

"Sounds like me on any given night," she said.

I nodded. Her personality shifted with each statement. She shifted from meek, to controlling, to extravert right before my eyes. It had to be my imagination. How many personas did she have? "Violet, can I ask you something?"

Her smile remained fixed, but her eyes darted to her watch again. "Of course."

"How well do you know Tommy Chen?"

The question caught her off guard. A series of emotions flashed across her face too quickly to interpret before settling back into careful neutrality. She was not good in masking surprise, but she was better than anyone I knew in shifting immediately back to calmness. I touched a nerve. "The security guard? Not well. I've seen him around, obviously, but our paths didn't cross much. Why?"

"He mentioned seeing Doctor Green at the theater the night Jerry was killed, but Green insists he was working all evening with you."

Violet's composure slipped for a fraction of a second. "Tommy must be mistaken. We were both at the lab that entire evening." She checked her watch yet again, the gesture becoming a tell. "I really should get going."

"Sorry to have kept you."

She nodded, her movements now precise and economical as she slid out the door. "Good night. I hope your migraine improves."

"Good night." I smiled. "Oh, and give my regards to Doctor Green. Tell him if he has questions about phoenix bonding patterns, my door's always open."

Her smile tightened, leaving me alone in the back of the room. Sleep would be even more elusive tonight. The encounter left me with more questions than answers. Violet's responses had been perfect - perhaps too perfect. There was a rehearsed quality to them, as if she'd prepared for exactly these kinds of questions.

Penny approached. "You ready?"

"Yeah," I said. The last traces of Violet's taillights vanished into the night. "I had an interesting conversation with Violet Newsome. You might want to put someone on her."

"She is still on the suspect list. Did something else happen to make you think she's involved?" Penny was alert.

I thought about Violet's expensive watch, her defensive posture, her carefully crafted answers. "I think there's more to her story than she's telling us. And right now, that's enough to warrant a closer look."

"I'll have Rivera follow her," Penny said. "Anything specific I should tell him to look for?"

I considered this for a moment. "Anything unusual."

"Got it. Let's go, still no word from Tommy."

I was already heading for the door, Penny right behind me. As we rushed out, I could hear the pixies enthusiastically planning their new anti-graffiti in the air campaign. Something about tactical glitter deployment and aerial surveillance. They were going to start right away.

"Mark," Penny said as we reached her jeep, "I'm officially deputizing you for this investigation. We need your gift, your knowledge of the sanctuary's systems, and your connection to the magical community."

"What about the clinic?"

"You can still work there. I want to make sure anything you find or do is covered under our legal protection." She smiled. "This is bigger than upset unicorns and dragon hiccups now."

She was right, of course. I looked at the empty space where Violet's car used to be. The jeep started up, and we were off. As we sped toward the security station, I couldn't help thinking about Ziggy, alone with Alice, his scales still dulled by grief. Whatever was going on here, someone had tried to frame an innocent creature for murder. And if there's one thing you learn growing up in a town full of supernatural beings, it's that people who hurt animals rarely stop there. Could Violet Newsome be one of those?

CHAPTER 16

The security station in the center of town loomed ahead. Its small building had no signage and hid in plain sight between a lawyer's office and a hairdresser. Officer Rivera was already there when we arrived.

"I have the boys out searching for him along his route," Rivera said as Penny and I approached.

"Thank you," Penny said. "Tomorrow we'll have the approval to search the labs for the egg. We can look there for Tommy as well if we don't find him."

"Will do."

"Have you been inside?" Penny asked.

Rivera shrugged. "I just got here a minute ago."

"No problem," Penny said.

"When was the last check in?" I asked.

"It's been three hours, and they have to check in hourly with the main gate." Rivera said.

"I thought he worked grave shift. It's only eight o'clock," I said.

"I asked," Rivera said, and he looked at his notebook. "Apparently, he switched shifts with a Chris Tremane."

"Thank you. Did you reach out to Chris?

"I did. Apparently, he is at an anniversary dinner with his wife in Nashville."

"I appreciate it. You can get back on the murder case. Mark and I will pull on this thread," Penny said.

"You got it, boss."

Penny and I walked up the small building's steps. The sanctuary's security office was empty when we entered, Tommy's coffee mug half empty on his desk. His phone lay abandoned next to a half-eaten donut, the screen showing an unsent text message: "Mark. I've made a mistake. I need to share some stuff with you. I know who killed Jerry and stole the phoenix egg. Need to talk to you ASAP."

Penny picked up the phone. "Do you know anything about this?" She pointed to the last entry.

"It never got to me. It's unsent."

"Did he send you any other messages like this?"

"No. I would have told you."

"We need to find Tommy. Seems like our instinct was correct. These two things are connected. Why did he reach out to you instead of me?"

"No idea. Maybe he was afraid of getting in trouble." I pointed to the phone. "This kind of thing does happen on TV."

"Not now." Penny spoke into her radio. "Harry, I need everything you can find on any logins for Tommy Chen for the past twenty-four hours."

Static crackled, then Harry's voice came through: "Already on it. You will not like this. He used his credentials near the south barrier twice. Once ninety-three minutes ago and another time about fifty minutes ago."

"Why would he use it twice?" I said. "It doesn't make any sense."

"Exactly." Harry's typing could be heard in the background. "And here's where it gets weirder. The same credentials were used to access the phoenix sanctuary fifteen minutes after that."

"Let me know immediately if it gets used again."

A sudden crash from outside made us both jump. Through the window, I could see several pixies zipping past, their wings leaving trails of iridescent smoke in the air.

"Um, Sheriff?" One sparkly pixie pressed her face against the glass. "We might have found something. You know that anti-graffiti surveillance we were planning?"

"Already?" I raised an eyebrow.

"Keep on it, Harry. Thanks." Penny holstered her radio and turned to the pixie. "What are they saying?"

"Hold on," I said.

"Well, we got eager about our new mission and started early. And we saw someone leaving Unit C about twenty minutes ago. They were carrying something that looked like a huge egg. It was a woman with red hair. She took it from the supply room there. I thought you would want to know."

"The pixies saw something suspicious," I translated.

Penny and I exchanged looks. "Violet?" she asked.

"Possibly," I said.

Another pixie zoomed up to the window, this one covered in what appeared to be tactical green shimmer dust in various camouflage patterns. *"We tracked the red-haired lady to the old maintenance tunnels behind Unit C! Some of us could fit through the vents and... Oh my, is that a pterodactyl coming back?"*

"They say she went into the tunnels behind Unit C," I said.

A roar shook the building, followed by the distinctive sound of pixies screaming *"Retreat!"* in very high-pitched voices.

"What the hell?" Penny rushed to the window. "What did your pixies do?"

Indeed, the pterodactyl was dive bombing the pixies and snapping at them with its oversized beak. The flying dinosaur was not a meat eater and normally very docile. The pixies did it this time.

"I think," I said, watching another bunch of pixie's dodge left. They were too fast for him. "The protest has caught the anger from our air graffiti offender."

The pixies had regrouped, now sporting what appeared to be tiny tactical vests made from paperclips and leaves. Their leader - the one wearing the most glitter camouflage - saluted as we passed.

"Operation Glitter Justice is a go, Sheriff! We told that foul creature you had asked us to get rid of the problem. We were firm with him."

"What did they say?"

"They told our graffiti artist you asked them to stop him," I said.

"Good work," Penny said with admirable seriousness. "But I didn't ask them to do anything of the sort. You need to go make peace with him before he eats all of you up."

"Peace? With what, anti-glitter spray?" A pixie scoffed. Then, more worriedly: *"Wait, is that a thing?"*

I stepped outside and screamed, "Come down here right now?"

The pterodactyl, a teenager, and pixies immediate froze in mid-air and came to the ground near me. They kept their distance as I stared the group down.

"We don't have time for this," Penny said.

"Just a second." I addressed the group. "Listen, this stops now before someone gets hurt."

The pterodactyl sent his vibes to me. "They started it. I was minding my own business, and they came at me."

"This stops," I reiterated. "You aren't innocent. Stop with the pictures in the clouds near the school. You can do it over your habitat, but no more. I would be happy to tell your parents or send you back to Arizona."

"Please don't, Doctor Green. I will stop."

"Yay," a pixie said.

I turned to them and snapped. "You, too. Stop. Work on kindness, not anger. You were supposed to protest, not attack. If you come at him again, and it is near his habitat, I won't be able to stop him from chasing you and he may catch someone. Then, someone may really get hurt. Got it."

All the cryptids nodded and flew off in different directions.

"Damn, you have a temper," Penny said.

"It's just been a bad few days."

"I hear you. We moved toward Unit C around the corner. The door was shut, and Penny scanned her credentials.

"Penny," I grabbed her arm, pointing to a small rectangle container next to me. I punched up the settings on its tiny display. "That box, it's the kind used for cold storage. But its temperature readings are all wrong. They're way too low."

"Cold storage," she muttered. "They're keeping the eggs in stasis for transport."

"Yes," I said, opening it up. "Empty. No one would have just left it here. We've to go find the lady in the tunnel. Seeing this container, I bet it's Violet."

"We don't know she did this. Especially with all the other potential suspects. The pixies only said it was a woman, right?"

"Correct. So, what now?"

"We're spread way too thin. Call mom. If there really is a phoenix egg down there, we'll need her expertise since she has recently been sneaking around. You wait here for her and then follow."

"Follow?"

"I'm going to see what I can find."

"Next time," I said, "maybe I should stick to treating unicorn horn anxiety and dragon hiccups?"

"Please." Penny smiled. "You'd be bored within a week."

She was right, of course. I wouldn't admit it. Especially not with a potentially murderous egg thief in the tunnel, Tommy missing, and an army of glitter-armed pixies above. Sometimes, dignity is all a veterinarian-turned-deputy had left.

I pulled out my phone, but before I could dial, Penny disappeared down the tunnel. Behind me, I could hear the pixies beginning what sounded suspiciously like a military cadence:

I don't know, but I've been told,
Pterodactyls are really slow,
Sound off - sparkle sparkle,
Sound off - glitter glitter."

I looked up and they were keeping their distance. I guess they found a loophole. I didn't say they couldn't yell at each other. They were annoying little cryptids. Though I had to admit, the tactical pixies were a new touch.

CHAPTER 17

Mom and I entered the tunnel. She had only taken ten minutes to meet me, which didn't give Penny too much of a head start. I wanted to yell to my sister that we were coming down, but I thought better of it when I realized the egg thief could be hiding somewhere. I would not take any chances with mom near me.

"And they were sure it was a woman?" Mom asked after I gave her a quick recap.

"That's what they said. It lines up with what Ziggy sensed and, more importantly, the cameras seem to confirm."

The beams of our flashlights swept across the damp stone walls, casting long shadows that danced and flickered. Each time I thought I saw a person moving, it ended up being a trick of light. We were literally chasing shadows.

The air in the tunnel was thick with the musty scent of age and abandonment, tinged with something else – something warm and spicy that reminded me of cinnamon and wood smoke.

Mom said, "Do you smell that?"

"I do, but I can't quite place it."

"That would be the phoenix egg. It's fiery, yet soothing."

"Yes, that's it. I knew I smelled it before."

"We should be able to follow that scent," Mom nodded to a thought she had. "Do you think this thief knew about these tunnels beforehand?"

"These passages weren't exactly a secret." I kept my voice low.

"Other than me, these haven't been used in decades and are kept locked. Maybe the person we're after has been in this town a long time?"

"That would narrow down the list, but I don't think so. The faked credentials on the gates and avoiding showing their face on cameras tells me they may just have planned out each step meticulously."

"I guess. Though I doubt many people are aware these passages extend this far under the town."

"Left, or right?" I asked, studying the diverging passages in front of us. The one on the left sloped downward, while the right-hand tunnel maintained its current level but curved sharply about twenty feet in and then up to a high grade.

Mom's eyes moved from side to side as she took in a deep sniff of the air and searched her memory. "I believe the left tunnel curves back around to another part of the sanctuary. There isn't really anything out that way. I would suggest we go right. We could split up."

Before I voiced my objection, a faint sound echoed from the right-hand passage. It sounded like a click and then footsteps. Without speaking and wide eyed, we both moved toward the passage, trying to keep our own footsteps as quiet as was manageable on the uneven floor.

We crept along for several minutes before stopping. Silence returned. I questioned whether we'd heard rats. However, I had another concern growing. We hadn't yet encountered or even heard Penny. Did she go down the other tunnel?

"How long do you think the egg has?" I asked.

"Assuming they know what they're doing and have kept it dormant at a certain temperature, I would say a few days if we're lucky. Less if the thief hasn't been keeping it at the correct status temperature." Mom's tone was worried. "And when it does destabilize it will not be good."

Mom didn't need to finish the thought. I knew an unstable phoenix egg ignited in a small burst of flame. The blast would injure anyone within ten feet, if not kill them. Further, if the egg was around anything flammable, it might start a fire that would be very difficult to snuff.

The tunnel curved again, and I caught another sound. This time, I recognized a footstep followed by a muffled curse. It was no rat this time. We were getting closer. The cinnamon and wood smoke scent were stronger now, almost overwhelming in the enclosed space.

Mom grabbed my arm, pulling me to a stop. Her flashlight beam had caught something on the ground. A person was crouched over.

"Stand up," I ordered, using my best authoritative voice.

The person turned. It was Penny. "Settle down there, little brother."

Mom rushed forward. "Are you okay, honey?"

Penny waved her off. "I'm fine. I followed the scent here, but this hatch is locked and I'm sure they went out this way. I tried my keys, but they didn't work. So, looking for an emergency release or something."

"Stand back, honey," Mom said. "These were built before all the regulations on emergency exits and such. As far as I know, there are only a few keys left for the door. The primary set hangs in the town's security office."

Penny and I looked at each other. Was this how our little adventure started? Did someone steal the keys and hurt Tommy?

Mom smiled and pulled out a key ring. She handed it to Penny. "Lucky for you, I am as old as dirt and still have my original keys. It's the green key."

"How can you remember that?" Penny asked. She found the key, slipped it in the lock and the bolt turned. She handed the ring back to mom, drew her side arm, and pushed on the door. "Does this have to do with your illegal plant harvesting?"

"No honey. Brain like a steel trap." Mom tapped the side of her head with an index finger.

"Stay back and protect that brain," Penny said. She climbed out ahead of us and surveyed the area and then waved us up. "It looks safe."

We climbed out of the tunnel and I almost gasped. We were behind the bushes across from the movie theater. Jerry's place, to be specific. "Holy crap."

"Another coincidence," Penny said. "They're adding up."

"I told you, get the hell out of here." A new voice joined the conversation.

We all turned towards the voice, yelling at us. Walking across the street, an older man was shaking his fist at us. His face was contorted in what could only be described as rage. The three of us stepped out from the shadows.

Mom spoke first. "What are you yelling about, Konas?"

The old man stopped in his tracks and blinked rapidly. He took in the three of us. You would think seeing the sheriff was enough to straighten him up, but it was mom that caught his attention. "Oh Clara. Kids. Sorry. I thought you were that crazy weird lady again."

I opened my mouth to speak, but penny put her hand over it, shook her head, and said, "Let's wait for what mom gets."

Konas ran the local apothecary shop. He sold herbs, CBD oils, and soaps he made himself. He had been in town for a little over a decade. Not as long as us, but still longer than most. Everyone knew he has a crush on Mom, and even though Dad passed away twenty years ago, she still refused to date anyone.

"No harm," Mom said. "Though I'm not keen on you yelling at people walking on the street. I thought you were nicer than that."

Konas ran his hand over his thinning gray hair, looked away, and then back, with a smile. "Oh, I am, but that stalker lady just doesn't listen."

"Stalker?" Mom asked.

"Yeah, poor Jerry. It had to be horrible for him. I mean, not as horrible as death, but still."

The town had a few thousand people, and it was no surprise everyone knew Jerry was dead. Still, it was pretty clear who he was referring to, but to Mom's credit, she still asked while feigning ignorance. "He had a stalker?"

"Oh yeah, she changes her hair color a lot. A wig, I guess, I don't know. But either way, it was still the same person. She was pretty, but crazy as a loon. We all call her crazy Crys. I caught her out in these bushes more times than I can count."

"What was she doing?" Penny asked. I guess the silence part was over.

Konas turned to her. "Writing in some notebook. She just watched and took notes."

Penny looked at me. We both knew who he was talking about, Crystal Lockhead. She searched her phone and pulled up a picture. "Just to be sure, is this her?"

Konas leaned in and squinted. He looked left, then right. "Yep, that's her."

"Have you seen her here tonight?" I asked.

Penny shot me a glare, and I mouthed, sorry.

"Not tonight, no. Last time I saw her was a few nights ago when the basilisk killed Jerry."

"Ziggy did not..."

"I will handle this," Penny said, cutting me off.

"We are still investigating the cause of death," she said to Konas. "Do you know about what time you saw her that night?"

"Around eleven, I believe. Yeah, that had to be. I was here finishing up my brew." He pointed to his shop next to the cinema. "She wasn't subtle about it. I saw her from across the street."

Penny nodded. "Thank you. Did you see anyone around this area tonight? Maybe a bit before us."

"I didn't, but I was in back most of the night. I only saw you when I was locking up."

"You have been a big help," Penny said. "You can head home."

"Sure. What are you doing out here, anyway?"

"Just investigating some strange reports," Penny said. She motioned us to follow her.

"It was great seeing you tonight, Clara." Konas was blushing. "Maybe, we can grab coffee some time."

"We'll see," Mom said. "Right now, I have to help my kids."

"Oh, I completely understand. Good night, all. And sorry again, for the early mistaken identity."

Frustrated, we started down the street. Whomever had the egg, eluded us, but couldn't have gone far. However, it wasn't all bad news. I smiled and said, "Crystal lied to us. Her alibi is blown."

"Yep. It's time we have a talk with her again." Penny looked distracted.

"What is it?"

"Just frustrated. Apparently, the deputies missed talking to Konas. I didn't know this information beforehand."

"This is the towns first murder."

"And I hope the last," Penny said. "Still, we have to be better than that. I guess more training is needed."

"One issue at a time," Mom said.

Walking back to the security station, I saw a shadow move. A tall figure hurrying down the street, casting nervous glances over their shoulder. I pointed to the distinctive silhouette of the phoenix researcher. "Doctor Green?"

"Shhh," Penny said. Her hand shot to my mouth before I could speak again. She really had no boundaries and this was getting old.

I pulled her hand away. "You could just say that. I don't know where your hand has been."

"Shhh," Penny repeated. "I have told you. Multiple times."

CHAPTER 18

Green was behaving oddly, but nothing criminal. There was no law against being out this late at night. Strange, but not illegal. He kept stopping behind bushes, checked something, and then moved on to another one. Ten minutes later, we were crouched behind a hydrangea bush.

I explored the tree base surroundings. I felt a tap on my shoulder and looked up. Mom pointed toward the gazebo at the town square. I followed her finger. I could see Green's flashlight beam dancing erratically among the shrubbery. He was on his hands and knees, his normally pristine khakis streaked with dirt.

"Has he found anything?" I asked.

"Not that I can tell. He keeps muttering to himself, though," Penny said.

I reached out with my gift, scanning the area for any cryptid presence. There was nothing out of the ordinary except a mildly annoyed garden gnome who'd been awakened by Green's digging.

"Humans," the gnome projected grumpily. *"No respect for decent sleep schedules."*

"Sorry about that," I sent back. "Anything unusual happen here tonight before this guy showed up?"

"Just the usual. Teenage pixies smoking dewdrops behind the fountain. A silkie singing off-key at the moon. Oh, and that woman who buried something over by the eastern hedge."

I stiffened. "Woman? What did she look like?"

"Didn't see her face. She was wearing one of those human head-hiders."

"A hat? A hood?"

"The second one. Dark clothes. Quick hands."

"When was this?"

"Two decent sleep cycles ago."

That's two days following the missing egg. I relayed this information to Penny, whose eyes narrowed.

"Could be our thief," she said. "Or an accomplice."

"What's he doing excavating the municipal plantings at midnight?"

"That's what we're trying to figure out," I said. "The gnome says a hooded woman buried something here two nights ago. Green seems desperate to find it."

Mom's expression shifted. "Well, we don't know that the two things are connected. I'm sure if we ask, there's a perfectly reasonable explanation. Victor is a respected scientist, after all."

Penny and I exchanged glances. That was Mom's diplomatic voice – the one she used when serving tea to visiting officials she secretly couldn't stand.

"Mom," Penny said. "Why are you defending him?"

"I'm not defending anyone. I'm suggesting we shouldn't jump to conclusions."

"Does this have anything to do with your illegal removal of plants from the reservation grounds?"

"We already talked about this, honey. I am just testing, not using it for criminal means."

"Still, I don't like secrets," Penny said.

Green's flashlight beam was still. He'd froze, head cocked, as if listening.

"Someone's coming," I whispered, pulling Mom further down beside us. She grunted as her muscles strained for her to get lower.

A figure emerged from the fog, walking briskly across the square. Even in the dim light, I recognized Violet Newsome's distinctive gait. She approached Green, who stood quickly, brushing dirt from his knees.

"Told you not here." I caught fragments of her hushed voice. "Risky."

"I had no choice." Green replied, his tone urgent. "Running out of time."

"They're too far away," Penny muttered. "I can't make out what they're saying."

"I can only get a few words. She doesn't sound so scared of Green. Maybe I can get closer," I said.

"No." Mom placed a restraining hand on my arm. "We need to be smart about this."

Penny was already reaching for her phone. "I'll call for backup."

"Wait," Mom said. "Let's not overreact. Victor may simply be conducting nocturnal research."

"Victor?" Penny raised an eyebrow. " By digging up town property? After the thief apparently buried something around here?"

"Perhaps he's looking for rare soil samples."

I studied her face in the darkness. "Mom, do you know something we don't?"

Before she could answer, Green and Violet began moving. They walked rapidly across the square, heads bent together in intense conversation. Silently, we three shadowed them, maintaining distance.

"Mom," Penny said. "Why are you so reluctant to suspect Green? You've been making excuses for him since we spotted him."

"I haven't been making excuses," Mom said, though her voice lacked conviction.

"Mother," I used the proper designation deliberately, a rare tactic that usually got her attention. "What aren't you telling us?"

She sighed, her shoulders sagging. "Victor and I, we worked together on collecting samples for my project. However, I don't know why he would be looking in town. It wasn't in our plan."

That stopped both of us in our tracks.

"You are working with Doctor Green?" I blinked. "You never mentioned that."

"It's a brief collaboration. Nothing significant."

Penny's eyes narrowed. "Is it just professional?"

In the moonlight, I caught the slight flush that rose on Mom's cheeks. "Penny Annette Sterling! That is none of your business. And no."

"Oh my god," I said. "Mom, are you dating Doctor Green."

"I did not say that," she said. "We have a friendship. That's all. You know how hard it is to find someone with my level of phoenix knowledge. Impossible."

"Any other secrets associated with the theft and murders we are investigating." Penny pressed, hands on her hips.

"No. If there was anything, I would tell you."

Before Mom could elaborate further, Green and Violet turned down a narrow side street. They were heading toward their lab. They stopped in front of the newest of the research buildings, building C. Heritage Crest was not very creative when naming things. The exterior work was done, but the modern set of labs hadn't opened since the interior was still under construction. They looked up at the darkened building and exchanged some words and head nods.

We slipped behind a construction gate and made our way across the weed-choked parking lot. Ahead, a beam of light moved behind one of the ground floor windows, Green's flashlight, presumably. They were looking in the building.

"This is getting serious," Penny said. "If they're involved in the theft we may catch them in the act."

"We don't know that yet," Mom said. "They could just be curious about how the build out is going."

"Mom," I said gently. "I understand loyalty to a colleague, but two people are dead. A phoenix egg was stolen. If Green is involved—"

"He's not," she said with surprising firmness. "Victor Green may be arrogant, infuriating, and occasionally ruthless in pursuing his research, but he's not a murderer or a thief."

"How can you be so sure?" Penny challenged.

Mom hesitated. "Because of his insistence on stricter protections for the phoenix's. He thinks they are still too exposed. We had a slight disagreement, but in the end, he was only concerned about their safety. I believe he would resign rather than compromise his ethical standards or cause any possible harm to those delicate creatures."

That gave us both pause. It didn't align with the person I'd been assuming Green might be.

"Then why is he sneaking around town in the middle of the night?" Penny asked.

"That," Mom said, "I cannot explain."

A sharp crash from the new building interrupted our whispered debate. Raised voices followed it. Violet and Green were arguing.

"We need to get closer," Penny said, drawing her service weapon. "Stay behind me."

"Penny," Mom said, "if you're wrong about this."

"Then I'll personally apologize to Doctor Green and his assistant for interrupting their midnight scavenger hunt." Penny's tone was firm. "But I'm not risking more lives on assumptions."

We approached the building. A side door hung partially open, spilling a thin line of light onto the cracked concrete. Penny motioned for us to stop, then advanced to position herself beside the entrance. With practiced efficiency, she peered around the edge.

After a moment, she beckoned us forward. "They're in the main processing area," she whispered. "I can see them, but can't make out what they're saying."

I joined her at the door, looking inside. The building's vast interior was a mess of construction machinery and building supplies. Green and Violet stood near the center, illuminated by a portable lantern set on an overturned crate. Between them lay what appeared to be a map spread across another crate. Green was pointing at it emphatically while Violet shook her head.

"Already searched there!" Violet's voice echoed. "It's not there."

"It has to be!" Green slammed his fist down. "There is nowhere else to search."

"We need to get closer," I said.

"Too risky," Penny replied. "They'll spot us."

I glanced around, then pointed upward. "Catwalk. It runs above where they're standing. We might be able to hear better from there."

Penny nodded. "Worth a try. Mom, stay here."

"Absolutely not," Mom said. "I'm coming with you."

The stare she gave us brooked no argument. Sometimes I forgot that beneath Mom's gentle healer exterior was the woman who once faced down a rampaging manticore armed with nothing but a wooden spoon and sheer determination.

We found the access stairs to the catwalk. Penny led, testing each step before allowing us to follow. The metal groaned softly beneath our weight, but the sounds from below masked any noise we made.

From our elevated position, we could see Green and Violet. Green looked disheveled, his customary composure replaced by barely contained agitation. Violet appeared calmer but kept glancing toward the doors.

"Running out of time," Green was saying. "If we don't find it before the window expires."

"I know the stakes," Violet said. "But we've searched everywhere on this map. The town square was our last option."

"Then we're missing something. We have to be." Green ran his hands through his hair in frustration.

"Unless it's already gone," Violet suggested.

"Possible," Green said. "But unlikely. This place was locked down."

I turned to Penny, mouthing silently: What are they looking for?

She shook her head, looking as confused as I felt. This didn't sound like two people who had stolen the egg themselves. It sounded like they were searching for it.

"What about the theater?" Violet asked. "The egg was stolen the night McKinnon was killed."

Green shook his head. "The sheriff's department has been all over that building. If it was there, they would have found it."

Mom touched my arm, pointing to a collapsed section of catwalk about ten feet ahead of us. Beyond it, the walkway continued above Green and Violet. If we could get past the gap, we'd be positioned to hear everything.

The gap wasn't huge – maybe three feet across, where several support struts had given way. I judged it. A simple jump would do it, but the noise might alert them to our presence.

Penny seemed to think the same thing. She motioned for us to stay put while she attempted the crossing. With a few steps back, she took a short run-up and cleared the gap with minimal noise.

The catwalk shuddered slightly, but held. Penny froze, but Green and Violet didn't look up, too engrossed in their discussion and moving things.

Mom was next, moving with surprising agility for someone in gardening boots and a nightgown. I followed last, wincing at the slight metallic groan as I landed.

Below us, Violet paused mid-sentence, looking up.

"What was that?" she asked.

"Probably just the building," Green said, still focused on the map.

We held still, hardly daring to breathe. After a tense moment, Violet returned her attention to the map.

"We need to consider that she might have already moved it out of town," Violet said.

"Impossible. No vehicle has left Heritage Crest with the appropriate cold storage capacity."

"What about non-vehicular transport? The maintenance tunnels run for miles under the old parts of town."

Green's eyes widened. "The tunnels. Of course." He refolded the map. "Some of them connect to the old railroad service station. However, I understood it had been walled up and closed tight."

"Maybe not. We should check it out," Violet said, already gathering their equipment.

They quickly packed up, extinguishing their lantern. We pressed ourselves against the catwalk railing as they moved toward the exit, their flashlight beams swinging wildly across the floor.

As soon as the door closed behind them, Penny straightened. "We need to follow them."

"Wait," Mom said. "I don't understand what's happening. Are they trying to find the egg or not?"

"Sounds like they are," I said. "But if they stole it, did they lose it?"

"Add it to the growing list of questions," Penny said, already heading for the stairs. "But whatever they're up to, they think the egg is being moved soon. We can't let that happen."

We descended and emerged into the parking lot just in time to see Green's car pulling away, gravel crunching under its tires.

"My car's closest," I said, breaking into a jog. "This way."

We piled into my truck, Penny taking the wheel without discussion. She was the better pursuit driver, having actually trained for it. I navigated while Mom sat tensely in the middle.

"The old railroad service station is on the east side of town," Mom said. "Near the county line. It's been abandoned for years."

"I know. We can't follow too closely here," Penny said, slowing down. "They'll spot our headlights."

We followed at a careful distance, headlights off. Green was driving fast but not reckless. After about fifteen minutes, he turned onto a road that wound through a dense corpse of trees.

"Pull over," I suggested. "We can proceed on foot. The old station can't be far now."

Penny parked behind a thick stand of evergreens, concealing the car from the road. We got out and started down the access road, staying close to the tree line. The night had grown colder.

After about a quarter mile, the trees thinned, revealing the silhouette of the abandoned train station against the starlit sky. The building, smaller than anticipated, was only one story and a loading dock beside the tracks. Green parked his car near the entrance; its engine still ticked as it cooled.

We crept closer, using the shadows for cover. A faint light glowed from inside the station – not electric, but the warm flicker of a lantern.

"I'll go first," Penny said, her hand resting on her service weapon. "Stay behind me and be ready to move fast if things go south."

"Be careful," Mom said. "Remember, we still don't know what's happening here."

Penny nodded and led us toward the building. As we approached, I reached out with my gift, scanning for any cryptid presence. There was nothing immediate, though I sensed something faint. It was a small voice emanating from the far side the station, but could be anything.

We reached the weather-beaten wall of the building, edging along it toward a broken window. Penny peered inside, then withdrew quickly.

"Three people in there," she said. "Green, Violet, and a third I don't recognize from the back of her head. Woman in her fifties, professionally dressed."

"Can you see what they're doing?" I asked.

"Looking for something. They've split up, searching different areas."

I risked a glance through the window myself. The interior was mostly empty except for a few abandoned crates and a collapsed ticket counter. Green was methodically checking behind loose floorboards while Violet examined a rusted control panel. The third woman was opening a series of metal lockers against the far wall.

"Do you recognize her, Mom?" I asked.

Mom leaned forward, then drew back with a sharp intake of breath.

"Elenor Pembrook," she said, her voice tight with surprise. "But no Sparkles."

That threw me. "She's involved in this?"

"It seems so." Mom frowned. "But why would they be operating covertly?"

Before we could speculate further, a distant whistle pierced the night – the sound alerting from a food dispenser that needed filling. Cryptids pushed a button to signal handlers to refill.

Inside, the three searchers tensed. The woman Mom had identified as Mrs. Pembrook walked to the center of the room.

"It's not here," she announced, her voice carrying through the broken window.

"That's impossible," Green said. "All our intelligence pointed to this being the last unsearched location."

"Intelligence can be wrong," Mrs. Pembrook said. "Or deliberately misleading."

"We need to get in there," Penny said. "Find out what's going on."

She moved toward the entrance, Mom and I following closely. Just as Penny reached for the handle, the door swung open from inside. Doctor Green stood in the doorway, his expression shifting from surprise to exasperation.

"Clara," he said, addressing Mom. "I might have known you'd complicate things."

"Victor," Mom replied coolly. "Imagine my surprise finding you sneaking around at this hour."

"It's not what you think," Mrs. Pembrook said over Green's right shoulder.

Green sighed, stepping aside to let us enter. "You might as well come in. We still haven't found the egg."

Mom's expression softened slightly. "So that's what you've been doing."

Green met her gaze. "Nothing is more important than returning that phoenix egg. You have to know that."

The feed whistle sounded again. A restless cryptid lurked nearby. If the situation wasn't so serious, it might have made me smile. The cryptids that slept at night would be pissed.

"I do," she said. "But why sneak around."

"You'll have some explaining to do." Penny's voice cut through the room like a blade. She stepped through the main doorway, her gun still drawn and steady at her side. Mom flanked her, looking every inch the formidable woman she was

"Sheriff Sterling!" Doctor Green's face drained of color. "This isn't what it looks like."

"Really?" I stepped into view from my position, effectively cutting off their escape. "Because it looks like a sophisticated phoenix egg trafficking operation. Complete with equipment for keeping the egg dormant until transport."

Mrs. Pembroke's expression hardened. "Doctor Sterling. We would never."

"Where's the egg?" Penny asked, her voice demanding.

"We don't know," Violet said. "We're looking for it just like you."

Mom stepped forward and turned to Mrs. Pembroke. "I believe you, but you have to admit, this is looking pretty suspicious."

Mrs. Pembroke's smile was brittle. "Just concerned citizens trying to help."

"Like murder?" I couldn't keep the disgust from my voice. Sparkles trusted this woman. We all had. Could we have been wrong?

Violet moved, reaching into her lab coat. Penny was faster, her weapon raised and tracked the movement. "Don't."

Violet withdrew her hand, revealing a small remote control. "Whoa," she said with a smile. "Just getting my phone. I wanted to show you pictures of areas we searched. I thought it might help prove what we're doing."

"There's no negotiation happening here," Penny said. "You're all under arrest for theft, conspiracy, and murder."

"And murder?" Mrs. Pembroke raised an eyebrow. "Is that what you think? That we killed Jerry McKinnon?"

The three of us exchanged glances. "Didn't you?" I asked.

Doctor Green laughed. "Why would we kill Jerry?"

"He was on to you. I saw all the papers on his desk."

"On to me? About what?"

"The theft."

Violet looked away. I couldn't be sure, but I thought I saw a smile. Was this funny to her?

"That's absurd," Green said. "We're trying to help you."

"Are we breaking any laws?" Violet asked.

Penny grunted. "Trespassing for a start."

"Come on," Green said, softer now. "We're just trying to help you. We can show you the search map. Please, just look at it."

A heavy silence fell, broken only by the persistent wail of the food alarm in the distance. My only thought being, would someone please feed the damn cryptid.

CHAPTER 19

Penny was satisfied by what she got from Doctor Green, Violet, and Mrs. Pembrook. She grilled them extensively. Even though they seemed to mean well, my sister was not hiding her suspicion. Something else was off. She let them go with a warning and a promise that going forward, they would coordinate with her team on their search. They agreed, and we parted.

Penny dropped mom off at her place close to midnight. We spent a few more hours searching the town for our egg thief and Tommy. The combined force of the sanctuary security and sheriff's office hadn't found any sign of either. They hadn't left the town and had to be here somewhere. It was just a matter of time.

With it being so late, Penny drove me home. I hoped to get a few hours of sleep before the next day. The schedule at the clinic was jammed pack until lunchtime, but after that I would be back to pretending, I was a detective.

We turned on my street and Penny said, "I may be hard to get a hold of tomorrow. We'll be searching every lab and building for most of the day for the egg and now Tommy. Sometime around dinner time we would go back to Crystal and find out if she has an explanation for lying to us about her whereabouts on the night of the murder. Thought you might want to go?"

"I should be free by then," I said. "Just text me. What about the employee he fired?"

"We can go to her after."

"Sounds like a plan." Penny stopped her jeep in front of my home. I turned to her. "What are you going to do now?"

"I'm going to check in on the kids, talk with the teams, and hopefully get some sleep. I can barely stand."

"You couldn't tell me that before I let you drive me home?" I gave her a half smile.

"Well, little brother. Last time I checked, I don't drive standing up."

"You're crazy." I got out of the jeep and headed in.

Within one minute, I was undressed, on my bed, and out cold. I wished I could've slept until seven, but my sisters call wouldn't let me.

CHAPTER 20

My phone rang at about five in the morning. My first reaction: Someone was joking; we couldn't possibly have another emergency. However, I looked over at my sister's face on the screen. Based on the time, I knew it was serious and answered. "Hey, what now?"

"We found Tommy near the north entrance, sector 319. Get here, NOW." The phone line clicked off. She needed to work on her wake-up calls.

I dressed and was in my car within five minutes. I hoped he was alive, but from the tone, I wasn't holding out much hope.

Driving to the sanctuary perimeter took less than twenty minutes, but it was enough time for my thoughts to arrange themselves into an unsettling pattern. The missing egg, Jerry's death, and now Tommy. The precise timing of the "maintenance" visits. These events were somehow connected.

I found Penny standing near the sanctuary's back fence, next to what looked like a crumpled heap of fabric. Her face was grim. A small cluster of officers huddled nearby, their hushed voices carrying an edge of unease that had nothing to do with the usual wariness around cryptids. As I got closer, I realized the heap was Tommy Chen. He wasn't moving.

"Thanks for coming so quickly," Penny said.

"Tell me he's just unconscious," I said, kneeling beside the body.

Penny shook her head. "Found by the morning patrol about forty-five minutes ago. Look at his hand. I wanted you to see it before we bagged it as evidence."

Tommy lay sprawled in the dewy grass, his security guard uniform darkened by what looked like scorch marks. He partially gripped something with his burnt right hand. Using a pair of gloves from my medical kit, I extracted what looked like a curved piece of shell. It was warm to the touch, thrumming with heat.

"Phoenix eggshell?" Penny asked.

I nodded, examining the fragment more closely. "But there's something wrong with it. It's... muted somehow. Like it's been exposed to some kind of dampening field."

"Cold storage?" Penny asked. When I looked up in surprise, she smiled. "I do occasionally listen to you."

I stood up, bagging the shell fragment. "We need to find that egg. A phoenix egg can't be kept in cold stasis indefinitely. It is already breaking. Eventually it has to be awakened to prevent damage to the chick inside."

"Today we start the building-by-building search. We'll find it. Any idea how long we have?"

"Not really, that is more mom's area. She said it was a few days, but I don't know all the details or if she could be more exact."

"No, worries. I'll ask her."

"Just be careful," I said. "Anyone willing to kill twice to protect this secret will not give up easily."

"Speaking of which," Penny gestured to Tommy's body as the forensics team arrived. "What do you think happened here? Did he catch them moving the egg?"

I examined the scorch marks on the ground around Tommy's body. They were like phoenix fire patterns, but not quite right - too uniform, too controlled. After years of treating burned handlers who got too close during regeneration cycles, I could see the difference. "Someone wanted to make us think the phoenix egg hatched. He isn't burned. They tried to make the ground appear the chick was freed. This wasn't a phoenix. Phoenix fire leaves traces of a green energy, even in death it glows. This is artificial somehow. Definitely staged."

"That's what I thought as well. Someone tried hard to make it look like a phoenix though. I think I know the answer, but I need to ask. Who would have the knowledge to do this?"

"Dr. Green has that kind of knowledge," Rivera's said from behind us, making me jump slightly. The deputy had an uncanny ability to appear silently, like a ghost.

"He would," I said. "But so would anyone with access to his research. Including, his assistant. Do we know how Tommy died?"

"Not sure yet. We can't seem to find any wounds or marks. It may be a tranquilizer gun, but we won't know until the autopsy, and then there's the matter of the eggshell fragment he was holding."

"Have you looked at his eyes? Anything unusual?"

She seemed confused, but using her gloved hand, she pulled up one of his eyelids and pointed. "What do you make of this?"

The white of the eye was now green. I recognized it instantly. "You said you found no wounds?"

"No. Why?"

"He was poisoned."

"Poisoned?"

"The green of the eye tells me he died from mapinguary spit."

"What now?"

"Essentially, a giant sloth. It is a mixture of a sloth and gorilla with long fluffy yellow hair and can walk on two or four legs. They smell terrible and are slow. There is one eye, and mouth is in their chest area."

"That sounds terrifying," Rivera said.

"I suppose you could see them that way. They are very docile herbivores. They keep to themselves and hide in trees. Tommy would smell them within a hundred feet and easily out walked their fastest pace. Plus, if they bit him, you would know. They have humanlike teeth."

"Even more terrifying," Penny said.

"Are there any of these mapi things in the sanctuary?" Rivera asked.

"Mapinguary. And yes, there are six on the south side. But it would've taken them ages to get over here. We would notice. Any footprints?"

"None yet," Penny said.

"Keep an eye out for three-toed prints. That would be them."

"Let's take a few steps back. You said they had saliva, and this was what killed him. Could it be fake, like the basilisk venom?"

"Maybe. But it looks legit. However, with no bite, it had to have been consumed by mouth."

"So, this mapi kissed him?" Rivera asked.

I glared at Rivera. "Mapinguary. And probably not. Most likely, it was slipped into a drink or in food. Konas might know more as well. He sells a cure if you are infected."

"This sounds premeditated," Penny said.

"Probably," I said with a nod. "I can't see how he could've accidentally ingested it. The mapinguary keep to themselves. And even if he did encounter one, it would take several hours to kill him. He would feel pain and sickness that would send him to the emergency room."

"I'm confused." Penny rubbed her chin. "How did you know to look at his eyes."

I smiled. "I treat lots of poisons and it's just a habit. The eyes can show most cryptid poisons or venom. The autopsy will have to confirm, but mapinguary is specifically green."

"Good to know."

"Could he have been poisoned and then the bird, having been so upset over her missing egg, attacked him and maybe he was unconscious and couldn't run from those things?" Rivera asked

"I don't believe so. Cryptids aren't like humans. They wouldn't seek revenge. Sure, they would defend themselves, but I don't see evidence of that here. Plus, there are no wounds."

Rivera looked skeptical. "With all due respect, Doctor Sterling, we can't base an investigation on what amounts to bird behavior."

"These aren't just birds," I snapped, my patience wearing thin. "They're highly intelligent magical creatures with a complex social structure and an understanding of temporal physics that would make Einstein's head spin."

"Poetic," Rivera muttered, "but not helpful for building a case."

"Mark," Penny said before Rivera could continue, "anything else.

"Not really. The doctor will need to confirm if I'm right. Why kill Tommy though? Was it the message he was going to send me?"

"I think he found something that proved what they were doing. It lines up with the text on his phone."

"I guess."

"This shows me they're getting nervous," Penny said.

I nodded in agreement. "Making mistakes."

"Good," she replied. "Because I'm getting tired of finding dead bodies in my town."

I looked at the eggshell fragment in the evidence bag, then at Tommy's body being photographed by the forensics team. Two people were dead, one egg was missing, and a killer who wasn't finished yet. Not the best way to start a day.

"Ok. I want to stay with the team here until this is processed and then we go to the doctor. Shouldn't be much longer." She put her arm around me and squeezed. "So, other than a few deaths and a missing egg, how's your morning going?"

"I'm tired."

While Penny stayed to complete processing the scene, I headed back to my car. I had free time before my eight am patient. I needed to check in on Aurora. She needed to know we were still searching. I was adamant that she wasn't involved, but it wouldn't hurt to ask the worried phoenix mom.

CHAPTER 21

The ancient phoenix's gaze pierced through me with the intensity of a thousand suns. Aurora perched atop her nest platform in the sanctuary's highest chamber, her iridescent feathers casting dancing patterns on the crystalline walls. After three days of searching for her missing egg with no results, this was the closest she'd let me get.

"I know you don't trust humans right now," I said both aloud and mentally, keeping my voice steady. "But I'm trying to help. How are you holding up?"

A wave of skepticism radiated from her, accompanied by flashes of memories - humans with clipboards, humans with cameras, humans asking endless questions about phoenix breeding patterns. Doctor Green featured prominently in her images, though something felt off about the timing.

"Humans always want." Aurora's thoughts crackled like embers in my mind. *"Want eggs. Want feathers. Want secrets. Never just help."*

"I want to find your egg. My sister will go through the remaining buildings today. Everyone is looking," I said, taking a careful step forward. "And I want to protect your remaining eggs as well. But I need your help to do that."

The mention of her eggs caused her feathers to bristle, small sparks dancing between them. The temperature rose several degrees - a warning sign I'd learned to recognize during my years of treating phoenixes. I took a step back.

"Just because you can talk, doesn't mean to speak truth. Why should I trust you, young-healer-who-speaks?"

"Because, unlike most humans, I can hear what you're trying to tell us." I gestured to the empty nest space where the missing egg had been. "Someone took advantage of our sanctuary's trust. They hurt Jerry, who we believe was trying to protect your family. And now, a second human has been killed in the search for your egg. I'm afraid they'll try again unless we stop them."

Aurora tilted her head, studying me with eyes that held centuries of wisdom. Phoenixes could live for millennia if they kept regenerating. This phoenix was ancient, even during my mother's youth.

"Your gift is strong, but do you truly care about righting this wrong?" she asked. *"Understanding our words does not mean you understand our ways."*

"Then teach me."

The request seemed to surprise her. Her feathers settled, and the temperature dropped back to its usual warm level.

"You would learn? Truly learn what it is to be Phoenix Life, not just gather information?"

"I'll take whatever lessons you're willing to give," I said. "Right now, I'm missing something important about this case. Something that connects Jerry and Tommy's death, the missing egg, and Doctor Green's research. I can feel it, but I can't see it. Maybe this can help me."

Aurora made a sound like wind through crystal chimes - a phoenix laugh. *"Then your first lesson, young healer, is this: Sometimes to see clearly, you must look through fire."*

Before I asked what she meant, she spread her magnificent wings and burst into flames.

I stumbled back, but the fire didn't spread. Instead, it formed a circle around us, creating a barrier of pure phoenix energy that somehow didn't burn. Through the flames, I saw the world differently - magical energies became visible as distinct patterns flowed through the sanctuary like luminous rivers.

"Watch," Aurora commanded. *"Remember. Learn how energy moves when undisturbed."*

I observed, fascinated, as the natural energy currents of the sanctuary swirled in complex but harmonious patterns. Then Aurora showed me memories of recent disturbances - places where those patterns had been redirected or suppressed. The flow parted and skewed in different directions. I could feel the disturbance. It made my stomachache.

"The egg-taker used stealth," Aurora explained. *"Disrupted the natural path to hide their actions. But fire sees."*

Through the flames, I watched as Aurora manipulated the fire to show me moments of disturbance in the sanctuary. It was like watching security camera footage, but instead of grainy video, I was seeing pure energy patterns. The spots where someone had disrupted the natural flow stood out like dark voids in the otherwise vibrant tapestry.

"There," I pointed to a strong disruption near the research facility. "That happened the night Jerry died, didn't it?"

"Yes." Aurora's mental voice carried centuries of disapproval. *"But you see only part. To understand fully, you must learn to look through many eyes. All Phoenix are connected within the flame."*

The flames dissipated, leaving me blinking in the suddenly ordinary light. Before I processed everything I'd seen, a familiar ring echoed from my pocket.

"Sterling," I answered.

"Your first appointment is here, and I wanted to check how close you were," Alice said.

I looked at the time. Two hours had passed in what felt like a minute. Crap. "Aurora, I need to go. Hang in there and thank you for showing me that. If it's okay, I would like to come back and learn more."

"We shall see friend-healer. Please find my child."

"I will." Deep down, I hoped it was a promise I could keep.

CHAPTER 22

"Doctor Sterling, your 9 AM is here," Alice said as I entered the clinic in a rush. "And the 8 AM is still waiting in room three. Also, mentally prepare yourself. Sparkles is on the docket again for today.'"

I groaned, rubbing my temples. The number of patients I was letting down was growing faster than a teenage dragon's appetite. I hadn't showered in two days, barely slept, and was starving. I couldn't keep up. I hoped this series of emergencies ended soon. My body couldn't take much more.

"Tell them I'll be right there." I shuffled into my office, grabbed my lap coat, and sprayed on some cologne from a small bottle in my top desk drawer. It would have to do until I could shower.

The next few hours were a blur of routine appointments interspersed with careful observation. Despite my focus on patients, I hoped Penny's search of the labs and other buildings went well. However, a part of me knew they wouldn't. Whoever was doing this was smart and clever.

I had one appointment left before I headed out to help her. We were going to talk to the ex-girlfriend again, and the fired employee. Proof was in short supply, but focusing on women only helped narrow our scope. Twelve cups of coffee held me over for the day, but I hoped somehow, some way, I'd be in bed by eight. A guy could dream.

With a high degree of dread and frustration, I entered the room with my last patient – Sparkles. She pranced in place, her horn wrapped in foil, but now with an elaborate chart being held by Mrs. Pembrook beside her. Upon seeing me, she got so excited she tripped over her own hooves and fell against the wall. Quickly, she righted herself and took on an air of embarrassment.

"Good afternoon Mrs. Pembrook, Sparkles."

"Thank you for seeing us," Mrs. Pembrook said. She looked embarrassed to be here, again. "I wanted to apologize for the other night. We went a little too far and I just didn't want you to think less of me."

"Do you mean trying to get Ziggy mutilated or investigating the egg? I have feelings about both, but now is not the time."

"I have another issue with the horn," Sparkles said. The unicorn was not going to let Mrs. Pembrook get any of my focus.

"Let me guess," I said, setting aside my agitation. "Your horn is experiencing seasonal allergies?"

"Worse!" Sparkles projected, her mental voice quivering with distress. *"I read on UniBook that exposure to artificial light can cause horn dulling. I feel less sparkly."*

I pinched the bridge of my nose. "Sparkles, you realize unicorns have existed under the sun, the biggest light source around, for millennia, right?"

"But the sun is natural lighting! These office fluorescents are draining my magical essence!" She gestured upward with her horn and Mrs. Pembrook removed the foil. *"You have to see the difference. Look how the light reflects off my horn at only 98.7% efficiency instead of the usual 98.8%!"*

"You can't measure that precisely."

"I downloaded a sparkle-measuring app!"

Of course she had. I was about to explain why trusting random unicorn health apps wasn't the best medical strategy when my phone buzzed.

"Sparkles," I said, "I promise your horn is fine.

"How can you be sure?"

"I'm a doctor. I hate to ask this." I motioned to Mrs. Pembrook. "What is the chart for?"

She pointed to Sparkles.

"Thank you for asking. Doctor Sterling!" Sparkles said. *"Look! I matched my horn's current hue to Pantone color 2685C. That's three shades more purple than yesterday!"*

"Sparkles," I said, "your horn is its usual pearlescent white. The purple tint you're seeing is just a reflection of the ink on your new chart."

"But I cross-referenced it with the International Scale of Unicorn Horn Luminescence!"

"The what now?"

"I found it on UniBook!" She projected an image of the unofficial social media post decorated with rainbow emojis.

Before I explained, for the hundredth time, why getting medical advice from social media was a bad idea, Alice appeared in the doorway. "Doctor Sterling? The sheriff is wondering when you might be there."

I glanced at Sparkles, who was now attempting to demonstrate her horn's supposed color change through an elaborate series of poses. "Tell her I'll be there in ten minutes, fifteen at the latest."

Alice nodded, understanding my meaning. The police station was two blocks away, which would mean this appointment was over. Unfortunately, Sparkles realized it as well.

"But my horn!" Sparkles protested.

"Tell you what," I said, already heading for the door. "Why don't you document any color changes over the twenty-four hours? Take detailed notes, make some graphs, and then we will talk."

"Ooh, graphs! I could use different colored highlighters for the data points!"

Sometimes, the best way to handle Sparkles was to redirect her energy into relatively harmless projects. By the time she finished her graphs, she'd forget about the alleged color change. I wanted to ask how she would even make the drawings with her hooves, but decided not to dive down that road of conversation.

"Is there anything I can do?" Mrs. Pembrook asked.

I leaned towards her and whispered, "I stand by my previous advice that you may want to get her to talk to Doctor Foster. She can translate as well and is better equipped for the more mental challenges that Sparkles may be having. If that doesn't happen, then at least limit her internet time. If at all possible, keep her off Unibook."

"That's her favorite site."

"I'm aware."

CHAPTER 23

The workday ended, and I was wiped. I would've loved to do nothing more than go home, crawl into bed, and sleep for a week. However, the missing egg and two murders drove me to continue. Two energy drinks and one cup of coffee later, I was off to talk to my sister.

The police station was only two blocks from my clinic, but I still had to dodge three different cryptids seeking medical advice on my way there. A pixie with alleged wing asymmetry (she was flying in circles), a young sasquatch worried about premature shedding (it was spring, and he was supposed to be shedding), and a garden gnome convinced he was shrinking (he'd slouched over from sitting all day).

I found Penny in her office, surrounded by stacks of financial documents and evidence containment boxes. My brother-in-law Harry was there too, his usual easygoing demeanor replaced by focused concentration as he worked on multiple tablets displaying complex data streams.

"Did you find anything today in your building searches?" I asked.

"We did an exhaustive search of all properties and found lots of pot. Who would have thought scientists liked to get high so much. But I digress, there was nothing related to the missing egg or the murders. Absolutely nothing."

"Seems you would have found something."

"My thoughts exactly. My guess is the delay in getting search permissions gave time for the bad guys to cover their tracks. They must have missed something crucial. We just need to find it. Harry found some stuff online though." Penny pushed a folder toward me. "It's the tip of the iceberg. We've got at least three different international buyers vying for an upcoming phoenix egg sale."

"Three?" I leafed through the documents, noting the astronomical figures. "Who has this kind of money?"

"A Saudi prince with a private supernatural menagerie," Harry said, not looking up from his screens. "A Chinese industrialist collecting 'magical investments.' And my personal favorite - a tech billionaire who pumps out electric vehicles thinks keeping cryptids near him will help him achieve immortality when he starts space travel."

"Please tell me you're joking about that last one."

"Wish I was. He's got a whole manifesto about harnessing phoenix regeneration energy." Harry swiveled one of his tablets to show me a webpage filled with bizarre theories about cryptid life extension.

"Guy makes Sparkles UniBook medical advice look reasonable," I said. They looked at me, confused. "Never mind, a story of another time."

"There is nothing specific to the source of the phoenix egg on the market, but that doesn't mean anything if they are working for a buyer," Harry added.

I frowned at the documents. "But how are they getting insider access to so many sanctuaries? The security protocols can't be that bad."

"They're only as good as the people enforcing them," Penny said.

"Is Green and his little search party behaving?"

"Seems so. I still don't trust him, but he is coordinating and putting in a lot of hours. So, I can't complain."

"I don't either. Plus, I still think Mom might like him more than a colleague."

"I don't even want to think about that." Penny stood up and grabbed her jacket from the back of the chair. "Ready to go visit the ex-girlfriend again and the terminated employee."

"Sure, but can we grab a sandwich first? I haven't eaten all day."

"I supposed we can stop by the deli." She smiled. "Harry, keep digging into those financial records and I'll probably be late, so tell the kids goodnight for me and that mommy loves them."

Penny kissed Harry on the cheek, and we were off.

"Do you kiss all of your employees?"

"I swear to God, Mark. I will throw you in jail," Penny said. I could tell she was fighting hard to not smile.

Thirty minutes later, I had finished a foot long sandwich, and we were pulling up in front of Crystal's house.

"What's the plan?" I asked as Penny pulled her jeep to a stop.

"The same as before. Let her talk, don't give any additional information, and only ask questions along the same subject we are on. I will guide the conversation. Remember she claimed she was doing her meditation witchcraft thing, but if Konas is right, she could have done something screwy with the time." She stopped, her expression softening. "Well, you know."

I knew. The image of Jerry's body, the blue slushy around the wound on his neck, burned itself into my memory. Almost as vivid was the recollection of Ziggy's grief, the basilisk's normally vibrant scales dulled.

"What I don't understand," I said, reaching for the car door, "is why Crystal would lie. She and Jerry broke up six months ago."

"Eight months," Penny corrected. "And it wasn't exactly amicable. She was furious when Jerry adopted Ziggy. Some people hold grudges. And if she's been hanging around the theater like Konas said, then, she had the opportunity to do it or at the very least she might have seen something."

"What I don't get is if she did it, why kill Tommy, too? Or take the egg?"

"Maybe, they aren't connected and we're wrong. I would hate to think we have two killers running around, but it could happen, I guess."

"I don't know what situation is worse." I clapped my hands. "So, want me to play bad cop this time?"

"Why do you keep saying that? This is not TV. Just stay muted. The best thing to do is let her talk. Don't make me pistol whip you."

I smiled. "I will do my best."

Penny shook her head, and we walked up to the front door. She knocked, and we waited. Several seconds passed, and she knocked again. No answer.

"Let's go around back," Penny said.

"Maybe, she's not home."

"Possibly, but I want to check if we can see any movement through the windows."

Rounding the house, we found Crystal. She was sitting in a lawn chair with a book and staring up at the clear night sky. She was in a lime green dress with purple sleeves. Around her waist was a bright red belt with what looked like broccoli hanging every few inches. She still looked like a vision from heaven, an odd angel, but an angel none the less. Damn. I had to get a date. We stood there for a minute as she took notes on something she was observing above.

Penny cleared her throat and Crystal screamed. She leaped from the chair and scrambled away. She turned, then surveyed us. She let out her breath and smiled. "You startled me. Sheriff Sterling," she said, gaze flicking between the two of us. "To what do I owe the displeasure?"

"Ms. Lockhead," Penny replied with professional courtesy. "We'd like to ask you a few questions about your whereabouts on the night Jerry McKinnon died."

Crystal's expression hardened. "This is bordering on harassment. I already told you where I was. I was live streaming. I have witnesses."

"May we go inside and talk?" Penny asked, though it wasn't a question.

Crystal hesitated, then, stood with obvious reluctance. "Fine. But I have nothing new to tell you."

"We'll see about that."

The interior of Crystal's home hadn't changed. She cleared off the couch and motioned for us to sit across from her. I noticed several pictures I hadn't seen before. Crystal was in different parts of the facility helping people in lab coats.

"You used to volunteer at the sanctuary." I gestured to the photos on the end table next to me.

"Until your mother rejected my application to work there full time," Crystal said. "She thought I lacked the 'proper temperament' for handling sensitive creatures. Whatever the hell that means?"

I bit back a defensive response. Mom had excellent judgment when it came to people, and if she'd turned down her application, there had been a good reason.

"Please, sit," Crystal gestured to the floral-patterned sofa. A small terrarium on the coffee table contained what appeared to be mini frogs with wings, but I recognized them as poison dart bees—harmless when properly housed, but capable of causing quite a light show if agitated. It was said that they could shoot their stingers at you when their butt lit up. "You said you wanted to talk."

Penny sat on the edge of the sofa, maintaining perfect posture. "Ms. Lockhead, we believe your statement about your whereabouts on Tuesday night was inaccurate, and we wanted to give you an opportunity to amend it if necessary."

"Excuse me?" Crystal's voice rose an octave.

"A citizen claims to have seen you in the bushes near their establishment at the time of the incident," Penny said. "Not here doing a live stream ritual or whatever you called it."

A flicker of unease crossed Crystal's face before she composed herself. "The ritual may have finished earlier than I remembered. It was a busy night, and I'd had a few drinks. I walked along the street, but came straight home. I didn't think to mention it since it was outside the time frame you asked about."

"Did you?" Penny asked. "Because the witness saw you in the bushes for quite a while. They are pretty reliable and have no reason to lie."

I watched Crystal, noting the way her fingers twitched toward the terrarium—a nervous habit, or something more deliberate? The poison dart bees stirred, their skin beginning to shimmer with faint bioluminescence. Luckily, they were behind the glass enclosure.

"That's ridiculous," Crystal scoffed. "Why would I go into the bushes near that theater? Jerry and I were on good terms."

"Good enough terms that you broke up?" I asked, earning a sharp look from Penny for interrupting her questioning.

Crystal's cheeks flushed. "We were going to get back together. I accepted the dangerous creature he kept as a pet. I even go these frog bee things to show him I had changed."

"Ziggy is a well-behaved, properly registered mini basilisk," I said. "Jerry followed every regulation to the letter."

Penny tapped me. The universal sign to hush. "You said you weren't in the bushes near the theater?"

"Correct."

"I never told you they saw you in the bushes near the theater." Penny leaned back and sighed. "I don't like to be lied to. You are interfering in an investigation by misleading us."

Something shifted in Crystal's expression—a calculated reassessment. "Fine. I may have gone in the bushes by the theater that night. Force of habit. I used to watch from there to make sure that monster didn't hurt my Jerry. I left when that hussy was going into the theater. But I didn't see Jerry."

The frog looking bees pulsed with brighter colors, responding to the tension in the room. As a veterinarian with the gift of supernatural communication, I could sense their agitation, their awareness that their owner was lying.

"You saw someone?" I asked.

"Some lady. She had red hair. She looked around, messed with the lock, and entered. I guess she had a key."

"Did you notice any of her features? Could you identify her?" Penny asked.

"Not really. I was too far away, and they had a hoodie pulled up."

"Ms. Lockhead," Penny said, her tone deceptively casual. "Are you familiar with the penalty for perjury?"

Crystal stiffened. "I'm not lying."

"This time." Penny glared.

"Okay, okay. I'm not lying this time. I was afraid before. I thought if you knew I was in the bushes, you would think I did it. But I didn't kill him, I swear. I loved Jerry." Crystal cried. The genuine tears revealed her honesty. But my intuition wasn't enough to clear her. I had been mistaken before.

"You just admitted to lying. Excuse me if I am struggling to believe you," Penny said.

"It's the truth. I wouldn't lie under oath."

"We're not in court," Penny replied, motioning to the bees. "And I'd like to point out that Doctor Sterling here has certain abilities that make detecting untruths in the presence of cryptids straightforward."

Crystal's gaze darted to the terrarium, then back to me. I kept my expression neutral, though Penny was bluffing. While I could communicate with supernatural creatures, I couldn't compel them to reveal their owners' secrets or use them as lie detectors. Crystal didn't need to know that.

"This is harassment," she declared, standing. "I want you to leave."

"We can continue this conversation at the station," Penny offered, remaining seated. "With a formal recorder and holding cells. Your choice."

The poison dart bees had reached an impressive glow now, their colors cycling through a rainbow spectrum. One of them locked eyes with me, projecting a simple but clear message: *She-who-feeds-us speaks true-words about that night of loud cry sounds from her mouth.*

I kept my expression neutral, but something in my face must have changed because Crystal lunged for the terrarium. "Stop that."

Penny, with reflexes honed from years of wrangling unpredictable cryptids, intercepted her, catching Crystal's wrist. "I wouldn't."

Penny yanked her arms free, but stepped back from the terrarium. "I was in the bushes that night waiting for Jerry. I wanted to talk to him about getting back together. What more do you want to know?"

Penny raised an eyebrow. "After eight months? After multiple complaints about his pet? You chose the night of his murder to go talk to him."

"It was a mistake, okay?" Crystal's composure cracked. "I realized I overreacted about the basilisk thing. I wanted to apologize and hope we could start fresh. I didn't know someone would hurt him."

The bees pulsed an alarming shade of magenta. *"Half-truths,"* one projected. *"Crying that night when she came back to her enclosure. Please don't take our food source away."*

"You talked to him," I said, not a question.

Crystal shot me a venomous glare. "I waited two hours for him to come out, but he didn't. Like I said, he wasn't alone. That woman was with him."

"What time did she enter?" Penny asked.

"Around midnight, I guess. I didn't check my watch."

My pulse quickened. This further confirmed a woman, not Doctor Green, entered the theater. I was confident now that Tommy lied to us about seeing Green. Which made little sense. "Did you hear anything?"

A flash of recognition crossed Crystal's face before she shook her head. "No, nothing specific. Just, loud arguing. I couldn't make it out. I heard the word egg every so often, but I don't know what that means. I heard that one was missing."

"What did you do next?" Penny asked.

"I came home, laughed at a sitcom, and went to bed."

The bees strobed with color. *"More untruths! She-who-feeds-us cried for hours! Please don't take her."*

"Ms. Lockhead," I said. They were turning out to be very forthcoming and probably not aware they were calling out their owner. "My little friends here seem to think you came home crying."

Crystal's eyes darted to the terrarium, then, to me. "You can't know that. That's not possible."

"Doctor Sterling has a rare gift," Penny explained, a hint of pride in her voice. "The creatures don't lie to him. And right now, they're saying you are lying again."

Crystal sank into her chair, deflating. "Fine. Yes. I was in hysterics."

"Because you killed Jerry?" I asked. Another stern look from my sister caused me to shrink.

"No," Crystal screamed. Her beautiful features contorted, and the tears flowed faster. "Because he was with another woman. When I love, I love deep."

"So, you left them arguing, and the next morning Jerry was dead." I crossed my arms and looked down my nose.

"And you lied about being there because?" Penny asked.

Crystal looked away. "I told you. Because I knew how it would appear. Ex-girlfriend shows up. They find him dead the next day. I'm not stupid."

"No," Penny said, "just dishonest. Which makes me wonder what else you're hiding."

"Nothing! I swear!" Crystal's voice took on a desperate edge. "I left them arguing and headed home. That's the truth!"

The bees had settled into a steady amber glow—not quite truth, but not outright deception either. *"She is truth speaking,"* one confirmed.

Penny made a note. "One last thing. Why did you fake the livestream?"

"I didn't," Crystal said. "I mean, I guess it would appear that way. I always prerecord them in case I screw up and then, replay on my screen to livestream. I do it all the time. I can show you."

Penny shook her head. "Not now. In the meantime, I need you to come to the station today or tomorrow and make a formal statement about what you heard that night and you can bring the live stream recordings."

"Am I under arrest?" Crystal asked, suddenly looking small.

"Not at this time," Penny replied, "but you provided false information to law enforcement a few times, which is a serious offense."

"We help truth-speaker," a bee said. *"She-who-feeds-us not bad-person, scared-person."*

"I understand," I assured them. Straightforward cryptid perspectives frequently proved insightful.

"That's all for now," Penny said. "Please make sure you come to the station. If I have to come back, I will arrest you."

"I will be there. Thank you."

We stood and Crystal showed us out. Inside the jeep, Penny turned, inquiring about the bees' comments and asked, "What did the bees say before we left?"

"That Crystal's scared, not malicious."

Penny nodded. "Makes sense. Finding yourself in the middle of a murder investigation would terrify anyone."

"The bees confirmed she's telling the truth about overhearing the argument."

"I figured as much," Penny sighed, rubbing her temples. "This case keeps getting more complicated. Too many things crossing each other."

"Too many coincidences," I said. "What are you thinking?"

She hesitated, organizing her thoughts. "What if Crystal isn't just a witness? What if she's involved somehow?"

"In the egg theft or the murders?"

"Maybe both," she said. "Seeing the love of your life with another person could send someone over the edge."

"Who's watching too much TV now. You big on soap operas, sis?"

"Don't make me hurt you." Penny started up the jeep, and we pulled away.

I frowned, something still not adding up. "If Crystal wanted Jerry dead, why frame Ziggy? She could have made it seem like an accident."

"Unless framing Ziggy served another purpose," Penny said. "Like distracting us from the actual crime—the egg theft. She hated the creature. Maybe, she hoped it would also end his life."

A sudden thought struck me. "Or creating a scapegoat to protect someone else."

My phone rang. It was Alice, her voice urgent. "Doctor Sterling, sorry to disturb you, but you need to get back here. Ziggy's missing. I brought him into the office to do some paperwork, but he chewed through his enclosure."

"What?" I felt a spike of alarm. "When did this happen?"

"Sometime in the last hour. I checked on him and he was gone. When we drove over, I left the window down and he became agitated. Almost like he smelled something."

"Basilisks are like blood hounds. He might've smelled the killer," I said. "I'm on my way."

"Ziggy's gone?" Penny asked.

"Yes, and I think he went after the real killer. He wouldn't have left if it wasn't for a good reason. He smelled something that night and maybe smelled it again."

"If any of those pixies see him, it will be game over for Ziggy. He is only safe while with a human. Plus, what if the killer realized he could communicate with me? They might hunt him down if he is out on his own."

Penny's expression hardened. "We need to find him. Fast."

Ziggy's life depended on it.

CHAPTER 24

A sudden, sharp cry—not human, but the distinctive keening of a distressed basilisk—cut through my mind as I walked through the town. Ziggy was alive and close by. Penny and I had separated to see if we could locate him. She agreed if we asked anyone else to help, it may get leaked that Ziggy was able to escape.

I had to resist the urge to rush blindly forward towards the cry. Instead, I reached out with my gift, trying to establish a mental connection. "Ziggy? Can you hear me?"

The reaction was feeble and lacked conviction. *"Friend-healer! Danger-woman-person who ended breathing! Same smell as night nice-warm-Jerry stopped moving! Lost it."*

"I'm here, buddy," I projected, trying to keep my mental voice calm and reassuring. "Can you tell me where you are? What can you see?"

"Warm-dark-trash. Big box of rotten food here. Smell of burning-ice gone."

I relayed this information to Penny via text, not daring to speak aloud. She responded: "He must be in a dumpster."

I texted back. "That's what I think. He's nearby. You can stop your search and head this way."

"Ziggy," I projected, "Keep talking and try to get on top of the dark box. I'm on my way."

"Yes, friend-healer."

I turned down the nearest alley and followed the sound of Ziggy trying to sing. It didn't take long. He was slithering erratically on the top of a dumpster. He was extremely agitated.

"I got you, buddy," I said, picking him up gently and tucking him close to my chest. "What were you thinking?"

"I smelled the Jerry-stopper and was following."

"Did you find them?"

"No, lost smell. Ziggy bad."

"Hey, hey." I stroked his back. "Stop that talk. You tried. No harm done, but let's get you back to Alice. She's worried about you."

We exited the alley, and I waved down Penny in her jeep. The streets were deserted, as they often were at this time of night. Climbing into her vehicle, I put Ziggy in the backseat.

"That was close," Penny said. "Did he tell you why he did that?"

"He smelled the killer. He was following the scent."

"Did he find anything?"

"Nah, but look where we are."

Penny realized the theater was next to us on one side and Green's lab on the other. "He does have a strong nose. If it wasn't gone, we could've searched the area."

"It gives me an idea though. What about if we got all our suspects in one room and see if he can smell one of them?"

"Great idea, but not admissible in court. The judge would never accept that my brother, who can talk to cryptids, is testifying that the basilisk detected them by their odor. Plus, we could have some serious problems if we let him near someone and they accidentally look in his eyes."

"Obviously, petrification is a danger. Just a thought."

"And a good one. If we get desperate, maybe we can try it." Penny smiled. "But we aren't there yet."

"Understood."

"Do you want me to drop Ziggy off somewhere before we go talk to Jerry's former employee?"

"That'd be great. Alice is at the clinic. Just swing by there."

We drove the remaining blocks, dropped Ziggy off to the loving arms of Alice, and were back on the road. The next interview site: a hill overlooking the town. Non-scientists primarily inhabited this area.

"Same as with Crystal?" I asked as we got out of her jeep. "No talking."

"Yes. I have never met this person, so let's tread carefully. I don't want to agitate or upset her if she isn't involved."

I saluted her. "Ma'am, yes ma'am."

"The pistol whip offer still stands," Penny said. She knocked on the door after ensuring I got a quick glare of annoyance.

"Are you sure about this?" I asked Penny. The ramshackle house looked like something out of a Grimm fairy tale - and not one of the cheerful ones.

"Jerry fired Roberta Boule three months ago," Penny said, checking her notes. "She worked at the theater for six years before that. We need to talk to everyone who might have had a grudge."

The distinct sound of off-key singing drifted through the door. I recognized the tune as "Don't Stop Believing" - or at least, a very creative interpretation of it.

"HOLD ON TO THAT FEEEEELING!" The voice inside had impressive volume, if not accuracy.

Penny and I exchanged glances. "Well," I said, "at least we know she's home."

My sister knocked on the door. This time, harder and louder. The singing cut off abruptly, replaced by the sound of something - several somethings - crashing to the floor.

"Coming!" A voice called out cheerfully. "Just as soon as I remember where I put the floor!"

More crashes followed, along with what sounded like a detailed conversation with a lamp. The door swung open to reveal Roberta Boule, Bob, former theater employee, and current one-woman party singer. She wore what appeared to be a burlap bathrobe, mismatched fuzzy slippers, and tangled silver tinsel in her hair despite it not being Christmas.

"Sheriff!" Roberta beamed at Penny, then squinted at me. "And... other Sheriff? When did we get two of you? That's... that's just excessive, if you ask me. Budget cuts and all that."

The odor of alcohol coming off Roberta was overwhelming. I couldn't be sure, but it was possible she bathed in it.

"Can we come in?" Penny asked, rubbing at her nose in hopes it would douse the stink. I didn't have the heart to tell her it wouldn't work.

"Did someone complain about my singing? I can turn it down." Her slurring was barely understandable.

"Ms. Boule," Penny said. "No one complained. I'm Sheriff Sterling, and this is my brother, Doctor Sterling. We'd like to ask you a few questions about your former employer, Jerry McKinnon."

Roberta's face lit up. "Jerry! Good old Jerry. He fired me, you know. He was professional, though. Wrote it down and everything. I have the letter somewhere." She patted her robe as if expecting to find it in a pocket, then, looked confused when she discovered the robe had no pockets. "Huh. Must have left it in my disco ball. I can check for it."

"May we come in?" I asked, catching Roberta as she swayed in the doorway.

"Of course! Mi casa es... um... my house! I took Spanish in high school. Or was it French? There was definitely a language. Words were involved."

The interior of the cottage looked like a thrift store had exploded. An eclectic collection of items covered every surface: porcelain cats with varying degrees of judgment in their painted eyes, at least three lava lamps in colors I'm pretty sure lava never comes in, and what appeared to be a life-size cardboard cutout of William Shakespeare wearing sunglasses and a Hawaiian shirt.

"That's Bill," Roberta informed us, catching my stare. "He keeps me honest. Well, he tries. Mostly, he just judges my poor life choices. But you know what they say - to thine own self be... something something. I forget the rest. Bill's probably very disappointed in me about that."

"Ms. Boule," Penny said, again. "We need to ask you about the night Jerry fired you."

"Bob, please. Ms. Boule is my father. No, no, my mother." She stopped for a moment and stared off into the distance. "Doesn't matter. Just call me Bob."

"Okay, Bob. The night Jerry let you go."

"Oh, that!" Roberta flopped onto a couch, the vibration sending several porcelain cats scattering to the floor in shards. "It was fair, really. I mean, who hasn't had a few drinks before the afternoon matinee and accidentally started doing commentary during 'The Silence of the Lambs?' The audience loved it! Well, most of them. That one guy didn't appreciate my impressions during the lamb scenes."

I caught Penny's eye. My sister's expression did that thing it did when she was trying hard to maintain her professional demeanor. Talking to a drunk was never easy, but this was kind of fun. It was hard to keep a straight face.

"And where were you two nights ago?" Penny asked, her voice steady.

"Two nights ago?" Roberta furrowed her brow in deep concentration. "Was that Tuesday? No, wait, Tuesday was when I taught my goldfish to swim the breaststroke. They're not good at it yet, but they've got heart."

I couldn't help myself. "You have goldfish?"

"Not anymore," Roberta said. "But if I still did, I bet they'd be great at synchronized swimming." She fixed me with a sharp look. "Very ambitious, but flawed. Fish just don't have the rhythm for synchronized anything and stop listening when they lay upside down."

I wanted to correct her, but kept my mouth shut.

"Ms. Boule," Penny pressed on, "Someone killed Jerry."

"Bob," she said.

With a deep sigh that said Penny was close to punching this lady, she calmed herself and said, "Sorry, Bob. Jerry McKinnon has been killed. Do you know anything about that?"

"Oh, no." Roberta looked to her left. "He was such a good guy. I'll have to stop by and say hi."

"I'm afraid he's dead."

"Oh. That's sad. Poor Ziggy."

Penny was tired of messing around. "It's important that you tell us where you were two nights ago."

"Home!" she said. "Definitely home. Probably. Unless I wasn't, in which case I was somewhere else. But I didn't kill Jerry, if that's what you're asking. I liked Jerry! He gave me a nice recommendation letter. Said I was 'punctual when conscious' and 'enthusiastic about film commentary, perhaps too enthusiastic.' Top-notch reference."

I studied Roberta. Sometimes humans gave off emotional queues similar to cryptids when they were lying or under stress. All I got from her was a jumbled mix of genuine affection, mild confusion, and an inexplicable desire to flatten her eyebrows. She kept licking her finger and rubbing it above her eyes.

"Also," Roberta said, picking up one of her porcelain cats and addressing it seriously. "Killing requires planning. And standing. I'm not good at either of those things right now. Mr. Whiskers here will vouch for me. Won't you, Mr. Whiskers?"

She held the cat up to her ear, nodding at whatever wisdom the painted feline was apparently imparting.

"Is everyone in this town crazy?" Penny asked in a hushed whisper.

I shrugged.

"Mr. Whiskers makes an excellent point," she said. "He says I couldn't have killed Jerry because I was here having a precious debate with Bill about whether hamburgers are just meat cookies. Bill was against the proposition, but I think that's just because he's a literature snob."

Penny pinched the bridge of her nose. "Ms. Boule... Bob, is there anyone who can confirm you were home that night?"

"The raccoons!" Roberta brightened. "They've been visiting my trash cans every night this week. Very punctual for bandits. I've named them all after the Seven Dwarfs, even though there are only four of them. The big one is Grumpy."

I couldn't help noticing that despite her apparent intoxication, Roberta's grip on the porcelain cat was steady, and her eyes, while unfocused, kept darting to the window with surprising alertness.

"Bob," I said. "Those raccoons wouldn't be part cryptid, would they?"

Roberta's expression momentarily blanked before a giggle escaped. "Magical raccoons? That's silly. Next, you'll be suggesting that Bill isn't the real William Shakespeare!"

"The cardboard cutout wearing Ray-Bans and a Hawaiian shirt? No, I wouldn't dream of questioning his authenticity."

"Good." She nodded. "Because he's sensitive about that. Aren't you, Bill?" She turned to the cutout, then gasped. "Bill! Language! There are officers of the law present! You know, Bill here was ahead of his time. He was into Hawaiian shirts centuries before they were invented. A true visionary."

"Do you know how to make origami birds?" I asked.

Penny looked at me, but it wasn't the angry glare I was expecting. Instead, it appeared to be thanks for asking because she had forgotten. I guessed she got distracted by Bill's shirt.

"I absolutely do," Roberta said. She leaped to her feet and just as quick fell back on her butt. "Balance is hard. I was going to show you some. In that drawer over there."

I followed her finger and opened the cabinet. The cabinet held some of the most beautiful bird art I had ever seen. She had swans, eagles, and what looked like vultures, but I couldn't be sure. "These are beautiful."

"I learned how to do those in prison. It helped focus myself and get over my addiction."

"What were you in jail for?" Penny asked.

"I used to have a drinking problem." Robert took a sip of the brown liquid from the tall glass on the table. I was fairly confident it wasn't coffee. "Made some mistakes and ended up in there for a year. But it was worth it. I learned how to do this beautiful art and got cured of my drinking problem."

"Did you give any to Jerry?" I asked.

"He didn't like to drink."

"No. Did you give any of the birds to him?"

"Oh sure. He loved them. He liked me to put a message on them and leave them around as surprises. He was a nice guy."

"Any of those messages, angry?"

She gazed into my eyes. Her face was stone cold. A few seconds passed, and she burped. "I'm sorry. Did you say something?"

"Yes, what type of messages did you leave for Jerry?"

"Oh. Motivational things like 'you got this' or 'hang in there.' Why?"

"You don't have any of those around, do you?" Penny asked.

"Sure." Roberta tried to stand again. This time, she was successful. Steadying herself, she crossed the room and pulled one off the top shelf and handed it to my sister. "This is one from the last day. He fired me before I had a chance to hide it."

Penny opened it up and read it aloud. "You rock. Let despair roll off you."

"That's sweet," I said.

"Thanks." Roberta sat down on the floor.

Penny looked like she was developing a headache. "Thank you for your time, Ms. Boule. Sorry, Bob. When you're sober, if you could come down to the station for an official comment, I would appreciate it."

"Sure, thing. I hope I can remember."

"See that you do. It's important. And if you think of anything else about that night, please let us know."

"I'll ask the raccoons!" Roberta smiled. "They're very observant. Except Doc. He needs glasses, but he's too proud to admit it."

As we headed for the door, Roberta called out, "Oh, Doctor Sterling? One more thing..."

I turned back. "Yes?"

"Your aura is beige. You need to get some sleep."

"Thank you, I'll work on that."

On the drive back to my house, Penny was quiet. Finally, she said, "You noticed it too, right?"

"That she was watching us the whole time. Yeah. And I'm pretty sure those 'raccoons' aren't real."

"Think we should look into it?"

I thought about Roberta's brief moments of sharp clarity. "Maybe. But not tonight. Tonight, I need to process the fact that even the town drunk has a relationship. It's with a cardboard cutout, but that's more than I have."

"Look on the bright side." Penny grinned. "At least she's off the market and won't show up in your dating pool."

I couldn't stop the feeling that our theatrical drunk was too happy about being fired for drinking on the job, but that investigation would have to wait for another night,

Just another odd day in Heritage Crest, where even our red herrings come with a side of porcelain cats and Shakespeare.

CHAPTER 25

After a full night of sleep, I walked into the clinic bright and early before my first appointment at eight. It took a few hours when I hit the bed for my mind to stop churning through the clues and suspects. Eventually, exhaustion overtook me, and I was out until my alarm sounded off.

"Good morning," Alice said, rising from the front desk. "How are you this morning?"

"Good morning. Other than seeing dead bodies and searching for a missing cryptid, just peachy." I smiled to ensure she knew it was my humor trying to help me adjust to the tragedy. "How's Ziggy doing after his little adventure?"

"He seems fine. He cuddled with me and fell asleep on my lap."

"That's good. The poor guy has been through a lot. So, who do we have up first this morning?"

"You have a gumtwod with a toothache."

"Wonderful." Gumtwods were one of the lesser-known cryptids. They were balls of fur about the size of a basketball that rolled around the forest. They excelled at concealing themselves, but when faced with danger, they transformed like a puffer fish with four-inch spikes in all directions. When working with them, I had to wear steel mesh gloves to avoid being skewered. They had a mouth and eyes hidden beneath their fur, but it was hard to find without feeling around. For some odd reason, they were prone to toothaches, and this was a pretty common exam. Once I found the mouth, I parted the hair to check their teeth. I had to make sure I didn't startle it and get the spikes. "I better get ready."

"There's fresh coffee in the breakroom if you want it."

I made my way down the hall, got a cup of coffee, and stepped into my office. It had been a while since I sat down to enjoy a drink and take a breath. My morning was full. I had lunch planned with Penny and Mom at noon. After that, a few more appointments and then, I'd get back to playing detective.

"You're eight o'clock is here, Doctor Sterling," Alice said over the intercom. "Room three."

I went to room three, then opened the door. I had to stifle a laugh. The gumtwod was on the examining table and the owner, Frank Jeong, was standing a few feet away. Bandages covered his hands, and stitches ran along his right forearm.

"How can I help today?" I asked.

Frank motioned to the gumtwod and then, to his injuries. "If we don't address his toothache, I'm afraid he is going to accidentally kill me."

"Let's see." I slipped on the chain mail gloves and started my examination.

The day moved forward quick after that. Lunch time came in a flash. I headed over to the sheriff's office to pick up my sister on the way to Rosie's. If I knew mom, she was ten minutes early and already had a table for us.

The sheriff station's lobby was empty. A row of seven seats lined one wall across from the lady sitting at the front desk. She had been with the department since before I was born and even after talking to her a hundred times, I couldn't remember her name.

"Have a seat Mark, the sheriff is finishing up and will be out shortly," the older woman said.

"Thanks." I took a seat, and my eyes wandered around the room. It was a simple room. A single desk across from the entrance, gray walls, no art, and a coat rack by the door. I would have thought the coat rack was their attempt at decoration, but it had a single coat hanging from it. Someone used it.

I didn't have to wait long. I heard the door to the back open, and I stood to greet my sister. However, it wasn't her. It was Violet Newsome, and she looked angry. She almost collided with me as she stormed towards the door. She wanted out of there, and it was her only focus.

"Good afternoon," I said.

She paused, looked at me, and became present. "Sorry," she said. "My mind was a million miles away."

"No worries, I don't like this place much either." I gave my signature calming smile. Everyone told me it made me look awkward, but I didn't care.

"I'm late to check in with Doctor Green. He's probably already upset that I'm not where I said I would be, but would you be free later to grab a cup of coffee? I'd like to talk about a few things."

"Sure, I can meet you at The Perky Pixies around five."

"Great, see you then." Violet rushed out the door.

Penny soon emerged through the same door. "You ready?"

"Yep. I saw Violet. How did that go?"

"Just following up on a few details Harry found. We can talk through it with mom."

"Cool."

We headed for the door, Penny motioned to the coat rack, and said, "Crap. She forgot her jacket. Screw it. She can come back if she wants it."

"I'm having coffee with her later. I can take it to her?"

"A date?" she asked. "I wouldn't date a suspect if I were you."

"Ha, ha. She's too young for me. Do you want me to grab the coat or not?"

"Nah, leave it. That way, if I have some more questions for her, it will give me an excuse."

CHAPTER 26

"So let me get this straight," Mom said, stirring her tea with deliberate slowness. "You found basilisk venom that ended up being blue slushy from the concession stand, security footage tampered with, and a dead theater owner who just happened to mention strange activities at Doctor Green's research facility the day before his murder."

"And a dead security guard, Tommy Chen, who went missing just before hitting send on a message to Mark about knowing who killed Jerry and stole the egg," Penny said.

The late afternoon crowd at Rosie's Diner had thinned out, leaving us relatively alone in our corner booth. Mom had insisted we meet here rather than at her cottage - something about "neutral ground" and "better pie." I suspected she was just craving Rosie's famous blackberry cobbler. "And that's all the evidence?"

"Don't forget the missing phoenix egg," Penny said, tapping her sheriff's badge. "And the security breaches during Violet Newsome's shifts."

"And Tommy Chen had an eggshell fragment in his pocket," I said, keeping my voice low despite the relative privacy of our booth.

Mom nodded, her silver-streaked hair catching the light. The tiny protective charms braided into it clinked as she moved. "Any other evidence?"

"Nothing solid."

"Classic trafficking operation, I think. Harvest the egg, keep it dormant in cold storage until transport, sell to the highest bidder." Her expression darkened. "I've seen it before."

"You have?" Penny and I asked simultaneously.

"1992." Mom's fingers absently traced the spiral pattern on her right palm - a mark from a wild unicorn. "A group targeting unicorn foals. They were using similar methods - tampering with security, creating diversions, using misdirection to hide their activities. But our technology wasn't as advanced."

I leaned forward. "What happened?"

"Three unicorn foals disappeared before we caught them." Her green eyes - the same ones Penny had inherited - hardened with the memory. "By then, the foals had been shipped overseas to private collectors. We never recovered them."

A heavy silence fell over our table. The implications were clear: if we didn't move quickly, the phoenix egg would face the same fate.

Rosie appeared with coffee refills, her eyebrow raising slightly at our somber expressions. "Everything all right with you Sterling's?" she asked, her Brooklyn accent still strong despite her time of living in Heritage Crest.

"Just fine, Rosie," Mom replied. "Just catching up on family business."

"Uh-huh." Rosie looked unconvinced, but knew better than to pry. In a town full of supernatural secrets, discretion was as important as good coffee. "Reach out to me if you need anything else. That phoenix cake just came out of the oven." She glanced meaningfully at the few remaining patrons before adding in a lower voice, "Special recipe."

After she left, Mom chuckled. "Rosie always knows more than she lets on. That 'phoenix cake' of hers really is just an apple pie with extra cinnamon, and some other ingredient that makes is spicy."

"So, should we order some?" I asked.

"It tastes great, but it will tear your stomach up. Unless you can investigate from the toilet, I would pass." Mom winked.

Penny shook her head in amused exasperation. "Let's focus."

"You don't want to talk about the toilet?" I asked.

Penny cleared her throat, frustrated, but unwilling to show it. Classic Penny in business mode. "So, Mom, what's your assessment of our suspects?"

Mom leaned back, considering. "Well, from what you've told me, Doctor Green and his assistant are the obvious focus. These other two ladies, the ex's, I guess you could call them suspects too."

"But which one?" I asked, flipping through my journal's pages. "Green has the expertise and access, but Violet's movements align more closely with the security breaches."

"Or they could be working together," Penny suggested.

Mom shook her head. "In my experience, traffickers rarely work in teams at the collection stage. Too many opportunities for betrayal." She took a sip of her tea. "Tell me more about Doctor Green. I still don't think he's involved. Convince me. In the spirit of full transparency, he's left me a few messages, but I haven't returned them yet."

Penny pulled out her notepad. "Doctor Victor Green, 56, internationally renowned cryptozoologist specializing in phoenix reproduction. He's published several papers on phoenix breeding cycles. Arrived at Heritage Crest on a research grant from Thorne University."

"Thorne?" Mom's eyebrows shot up. "That's interesting. He didn't mention that."

"Why?" I asked.

"Thorne University has impeccable credentials on paper, but there have been whispers about their private funding. Their endowment comes from some questionable sources, including several private collectors with less than ethical reputations."

I frowned. "So, Green could be legitimate, but unknowingly funded by people with ulterior motives?"

"It's possible," Mom said. "What about the assistant?"

"Violet Newsome," Penny said. "Master's degree in cryptozoology from Stanford. Previous intern positions at three other reservations, all studying rare breeding species. Joined Green's team just before his arrival here. Excellent references, though..."

"Though?" Mom prompted.

"We haven't been able to contact her previous supervisors. They're all conveniently on sabbatical or field research."

Mom's expression turned thoughtful. "Three other reservations, you say. Were there any reported thefts or security breaches during her employment?"

Penny and I exchanged surprised glances.

"We didn't check that," I admitted. "Plus, she told me this was her first internship. I could have misheard her. I guess."

"The '92 unicorn traffickers had a pattern of moving from reservation to reservation, never staying long enough to arouse suspicion."

Rosie arrived with our food – sandwich and chips for each of us. "On the house," she said with a wink, sliding the plates onto our table. "Family discount."

I nodded while mom tried to convince Rosie it wasn't necessary.

"More about the evidence," I said.

For the next twenty minutes, Penny explained every piece of evidence we had, again. It wasn't much, but what we had was solid. The eggshell on Tommy's body, the poor cover up of Jerry's death, and the temperature changes in the phoenix environment. We reviewed the other details until we were exhausted.

Penny frowned. "So, evidence could be more abundant, but we are still waiting on results from certain particulates?"

"Sounds like this killer or killers are sloppy. I don't think they planned to kill anyone. Like I said before, they had to have been unexpected loose ends or somehow got in the way," Mom said.

I thought about Tommy Chen and the eggshell fragment in his pocket. "Could that explain why the scorch marks at Tommy's crime scene didn't quite match phoenix fire patterns?"

"Very possibly." Mom nodded. "If someone was trying to replicate phoenix fire using conventional means, they'd miss those flare aspects. It would look similar, but not quite right, to someone familiar with the real thing. Your catch on the color was right on. I don't think Doctor Green would make that mistake."

"If Violet or Green is working for one of these collectors," Penny said, "they'll have resources, and backup plans we haven't even considered."

"And they won't hesitate to eliminate obstacles," Mom said. "Like theater owners who see too much, or security guards who stumble upon their operation."

"So, how do we catch them?" I asked. "If they're as professional as you say, they'll be careful."

Mom smiled. That smile always preceded her most ingenious solutions to seemingly impossible problems. "Every smuggler has one critical weakness."

"Which is?" Penny prompted.

"Deadlines." Mom tapped the table for emphasis. "Their buyers are not patient people, and the black market operates on strict timetables. If a delivery is promised, it must be fulfilled or there are consequences. Plus, with the phoenix egg specifically, there is a little timer on hatching."

I thought back to the timeline we'd pieced together. "The egg went missing approximately four days ago. How long would they keep it in cold storage before transport?"

"For a phoenix egg?" Mom considered. "No more than a week. Like I said the other night, we only have a few days left. Any longer will risk premature hatching. Which would be catastrophic for their operation."

"Because a newly hatched phoenix bonds with the first being it sees," I said, remembering my training. "And once bonded, it can't be separated for a few years without serious mental consequences to the chick."

"Exactly." Mom nodded. "So, if we assume a one-week timeline, they'll be moving the egg within the next three days."

Penny straightened, her sheriff mode fully engaged. "That gives us a narrow window and a deadline. We need to find that egg before they transport it."

"Unfortunately, if they keep it in the cold too long, it could also damage the chick," Mom said.

Penny, who had been taking diligent notes, glanced at her watch. "We should wrap this up. I need to get back to the station. I still have to follow up on one last lead to see if they have any of Violet's employment history."

A comfortable silence fell as we finished our lunch. Despite the seriousness of our discussion, I felt a warm sense of rightness sitting here with my family, working together on a problem that mattered. Mom must have felt it too, because she smiled at us with that blend of pride and love that always made me feel about ten feet tall.

"You know," she said. "Watching you two now, it's like everything's come full circle. Penny with her evidence-based approach and Mark with your creature communication - you balance each other perfectly. Your dad would be proud."

A subtle smile played on Penny's lips despite her eye roll. "Save the sentimentality for when we actually solve the case, Mom."

"We need justice for Ziggy, too," I said.

"Exactly." Mom nodded. "Speaking of which, how is the little fellow doing?"

"Good. Alice has adopted him."

"That's excellent. Basilisks need stability after emotional shocks." Mom gathered her things, somehow fitting everything back into that miraculous bag of hers. "I should get going as well. I'm meeting with the sanctuary board tonight to review a proposed new area around the Evertine Cat zone."

"Thanks for all this," Penny said, gesturing to her notes. "It's... well, it's invaluable."

"Just be careful," Mom said, her expression momentarily vulnerable. "Both of you. This isn't just about a stolen egg anymore, it's about two murders and potentially a global trafficking network. Don't take unnecessary risks."

Coming from the woman who once faced down a rampaging manticore armed with nothing but a wooden spoon and sheer determination, this was significant. "We'll be careful," I promised.

"Good." Mom stood, adjusting her shawl. "And Mark? One last thing about communicating with traumatized creatures like Ziggy."

"Yes?"

Her eyes softened. "Sometimes, the best thing you can do is just listen. Don't push for information. Create a space where they are safe enough to share what they know in their own time."

"I was curious. You know basilisks pretty well. How accurate is their sense of smell?"

"Excellent, why?"

"We didn't mention it before, but the scent Ziggy caught when Jerry was killed, he detected it again. He escaped and chased after it."

"Oh, hell," Mom said. "Ziggy is runny around out there somewhere?"

"No, no," I assured her. "We found him, but he was positive he identified the same woman from the night Jerry died. Could his olfactory senses be that reliable?"

"Absolutely. They're better than blood hounds."

"We talked about this," Penny said.

"I know. Just wanted Mom's opinion."

"Hear me out. Ziggy is sure it is a woman. We have three suspects that are women, and we are running out of time to figure out which one it is. Could he be that accurate on the sex of the person?"

"We know all this." Penny was getting angry.

"Yes, absolutely," Mom said.

"It would not work," Penny said. "I told you this already, Mark."

"Right, but I am saying it would work if I could hide him and do it."

"The same answer applies. First, not admissible in court and walking a basilisk by three suspects, even hidden, would be bad if he stuck his head out and someone looked him directly in the eye. We can't do that. It's illegal."

"What about," Mom said. "We have Ziggy on the other side of an open door. He should be able to tell you if they are in the room. And that way, you don't have to worry about them being hurt. You would at least feel like you're on the right track."

"That might work," Penny said. She thought for a minute. "Let me think about it a little more. We would have to do it in the lobby because the exam rooms are cinder blocks and would probably not be easy to smell through."

"Sure. At least we would be aware if we had the right people." I smiled, hoping to defuse Penny.

"Let me think about it and I'll let you know."

"Don't think too long, honey. The clock is ticking." With that last piece of wisdom, mom left, the tiny charms in her hair tinkling as she moved. Penny and I remained, looking at the various magical items now spread across our table.

"Well," Penny said after a moment. "That was a lot."

I chuckled. "That's Mom for you. Always prepared."

"Think any of this will help?"

As we gathered our things to leave, I felt a strange mix of apprehension and excitement. "I hope so."

"And you have to stop with this Ziggy thing."

"Come on sis. I'm just trying to help move things forward."

"I know." Penny shook her head. "I'll admit it, he makes me nervous. I just don't want any accidents that could have been prevented by common sense. Especially, if those ladies are innocent. I know you mean well. Let me think some more on it."

We stepped out into the misty afternoon air. "Do you ever think about how weird our family is? Most siblings bond over sports or movies, not cryptid trafficking investigations."

Penny laughed, a rare, full sound that reminded me of when we were kids. "Would you have it any other way?"

We hugged and walked in two different directions. I had a few more appointments and then coffee with a potential thief and killer. If Violet wasn't responsible, someone else faced an imminent deadline. We had three days to find them before the egg disappeared forever or suffered irreparable damage.

CHAPTER 27

The workday ended and, to my surprise, I was on time for my coffee date with Violet. No, not a date, appointment. Yeah, that felt better.

Maintaining a poker face while having coffee with someone you suspect of murder is significantly harder than treating a hypochondriac unicorn. At least Sparkles only threatened to leave critical reviews on RateMyVet – she wasn't likely to make me disappear if she caught on that I was investigating her.

I took a sip of my coffee, met her eyes, and asked, "You mentioned you wanted to chat. What's up?"

"You seem distracted," Violet said, stirring her latte with practiced grace. We were sitting in a booth at The Perky Pixies, the local coffee shop that catered to both human and cryptid pets. It reminded me of the trend of Cat Cafes in the major cities. A family of pixies had made their home in the hanging plants above us, occasionally sprinkling sparkly dust into people's drinks when they thought no one was looking.

"Just a busy day," I replied. Everything about Violet was precise – her movements, her schedule, her carefully crafted stories about late-night research observations. She aligned her spoon with the edge of her saucer. "Had to treat a griffin with aspirational acrobatic tendencies. Again."

She laughed, the sound falling a fraction too late to be natural. "The same one I saw trying that triple spiral last week?"

"Different griffin, same poor life choices." I took another sip of my coffee, using the moment to study her reflection in the window behind our table. She maintained eye contact with a practiced, mechanical precision. "Speaking of poor life choices, how's Doctor Green's research going?"

"That's what I wanted to talk about," Violet said. "I thought if I asked your sister, she might feel compelled to do something, so I wanted to ask you."

"About what?"

"Doctor Green is intelligent and wants everyone to know it. He is mean, secretive, and seems to always be up to something that he doesn't want to share. I'm not there yet, but if I wanted to file a complaint about him how would I do it?"

I leaned back. This, I wasn't expecting. "Heritage Crest has a council that oversees the day-to-day activities. They have a form in the government building next to the grooming salon. You can fill it out and they will contact you."

"Are they discreet? I don't want to get in trouble for making a report. I can't find him half the time and then, he complains, I didn't do something he never asked about. Plus, he keeps telling me he should replace me."

"That sounds hostile. Have you tried telling him how you feel or to stop?"

"I have. He tells me I'm overreacting and even once suggested that it was my hormones making me overly sensitive to his words."

"Oh boy." I rubbed my chin vigorously. "That's not good. You should formerly complain."

"I will. Thank you," she said. "I love the work we're doing with the phoenix, and I don't want to jeopardize the experience."

"It doesn't give him the right to behave poorly." I studied her face. Something was off. She could have easily found out how to file a complaint from anyone. Why me? It didn't feel right. "You wouldn't be the first to call a scientist out on their lack of social skills."

"Thank you, that helps." She took a sip of her drink. "Listen to me going on and on about my issues. How are you? Any closer to solving the mystery?"

"Which one?" I smiled. "Between the murders and the egg being stolen, things are busy."

"Any clues or ideas about who did any of it?"

"We're close," I lied. "Waiting for a few more details."

"That sounds promising."

"We shall see." I realized she was fishing. I couldn't determine if their interest was in my details or morbid curiosity. Could she be worried we were close to discovering it was her? "I really shouldn't talk about it until we make the arrest."

"An arrest? That sounds like you are close. I'm worried about the egg," she said.

"Everyone is. I just hope we can keep Aurora in her habitat. The closer it gets to a possible hatching time, the harder it will be. If she wanted to break out and look for her child, it would be a mess."

Only a subtle tightening of her eyes betrayed her. The arrest comment had her distracted and looking guilty. After a few seconds, she said, "Oh, you know how it is with phoenixes. They're quite docile unless pushed. Hopefully, it doesn't come to that." She glanced at her watch. "Actually, I should head back. We're monitoring some interesting flight patterns in the nesting area."

"I bet you are." I kept my expression neutral. "Need any help? I could stop by later if you want."

"No!" The word came out sharp and immediately realized it. "I mean, Doctor Green prefers to minimize outside interference during this phase. You understand."

"Of course." I smiled, channeling my inner Sparkles-dealing patience. "Another time then."

She gathered her things, and a small round device fell from her bag, a temperature monitoring device, the kind we used for cold storage units. She snatched it up, but not before I caught a glimpse.

"Dropping and forgetting things. I must be more tired than I thought." She laughed, but there was an edge to it now. "Thanks for the coffee, Mark. We should do this again soon."

"Looking forward to it," I lied, again. "I almost forgot. You left your jacket in the sheriff's office."

"I was wondering what happened to that. Please tell your sister I'll stop by when I get a break over the next couple of days if it's okay."

"It should be fine. I'll let her know."

As soon as she left, Mrs. Pembroke materialized at my table, coffee pot in hand. I didn't know she worked here. "Well, that was more tense than a unicorn not getting the attention they want," she said, topping off my cup with a smile. "And I have some experience with that."

"You noticed?"

"Honey, even the pixies noticed. They stopped spiking drinks to watch the show." She nodded toward the hanging plants. Tiny faces ducked behind leaves. "Though I have to say, your poker face has improved since that time you tried to convince me Sparkles' horn wasn't actually turning plaid."

"In my defense, she had painted it while I wasn't looking." I lowered my voice. "Did you manage to...?"

Mrs. Pembroke slipped me a small notebook. "Every phone call she's made from my shop in the last week, complete with timestamps and any snippets of conversation I could catch. That woman has more phone calls than a Dooey Gobler has teeth. She was acting suspicious. I know we had a mix up with you and your sister the other night. I really do want to help. Not sure where her head is though. She was acting strange during our lone search for the egg."

I slipped the notebook into my pocket, wondering if she had one of these on everyone. Before I could ask her, my phone buzzed – the clinic's emergency line. "Doctor Sterling. Slow down, Alice."

"One of those giant frogs is trying to unionize."

"What do you mean?"

"I was checking on a Duffy bird we treated yesterday. I wanted to make sure the splint on its leg was still good. As I was getting ready to leave the enclosures, I was stopped by a furious Loveland frog."

The Loveland frogs were humanoid bipedal frog-like cryptids and one of only three species in the sanctuary that had vocal cords. Several had learned some broken English and could communicate with normal people. They stood about four feet tall and were from an area in Ohio. The news of their rage was quite peculiar. They were normally friendly. "What happened?"

"Apparently, he's organizing a protest over the 'inhumane living conditions' of having to make an appointment for medical care," Alice explained, sounding like she was one dramatic frog away from a career change. "I explained to him we are closed for the day and if it wasn't an emergency, he would need to schedule an appointment. He's got three others convinced they're being discriminated against and should fill our lobby with their bile."

"Did they threaten you?"

"Not exactly. But getting yelled at by a giant standing frog is enough to shake anyone up."

I pinched the bridge of my nose. "Tell him I'll be there in ten minutes and remind him there is nothing to unionize. They don't work."

"I tried that." She gave a nervous laugh. "He said it was speciesism and demanded to speak to the manager."

"I am the manager."

"I told him that, too. He's now insisting on speaking to your inner manager."

The things they don't prepare you for in vet school. What the hell was an inner manager? "Just keep them occupied. If you're near a media station, maybe put on that documentary about frog history. The one narrated by Morgan Freeman."

"Already did. They're fact-checking it in real-time and plan to write a strongly worded letters to the production company."

"Which section of the reservation are you in?"

"Alpha, three, three."

"Tell them I'm on my way."

No sooner than I hung up, my phone rang again. I ignored the caller ID before answering. "Sterling."

"Hey little brother. You got a second," Penny said.

"I'm heading over to stop a union being formed?"

"Do I want to know?"

"No." I laughed. "Can I call you after?"

"Why don't you come by," she said. "I'll be here."

"Everything okay?"

"Yeah. I had a two-hour meeting with the city council, and we are getting pressure to solve this. I'm out of options to move this along faster. I think I want to try your idea with Ziggy."

"Excellent. Hopefully, this won't take long. See you soon."

I hung up and prepared for a new kind of chaos in Heritage Crest. Our first bipedal frog union.

CHAPTER 28

The Loveland Frog union ended as quickly as it begun. I showed up, listened, ensured there were no emergencies, and reminded them we could always put them back in their natural habitat if they were unhappy. It seemed the thought of being chased and killed by hunters back in Ohio reminded them of their normal kindness. The courtesy returned to the cryptids, and they went about their business.

More annoyed than anything, an hour later, I was walking into Penny's office. "Sorry about the delay."

"No worries," Penny said. "Who was unionizing this time?"

"The walking frogs, but everything is okay now."

"Let me guess. You reminded them of the healthcare they don't get in the wild?"

"Something like that." I gave a slight smile.

"Classic tactic."

Penny was able pull me out of a bad mood as quickly as she could put me into one. "Enough about that. So, rough council meeting?"

She tightened her ponytail. A tick she had that meant nervousness. "Yeah. They're nice enough about it, but I agree with them - we are running out of time. Losing an egg will jeopardize the feeling of safety for all our cryptid residents and, more importantly, cause more scrutiny for our operations."

"Yikes." It was the only thing I thought to say. I had no desire for more oversight, either. Our little town was peaceful and had the right amount of leadership. "It makes sense why you want to try Ziggy now."

"Exactly. Here are my thoughts. Instead of you being on the other side of a door, you could walk through the lobby with them all sitting in there. If you cover a cat carrier or something like that with a towel, then they won't have a clue Ziggy is even in there and he would get a better sniff. Plus, if the cage is shut, I won't have to worry about him accidentally sticking his head out and petrifying someone. What do you think? Will Ziggy agree to be good?"

"Should be fine. I will talk to him."

"His confirmation isn't able to be used in court, but at this point, I need to at least know I am focused on the right people."

"I get it. What time do you want me here?"

"Let's do it in the morning. Say ten?"

I looked at my phone. I had an appointment at eight and another at nine, but those would be quick. "That will work. I'll ask Alice to bring Ziggy in with her tomorrow."

"Great. If you're early, wait outside. I'll tell them to be here at 9:45 and they should be settled before you come in."

"Sounds like a plan." I stood and started to leave.

"Hey, I forgot to ask you. How was your date?" Penny was grinning.

"Date?"

"Yeah, with Violet."

"It wasn't a date."

"She's a few years younger than you. If she turns out to not be a serial killer, you two might be a splendid match. When this is over, I can try to make it happen."

"Please, stop."

CHAPTER 29

The next day, after my morning appointments were as routine as I had hoped, I headed to the sheriff's station. I was a minute early and hung out in the parking lot until ten. There was a lot riding on this sniff test. I was nervous and so was Ziggy. He agreed to be good, but the unfortunate part about basilisks is they moved uncontrollably when emotional. I couldn't compel him to remain still in the carry kennel and ignore his natural reaction. I had to hope if he smelled the killer, he would stay calm enough to not cause any suspicion.

"Friend-healer. What do you want me to do if I smell the person who made warm-Jerry go cold?"

"Just let me know."

"Ziggy can do it."

"No worries. I trust you."

"Ziggy is scared," he said. *"What if the cold maker sees Ziggy? Cold-maker made warm-Jerry into cold-Jerry. Could make Ziggy cold too."*

"I won't let that happen," I said, projecting as much confidence as I was able to muster. "Penny and I will keep you safe. You're going to be our secret weapon. No one will know why you're there. Please just do your best to stay still."

His scales rippled – the basilisk equivalent of a nervous shrug. *"Ziggy trusts friend-healer."*

That simple statement of faith felt heavier than the entire weight of Jasper the dragon after she'd eaten too many magical fireflies. I wouldn't let him down.

I pulled open the heavy glass door and stepped into the lobby. I shut the door behind us, and I was slightly taken aback. There were only two people in the lobby, Crystal and Bob. Violet was missing. "Good morning, ladies."

Both ladies looked up at me and, almost in sync, responded with, "Good morning."

"Morning, Doc. Sheriff's expecting you." The older woman behind the check-in desk smiled. Damn, what was her name?

"Thanks. She in her office?"

She nodded, then, peered curiously at the carrier. "What've you got there? Don't tell me that damned unicorn managed to dull her horn through sheer force of hypochondria, and it fell off."

I forced a laugh, keeping my tone casual. "A stray I picked up. Thought Penny might want to see it before I take it to the sanctuary."

Her attention was already shifting to the ringing phone on his desk, allowing me to scan the lobby without appearing too obvious about it.

I was only a few steps toward the door leading to the back of the station when Ziggy started bumping the sides. A subtle vibration initially touched my hand. Then, it intensified, the plastic walls rattling as the basilisk inside thrashed. The carrier was visibly rocking. I grabbed it with both hands to steady it, but it was obvious.

"Cold maker is here. Warm-Jerry killer here. My body won't stop moving. I can't control it."

Crystal pointed at the carrier, the sleeve of her bright purple dress covering all but her index finger. "What's in there?"

Her beauty was so distracting, I forgot for a moment where I was and any worries or tension I was feeling. It was an out of body experience to hear her voice and see her perfect features. What was happening? I needed to get Ziggy out of there before his reaction became even more obvious.

"Sorry," I said with forced cheerfulness. "Rescue. Not quite socialized yet. I should get him to Penny's office."

"What kind?"

"Oh, just a stray cypher cat I found." The box was shaking more violently. I had to get out of there. "Sorry to be rude, but I have to run."

"Can you tell your sister that we have places to be?" Bob asked. She was not as pleasant sober.

"Sure will." I rushed through the door into the back area of the station, heart pounding as loudly as Ziggy was thrashing. Penny was waiting in the small conference room, and her eyes widened as I burst in and placed the violently shaking carrier on the table. I sent the basilisk calming thoughts until the erratic movement stopped.

"Well," Penny said.

I nodded, still focusing on soothing the traumatized basilisk and figuring out what the hell was happening to me every time I was around Crystal. "Someone in that lobby triggered him. He's saying 'cold-maker is here' and 'warm-Jerry killer here. Ziggy confirmed she's in there."

"Yes!" She stood and was visually excited.

Something struck me. A thought that didn't seem to be real. I asked, "I guess we were wrong about Violet."

Penny already considered this. "Yeah, she couldn't make it. Doctor Green called me and demanded that I let her work. He really is an ass. But yeah, now that we've narrowed it to one of these two, we can focus our digging there and hope Violet files a complaint against him."

"She asked me about how to do it. I'm sure it's coming."

"Good. You know what this means for you?"

I shrugged. "No?"

"Violet is clear for you to date."

"No...just no. I will find my person when I'm ready."

"Your loss." Penny started towards the door. "I need to chat with the ladies and let them go. At least now, I can put someone on each of them until we can build a case. Crystal lied to us once already, so I am putting my money on her. Let's see them sneak around with a watcher."

Something was still bothering me. Our two suspects might be capable of murder. Anyone was, but did they have the ability or knowledge to pull off the phoenix egg theft. I couldn't see it. One was beautifully strange and the other lived a drunken existence. Neither struck me as a criminal mastermind. What if we are wrong, and the theft is unrelated to Jerry or Tommy's death? What if someone different killed Jerry than Tommy? There were still too many questions, and the pieces were not fitting together. I'm sure Penny thought through all of this as well, but she was right. We were closer now than before.

CHAPTER 30

I woke up on day six since the phoenix egg went missing. The poor chick only had less than two days before it could start suffering permanent damage from extended cold storage. It was a rough estimate from mom and if we could find it sooner, we should.

I dressed and took a shower at a reasonable pace. The stress of events and impending deadline were taking their toll. I had to keep moving. Aurora and so many others were counting on me.

My phone vibrated. It was Penny. Part of me didn't want to answer it. I couldn't bear another death. That thought jolted me. Whatever depression or funk I was in from lack of a solution would not bring me down. I was better than that.

With a metaphorical splash of cold water waking me up, I answered, "Good morning, sis."

"Hey. Do you have some time this morning to stop by? Say around nine."

"What's up? Did something happen?"

"Not that I'm aware of. The night shift I assigned to watch our two leading ladies is stopping by to report in after shift change."

I looked at the clock. It was a few minutes past seven and my first appointment was at half-past nine. I couldn't remember who it was for and said a silent prayer it was not Sparkles. "Sure, I'll be there."

"See you then," Penny said. The line disconnected.

Grabbing a bagel loaded with cream cheese, I headed into the clinic before our meeting. I arrived before Alice for the first time this week. She would be in soon, but it still felt good. I started a pot of coffee and retired to my office. I needed to sit quietly and think through what we had so far on Bob and Crystal.

Alice arrived at the clinic, waved at me as she passed the door, and headed right to work. Desperate to find some uncovered clue, I engrossed myself in the notes and ignored my surroundings. I noticed her only when she stopped at my door and said, "Good morning. Thanks for making coffee."

"No worries. It's about time I got in early at least once. I have to step out in a little while, but I will be back for the first appointment."

"Got it. How is the investigation going?"

"Exhausting." It was the only word I could think of. "But we are getting closer."

"That's good to hear. Well, I need to get to work in examination room three."

"The pixies again?" I asked, directing my attention back to the notes on my screen.

"You know what the worst part about cleaning pixie sneezes off the ceiling is?" Alice said, nodding. "The glitter never really comes off. It's like supernatural herpes."

I looked up from Doctor Green's research notes online. The language changed between pages—something I might not have noticed if I hadn't spent years looking up some big words Mom often used. The words shifted in the notes from scientific terms to layman and back again. "Have you tried an energy drink? Mom swears it works better than regular cleaning solutions."

"Oh sure, because an energy drink is such a logical jump from bleach," Alice retorted. "Besides, I think some pixies are doing it on purpose now. That one with the purple spotted wings keeps aiming for the light fixtures."

Alice shuffled off, and I went back to the notes. Something caught my attention. The detailed temperature logs for the phoenix sanctuary showed minute variations going back much further than the technician Julie Niman had mentioned - nothing that would trigger alarms, but enough to acclimate eggs to slowly colder temperatures. Did we miss a suspect in the timing? Could Bob or Crystal know how to make the changes?

"Doctor Sterling?" Alice poked her head back into the office. "Um, Violet Newsome is here. Says she needs to discuss some research protocols?"

I closed the note file. " Send her in."

Violet swept into the office like a cool breeze, her lab coat impeccably pressed, and her auburn hair pulled back in a professional bun. Not a strand out of place, unlike my perpetually windswept look. "Mark, I hope I'm not interrupting?"

"Not at all. I was just reviewing some stuff online." I watched her face. "Fascinating stuff about temperature regulation in phoenix habitats."

Something flickered behind her eyes - there and gone so fast I might have imagined it. "Oh yes, Doctor Green is quite meticulous about his documentation. I help him organize everything."

"I guessed that. Do you enter all his notes or just some?"

This time, the flicker stayed longer. She seemed confused. "I'm sorry?"

"The entries. The wording just seemed a little different at times. I figured you both enter his notes."

"Ah, yes." Her smile didn't quite reach her eyes. "I just try to make things understood by all the levels of science knowledge. It was a requirement for my last internship. Old habits die hard."

"Where was that?"

"Oh, several actually. I did a sort of tour of programs at a few sanctuaries."

"I thought you previously mentioned that this was your first program involvement."

She glanced at her watch. "Not sure I said that. Speaking of programs, I should really get back to the sanctuary, but I had to stop by to ask you something. Aurora's been quite agitated lately, and we're monitoring her closely. Am I okay to resume our normal schedule and research?"

"Is this you asking, or did Green send you?" I asked.

Violet's professional mask slipped for just a moment, revealing something harder underneath. "He didn't want to be a bother."

"Tell him," I said, taking a deep breath, "I'll let him know. You should be able to start again in the next day or two."

"I will tell him. Thank you. I enjoyed our talk the other night. Maybe, we can do it again sometime." Violet looked nervous as she rushed out. Was it the thought of giving Green bad news or something else? Was she aware I caught her lying about her previous experience?

We eliminated her as a suspect, but something about her behavior seemed off. Green's behavior might have been inappropriate, I wasn't sure. A previous alarm I set on my phone sounded off. It was time to go see my sister.

Fifteen minutes later, I was sitting in Penny's office, and we were both staring at four pixies perched on the corner of her desk. The small cryptids seemed to always be energetic, but not these few. They looked tired and seemed to be fighting the closing of their eyes.

"You used pixies?" I asked.

"They wanted to help and are hard to spot unless you know what you are looking for. I figured, why not."

"How did you ask them?"

"You said they could understand me. So, I just asked. They saluted me and were off."

"Wow, look at you," I said. "We'll make a translator out of you yet."

"That's why you're here." One pixy was on his back and snoring. Penny tapped the desk to wake them. "I need you to hear their report. Let's move this along before they all fall asleep."

"Thank you so much for your help," I said, motioning to the pixies. "We really appreciate you staying up all night. You must be wiped out."

"*You have no idea,*" the shortest of the pixie said. He appeared to be their leader. In their world, the smaller you were, the more power you had. Odd, but funny in a weird sort of way. *"These two humans are probably the most boring we have ever watched."*

"You watch humans often?" I asked.

The pixie leader cleared his throat and looked away. *"No."*

"Right. Start at the beginning and I will translate for the sheriff."

The tiny pixie put his arm around the one sitting next to him. *"Meegoo and me had the one you called Cryssy."*

"Crystal," I corrected.

"Whatever. Anyway, this lady is not like other humans."

I translated for Penny and then she asked, "How so?"

"She walks around her house talking to objects with no life. For almost an hour, she had a conversation with the clock on the wall. And I couldn't be sure, but we think it answered back."

"Oh," I said, though I wasn't surprised. Crystal was different. Beautiful, but different still the same. "What about regarding the case? Any visitors? Did she go anywhere, phone calls, etc."

"Nothing. It was actually quite sad. She eventually headed to bed around eleven and...." He stopped to check the writing on a tiny notebook in his hands. *"She peed two times during the night."*

I conveyed the information to Penny.

"You gave her privacy while in the bathroom, right?" Penny asked.

The pixie nodded.

"Anything else?" I asked.

"Not for us. Feewed, tell him what you two did."

Feewed opened his eyes and sighed. He sat up and yawned. *"It was so boring. Boob sat around the entire night and kept drinking that brown liquid directly from its large bottle. She fell asleep on the couch for a bit and then started drinking again. She repeated this until our shift change."*

"It's Bob." I fought back a smile. "Same question for you. In all of that, what about in reference to the case? Any visitors? Did she go anywhere? Phone calls?"

"None. It was quite sad."

I translated for Penny.

"I wasn't expecting much," Penny said. She stood. "Thank you so much for helping with this."

The pixie's stood and bowed. The leader said, "*Anything for the town and sanctuary. We will have the next shift reporting to you at six tonight when we take over.*"

"Thank you," I said. "Talk to you then."

Departing the room, the pixies then left the station.

"Not sure what I was expecting," Penny said. "But I had hoped one of them would have done something suspicious or at least help us lean towards one over the other."

"Yeah. Hopefully, the day shift will catch something. They said they will report back here at six."

"I hope so. We are down to two days."

"I'm aware."

"We need to find something that we're missing. The video is no help. The logs and entry led to Tommy and, well... he can't help us. The egg has to be here somewhere here, but we have looked everywhere."

The angst, depression, and funk creeped back into me. We really needed a clue.

CHAPTER 31

I completed my morning appointments, and I asked Alice to reschedule the afternoon ones. I had to prioritize finding the egg over everything else. After no new information from the pixies, Penny had started the search all over again. No stone left unturned.

I stepped into the lobby to find Alice sitting at her desk, organizing a stack of patient files. Ziggy nestled in his carrier on the corner of the desk, his blue scales shimmering in the morning light.

"I'm heading out," I said, setting down my coffee. "Ziggy, you ready to go?"

"Ziggy ready."

"Thank you for bringing him in," I said.

Alice looked up with a smile. "No problem. He's been quite the gentleman this morning. Just don't let him get in any danger."

"He'll be perfectly safe," I assured her. "I just need his unique perspective on something."

"His sense of smell, you mean?" Alice raised an eyebrow.

"Exactly. His nose might help us narrow down our suspect list."

"Go with friend-healer? Help find bad person who hurt nice-warm-Jerry?"

"That's the plan, buddy," I said. "Thanks, Alice. I appreciate it."

"Just doing my part to help solve a murder," she said with a grin. Alice reached into the carrier and rubbed her hand down the base of Ziggy's neck. "You be good. I have grown attached to you."

"Don't worry. This is a great idea and it's safe."

"This is a terrible idea," I said to no one in particular. I parked my truck across the street from Crystal Lockhead's cottage. The place looked deceptively normal in the pale morning light—white picket fence, well-tended garden, and only minimal evidence of the resident's eccentricity in the form of wind chimes made from what appeared to be doll heads and silverware.

"Why watch Shiny-Hair Lady?" Ziggy said sleepily from his carrier. He'd taken to giving everyone nicknames: Penny was "Badge-Sister," Mom was "Wise-Healer," and Crystal had apparently earned "Shiny-Hair Lady" during our previous encounters.

"Because something doesn't add up," I said. "You smelled our killer when we brought you through the sheriff's station. With Crystal and Bob being the only ones in the lobby, I want to narrow it down."

My decision to follow Crystal had come after reviewing my notes and the less than a stellar report from the pixies. Crystal had lied about her whereabouts the night of Jerry's murder. She had an unhealthy obsession with him. She exhibited puzzling behavior even though Ziggy didn't outright accuse her of being the killer. Penny would definitely yell at me if she knew I was conducting unauthorized surveillance. But what she didn't know wouldn't hurt her. Plus, this was how they did it on TV.

"We catch a killer?" Ziggy said, his increased enthusiasm causing the carrier to warm several degrees.

"Not yet, buddy," I said. "And remember—no loud noises. Just stay calm. We're supposed to be inconspicuous."

"Inconsp... inconsp..."

"Hidden. We don't want Crystal to see us."

"Sneaky-sneaky," Ziggy settled down again.

I didn't have to wait long before Crystal emerged from her cottage, and when she did, I nearly dropped my coffee. Gone was the disheveled woman with feathers stuck to her clothes and cat faces pinned to her wedding dress. In her place stood someone almost dressed normal. She had tamed her hot pink hair into a sleek bob, and she wore a simple floral dress with sensible shoes. The only hint of her usual eccentricity was a necklace made from what appeared to be tiny forks and spoons.

She walked down her garden path, carrying a wicker basket covered with a checkered cloth. Whatever I'd been expecting, a ritual dance in the front yard or conversations with garden gnomes, this wasn't it. Was she going on a picnic?

I waited until she was halfway down the block before starting my car and following at a discreet distance. Crystal's first stop was the grocery store. I parked across the street and pretended to be engrossed in my phone while keeping one eye on the entrance.

"Hungry," Ziggy announced.

"We just ate," I reminded him, pulling a small container of spicy crickets from my pocket. Basilisks had metabolisms that would make hummingbirds jealous.

"Growing scales. Need fuel."

I slipped a cricket into his carrier and immediately regretted it when the scent of secreted enzymes digesting the insect filled my car. It reminded me of sulfur. "Try not to regurgitate, please," I said, rolling down a window.

Crystal emerged with her basket held lower, now fuller under the cloth. She continued down Main Street, greeting several townspeople with a normal cheerfulness that seemed at odds with the woman who had proudly shown us her collection of Jerry's dental floss.

Her next stop was the apothecary shop, where Konas had been working the night, he'd spotted her near Jerry's theater. I frowned. Was she returning to the scene of the crime? I thought he had yelled at her.

I couldn't follow her inside without being spotted, so I stayed in my car, drumming my fingers nervously on the steering wheel. What was going on?

"Shiny-Hair Lady hiding something," Ziggy said, peering out through the grates of his carrier.

"Maybe," I said. "Or maybe she's just buying herbs."

Crystal emerged from the apothecary with her basket looking suspiciously bulkier. She checked her watch, picked up her pace, and headed toward the park.

I followed on foot now, keeping a respectable distance and trying to look like a vet enjoying a morning stroll with his covered pet carrier. Perfectly normal. Instinctively, Ziggy's scent repelled the other cryptids. Humans couldn't detect the pheromones with their noses, but other cryptids took it as a warning to stay away.

I kind of liked people avoiding me and not being inundated with questions. I may have to ask Alice if I could take Ziggy with me everywhere. However, that was a problem for a different day.

The park was one of Heritage Crest's most beautiful features. It had sprawling green spaces with sections designed for both human and cryptid recreation. Trees and bushes isolated parts of the large area. In the center stood a massive oak tree, rumored to be as old as the town itself, its branches spanning wider than most buildings.

Crystal made her way to the oak, glanced around to ensure she wasn't observed, and then ducked behind it.

"That's not suspicious at all," I muttered, quickening my pace.

"Careful," Ziggy warned. *"Might be trap."*

"It's Crystal, not a supervillain," I said, though I did approach with caution.

Peering around the massive trunk, I expected to find Crystal performing some bizarre ritual or perhaps burying suspicious evidence. Instead, I found her arranging what appeared to be tiny plates of food at the base of the tree. Crystal must have heard me, because she whirled around, almost dropping the miniature cupcake in her hand. Her eyes widened at the sight of me.

"Doctor Sterling! What are you? I mean, this isn't what it looks like!"

I stared at the elaborate spread she'd laid out: tiny sandwiches cut into heart shapes, thimble-sized cups of what smelled like honeysuckle tea, and an assortment of sweet cakes barely bigger than quarters.

"Actually, I have no idea what this looks like," I said.

"She no smell like Jerry killer," Ziggy said.

I smiled. Mission accomplished. Now, how to get out of here. But first, I just had to know what was happening.

Crystal's face flushed pink to match her hair. She glanced around before leaning in closer. "You can't tell anyone. Promise me."

"I promise," I said, curiosity overriding the excitement of telling Penny that Bob had to be the killer. "But I'm not sure what I would say to anyone anyway."

Crystal's eyes softened at the sight of the pet carrier. "What's in there? I hope not the same cat you had at the sheriff's station," she said.

"No." I laughed. "Something different."

She straightened her back and decided. "Well, you're already here. You might as well meet them."

"Meet who?" I asked, but Crystal had already turned to face the oak tree.

"It's okay," she said. "He's the nice doctor I told you about. The one who can talk to you."

For a moment, nothing happened. Then, one by one, tiny heart-shaped faces peeked out from knotholes and from behind roots. The faces belonged to creatures no larger than grasshoppers, with delicate translucent arms and legs. Their bodies glowed with a soft inner light.

"Tree folk sprites," I said, amazed. They were one of the rarest and most secretive cryptid species. They were thought to exist only in the deepest forests of northern Europe. "I didn't know we had a colony in Heritage Crest."

"Almost nobody does," Crystal said, kneeling to place the last of her offerings. "And it needs to stay that way. They came here many years ago and most people who knew about them have moved on or died. They became forgotten. Which is exactly how they like it."

The sprites ventured out, their curiosity overcoming their fear. Several approached Ziggy's carrier, chattering in a language of clicks and bell-like tones.

"Tiny glowing friends!" Ziggy said from a crease in the blanket covering the carrier. *"Can I eat them?"*

"Absolutely not," I said. The last thing these endangered creatures needed was to be a meal. "They're extremely rare."

Crystal looked at me with newfound respect. "You really can understand them, can't you? Like your mother."

"It's a family gift," I said as the sprites sampled Crystal's offerings. "How did you find them?"

"Three years ago, I was having a terrible day. Jerry and I had our first big fight, and I came here to cry where nobody would see me." Her expression grew distant with the memory. "I was sitting under this tree, sobbing my eyes out, when I felt a tiny hand pat my cheek. At first, I was sure I was imagining things, but then I saw them—dozens of them, all concerned about the big crying human."

The image of tiny sprites comforting a distraught Crystal was unexpectedly touching.

"They've been my friends ever since," she said. "I bring them snacks twice a week. Honey cakes are their favorite."

A bold sprite had climbed onto Crystal's shoulder and was now attempting to braid a strand of her pink hair. She smiled, staying perfectly still to allow the tiny creature to work. Another sprite was weaving a leaf into a seam in her dress.

I asked, "The night we interviewed you had you visited them?"

Crystal smiled. "Yes, they made me that dress and other clothes. Sometimes they stop by to do my hair."

"They are amazing. So, no one else know about them?" I asked, sitting down on a nearby root. It was sweet she let them do that. I had misjudged her.

Crystal shook her head, mindful of her sprite passenger. "Only the former head of the tree preservation committee, and he died last year. These sprites have been living in this oak for over a century, but they're incredibly shy. If too many people knew about them it might become very dangerous. They are very skittish."

She didn't need to tell me. Rare cryptids often became targets for collectors—something we'd learned all too well with the phoenix egg theft.

"Your secret's safe with me," I assured her. "But this doesn't explain..."

"Why was I stalking Jerry?" She sighed. "After we broke up, I was in a bad place. The sprites were worried about me—they can sense emotions, you know. One of them followed me to Jerry's theater and saw his basilisk. The sprite thought it was dangerous and tried to warn me."

"Ziggy wouldn't hurt a fly," I said.

"I know that now," Crystal said. "I misunderstood what they were trying to say. I can't hear them like you. However, at the time, all I knew was that my ex had replaced me with a creature that could kill with a glance. I convinced myself he was in danger and needed protection." She winced. "Hence the, um, surveillance."

"And the dental floss collection?" I couldn't help asking.

Crystal had the grace to look embarrassed. "That might have been taking things a bit far," she said. "I'm working on establishing healthier boundaries. My therapist says it is important." She broke off, blushing again. "Yes, I have a therapist. Three sessions a week and probably will do more since Jerry died."

Crystals realization that she needed help and was in the process of getting it was admirable. I felt horrible for judging her as a nut. She was eccentric, that was for sure, but a lot saner than I gave her credit for. Pieces were falling into place. "So, the night of Jerry's murder, you were outside the theater?"

She nodded, accepting a tiny acorn cup of nectar from one sprite. "I was truthful about that. I thought you might think I was crazy if I was honest with you at first."

I tried to keep my mouth shut, but couldn't. "After everything else, you thought that would be the thing to make us think you were crazy?"

"What do you mean?"

Crap. She may still think the other behaviors were normal. I backpedaled and lied again. "I just mean, caring about someone is not crazy."

"Ah, yes. I suppose so. I didn't lie about what I saw, though. A woman went in. I heard arguing, but was afraid of being spotted, so I left." Her eyes filled with tears. "If I'd stayed, maybe I could have saved him."

"Or you'd have been killed too," I pointed out.

The sprites, sensing Crystal's distress, gathered around her, their soft glow brightening in apparent concern.

"After Jerry died, I sort of..." She wiped her cheeks. "The sprites were the ones who convinced me to get help. They led me to a pamphlet for grief counseling that someone had dropped in the park. I've had two appointments already." She smiled and waved to the tiny cryptids. "They're sneaky like that."

"So, the whole 'he's not really dead' thing?"

"Denial is a stage of grief." She shrugged. "I'm mostly past that now. Mostly."

The sprites finished their meal, several of them performing what appeared to be a thank-you dance around Crystal's offerings. They moved with a fluid grace that reminded me of leaves floating in a gentle breeze.

"I know what the town says about me and my nickname of Crazy Crys. I'm just different." Crystal allowed a sprite to kiss her cheek with a small smile that accented her beauty. "But not dangerous. I show up as my authentic self every day and make no apologies. I cared about Jerry, probably too much, but I would never have hurt him."

I believed her. The woman sitting before me, surrounded by rare woodland sprites that trusted her enough to reveal themselves, was not the unhinged stalker we'd assumed her to be. She was just someone who cared deeply and expressed it in ways that seemed absurd to others.

One by one, the sprites began returning to their homes in the oak tree, their little feast concluded. The last one placed a tiny flower in Crystal's hair before disappearing into a knothole.

"Same time Thursday?" she asked, softly after them. A faint chorus of bell-like chimes answered in what I assumed was affirmation.

"Your secret is safe." I promised again as she packed up the remnants of the sprite picnic. "But you could be a little more straightforward with the sheriff's department in the future? Penny's just trying to do her job."

Crystal nodded, looking chagrined. "I will. My therapist says honesty is the best policy, even when it's uncomfortable." She paused. "Especially when it's uncomfortable."

We walked back toward the park entrance and Crystal stopped short of the gate. "There is one more thing you should know, Doctor Sterling."

"Mark, please," I said.

"Mark, then." She took a deep breath. "The night Jerry died, when I was watching the theater, I saw something else. Something I didn't tell your sister because I wasn't sure it was important."

I felt my heartbeat quicken. "What was it?"

"There was someone else watching the theater that night. A man in a security uniform. He was standing on the corner opposite from where I was hiding. I only glimpsed him when a car drove by."

"Did you recognize him?"

Crystal shook her head side to side. "It was too dark, and he was wearing a hat pulled low. But he was studying the theater intently. And after the lady went inside, he walked away."

I frowned, mentally reviewing the case. "Do you think it might have been Jerry?"

"Not sure who that is."

Crystal hesitated. "The thing is he was in a uniform. I've not seen him around town since."

"Believe Shiny-Hair Lady," Ziggy said.

"I believe you," I said, both to Crystal and to my hidden companion.

"If you see him again, call Penny immediately," I said. "And don't tell anyone."

"Who am I going to tell? The sprites are my only friends," Crystal said. "Everyone else thinks I'm the crazy lady who collects dental floss."

I sighed, already knowing I'd regret what I was about to say. "Give me your phone."

She handed it over, and I typed in my private number. "If you feel unsafe, call me. Day or night."

Crystal's expression brightened. "Really? You'd do that for me?"

"Professional courtesy." I had to keep thinking of the missing egg. It was the only way to distract me from her beauty. I would never tell Penny, but I was crushing hard. "As Heritage Crest's veterinarian, I have a duty of care to all creatures, including eccentric humans who feed endangered sprites."

"Thank you, Mark," Crystal said, slipping her phone back into her pocket.

We parted ways at the park entrance—Crystal heading back toward her cottage, while I opted to take the long way around to the parking lot.

"Well, that was illuminating. And not at all what I expected."

"Shiny-Hair Lady not bad-person. Just different person."

CHAPTER 32

I rested my forehead against my steering wheel and silently questioned my life choices. For the third time, I reset the timer on my phone. Another thirty minutes of surveillance, watching Bob's cottage for any sign of suspicious activity.

"This seemed like a much better idea at noon," I said to myself.

"Why are we still sitting in the box?" Ziggy chirped from the makeshift nest on the passenger seat. The basilisk had refused to stay in the carrier, throwing what could only be described as a tantrum when I tried to get him to quiet down.

"We're spying on a suspect," I explained, adjusting the binoculars. "Though 'suspect' might be stretching it. Before I tell my sister what I've been doing, I just need you to verify that we're right about Bob. There's no other option, but we have to be sure. Consider her a person of interest."

"Ziggy heard that on TV. Is she a cold-maker?"

"Maybe. Or she's just an alcoholic with a cardboard cutout of Shakespeare. Heritage Crest is full of weird people."

"Human is weird people."

"Thanks for that." I sighed, checking my watch again. It was getting late, and this was not helping.

The lights in Bob's cottage had been on the entire time, occasionally flickering as shadows moved across the curtained windows. Once, about an hour ago, I'd heard what sounded like Journey's 'Don't Stop Believing' being belted at an impressive volume, but nothing suspicious. No phoenix eggs, no murderous activities, just the normal behaviors of our town's resident functioning alcoholic. Since then, nothing but quiet.

Ziggy fluffed his scales, sending tiny sparks drifting through the car's interior. *"Hungry."*

"Me too, buddy," I said, not taking my eyes off the house.

Just as I was considering calling it a night, the front door opened, and Bob stepped out wearing a muumuu, partially tucked in her underwear. Her disheveled appearance had somehow elevated to a new level of chaos with her hair pointing in several directions at once and held in place by what looked like chopsticks.

I ducked down, watching as she stumbled to her mailbox, opened it, peered inside, closed it, patted it affectionately, and then began a conversation with it that involved expansive hand gestures and occasional bows.

"What the hell?" I whispered.

"Mailbox speak back?" Ziggy asked, curious.

"Not typically, no."

Bob finished her conversation with a final pat to the mailbox, turned, and then froze. For a terrifying moment, I thought she'd spotted me. Instead, she tilted her head back and appeared to be arguing with the sky. After about thirty seconds of this, she shrugged, as if accepting its rebuttal, and stumbled back inside.

The cottage fell silent again. I waited ten minutes, then decided to take a closer look. If I was going to waste my time on surveillance, I might as well be thorough.

"Stay here," I told Ziggy. I was running out of patience. "And I mean it. That's not a suggestion."

"I be good. Promise."

I slipped out of the car and made my way toward Bob's cottage, staying in the shadows of the overgrown hedges that lined her property. The curtains in the front window were partially open, allowing me to peek inside without getting too close. The living room was dimly lit by a single lamp with a tasseled shade and what appeared to be at least a dozen candles arranged in a pattern that resembled a pentagram – or just a star; geometry didn't seem to be Bob's strong suit.

Bob sprawled across her couch, with one arm dangling toward a bottle on the floor, snoring. The William Shakespeare cutout stood sentinel nearby, now sporting what appeared to be a party hat and a feather boa. She had arranged several of her porcelain cats in a misshapen circle on the coffee table, facing inward as if conducting a feline seance.

I was about to turn away, convinced there was nothing to see here beyond the drunk habits of a woman who clearly needed a hobby that didn't involve alcohol or ceramic animal figurines, when a notebook on the table caught my eye. I saw what seemed like a list, though the document was some distance away.

Curiosity got the better of me. I tried the window – locked. The back door was my next option. I crept around the side of the cottage, avoiding a garden hose arranged in the shape of a question mark.

An unlocked back door presented a fortunate yet worrying situation. I eased it open, wincing at the slight creak of the hinges. Inside, the kitchen was a testament to creative chaos – dishes stacked in precarious towers, refrigerator magnets spelling out what appeared to be Shakespearean insults, and enough empty bottles to suggest that Bob's relationship with recycling was as complicated as her relationship with sobriety.

I moved through the kitchen toward the living room, stepping over a small pile of books about stage makeup and what appeared to be a half-completed papier mâché model of the Globe Theater.

Bob's snoring guided me. She hadn't moved from her position on the couch, though now I could see she was clutching something – a small, framed photograph. From my angle of view, I couldn't make out the image.

The notebook that had caught my attention sat on the coffee table, surrounded by the circle of porcelain cats. I approached, ready to retreat if Bob showed any signs of waking. The top page was written in neat handwriting:

The title of the page read, 'How to Get Your Life Together.' It comprised items she needed to do to move forward. The top item was 'stop drinking.' It made me very sad. She needed help. I couldn't imagine her killing anyone but maybe herself.

A loud snore made me jump. Bob shifted but didn't wake. The frame she'd been clutching slipped from her fingers and clattered to the floor. I froze, but she mumbled something about 'tomorrow's porridge' and continued snoring.

Breathing a sigh of relief, I crouched to pick up the frame. Turning it over, I looked at a photo of Bob, except she looked different. She had neatly styled hair, professional clothes, and a serious expression. She stood next to a woman I recognized: my mom. Both wore lab coats with the logo of the sanctuary.

The puzzle pieces started clicking into place. Bob's drunkenness had cost her a lot. At one point, she must have been sober enough to volunteer or work at the sanctuary. I set the frame down and returned to the notebook. As I turned the page, I found a letter addressed to "Roberta Boule" from a crypto zoological sanctuary in Oregon, accepting her application for a position in their research division. The letter was dated last week.

I needed to leave. This was wrong. Ziggy had to have been mistaken. It wasn't either Crystal or Bob. I backed away. My movement sent one cat toppling. I caught it before it hit the floor, but the disruption of their arranged circle violated some unknown law of ceramic cat physics. Like dominoes, they fell, each knocking into the next with a series of increasingly loud clinks.

Bob stirred on the couch. I rushed into the kitchen.

"What?" Bob's voice was thick with sleep and alcohol. "Who's there? Bill, did you invite the moon over again?"

I froze, hoping the shadows would conceal me. Bob sat up slowly, rubbing her eyes. She looked around, then focused on the coffee table with its disrupted circle of cats.

"Oh no," she said, slurring with distress. "The protection circles broken. Now how will they guard against the influence of the raccoons?"

She stood unsteadily, gathering the fallen cats and setting them upright again, muttering apologies to each one. Then she paused, sniffing the air.

"Do you smell smoke?" she asked the Shakespeare cutout. "Have the raccoons progressed to arson?"

My throat went dry. Shakespeare must have responded to her because she nodded and collapsed back onto the couch and, within seconds, appeared to be snoring again. I stood there for a moment, uncertain whether this was an act, then decided not to press my luck.

I slipped out the back door, making sure it locked behind me, and hurried back to my car. Once inside, I thought about everything I learned. I had all but eliminated Crystal and Bob. Ziggy couldn't be wrong, but how did that make sense.

As I started the car, Ziggy said, *"Friend-healer sad."*

"Yeah, buddy. I am more confused than ever."

"No give up."

"I won't."

Ziggy wiggled excitedly from the passenger seat. *"Adventure continues! More sneaking!"*

I couldn't help but smile despite the tension. "Unfortunately, this is the end of the road for you."

"Where we go for fun now?"

"This isn't fun," I said and took a deep breath. "I'm going to take you back to Alice and then I need to figure out what to do next. "

I called Penny and it went directly to voice mail. Why was there never a cop around when you needed one?

CHAPTER 33

It was going to be another long day and night. I stopped by Rosie's, grabbing a quick sandwich before jumping back in on the investigation. I would be no good if I passed out from hunger. I sat down and ordered the usual and let Rosie know I needed it quick. I tried to call Penny again, and like before, it went to her voicemail. I left a message and hoped that whatever was keeping her busy was helping solve this case.

I was halfway through my grilled cheese sandwich when the little bell above the door jingled. I didn't look up immediately—I was busy reviewing my notes, trying to figure out anything I might have missed, but the sudden sensation of being watched caused me to glance toward the entrance.

Violet stood in the doorway. She scanned the diner with an intensity that made me uncomfortably. When her gaze landed on me, something flickered across her face—surprise, perhaps, or irritation. She smoothed her expression into a pleasant smile. Too pleasant. Like someone who'd practiced smiling in a mirror and hadn't quite mastered the technique.

"Doctor Sterling!" she said, making her way toward my booth. "Sorry, Mark I mean. What a coincidence! I was hoping to speak with you."

"Were you?" I asked, sliding my notes under my plate with what I hoped was casual nonchalance. "I thought you'd be at the sanctuary with Doctor Green today."

She slid into the booth across from me without waiting for an invitation, her lab coat catching on the edge of the table. "Oh, he's running tests on the adult phoenix feathers he collected. Boring stuff, really.

I much prefer fieldwork." She leaned forward and lowered her voice. "Speaking of which, I've been meaning to ask you if there were any updates on the recent unpleasantness."

"You mean Jerry's murder?" I kept my voice neutral, watching her reaction. "Or the egg theft?"

Violet flinched at the bluntness. "Yes, all of that terrible business. Any findings yet? By the way, it's so cool that you are helping the sheriff with the investigation."

"She's my sister."

"Of course." She glanced around before leaning in even closer. "Any progress? Doctor Green is quite concerned. He and Jerry had scheduled a meeting the night of the incident."

That was news to me. "Had they? Doctor Green didn't mention that. He actually stated the opposite."

A flash of alarm crossed her face before she recovered. Whatever was going on in her head was complicated. I wished Ziggy hadn't eliminated her a suspect by smelling the killer when she was nowhere nearby. She was suspicious.

"Oh? Well, it was only an informal chat. Something about noise complaints from the theater. Probably didn't seem relevant. Anything I can help with?"

"Not really. We're close, but nothing yet."

Rosie appeared at our table with a mug and the coffeepot. "Coffee for you, hon?" she asked Violet, her tone considerably less warm than the beverage she offered. Rosie narrowed her eyes at Violet. Rosie had a sixth sense about people—not supernatural, just good old-fashioned small-town intuition honed by decades of serving coffee and pie to everyone in Heritage Crest.

"No, thank you." Violet's smile tightened. "Actually, I don't think I'll be staying. I just remembered there are some samples to process."

Violet was already sliding out of the booth, nearly knocking over my water glass in her haste. Rosie smiled and headed back to her counter.

"What did you need?" I asked.

"I'm sorry," Violet said.

"What did you need? You came in, but ordered nothing, and now you're leaving. Why did you come in?"

"I was hungry, but just realized I must get back to those samples. No time to eat. Perhaps we can continue this conversation another time." She turned to leave, then, paused. "Oh, by the way, I noticed you've been spending more time at the phoenix sanctuary. Any reason?"

The question was casual, but her eyes were sharp.

"Are you asking or Doctor Green?"

"Both, I guess."

"Just handling routine checks," I said, matching her casual tone. "I want to make sure Aurora is doing well."

"Seems unusual," Violet said. A half smile spread across her face. "I was wondering if your sister had questioned you as a suspect."

Before I could respond, a loud crash came from the kitchen, followed by Rosie's colorful cursing. Violet used the distraction to leave, the bell jingling as the door closed behind her. I signaled for the check, my appetite gone. As Rosie approached, she glanced toward the door where Violet had exited.

"That one's trouble," she said, wiping her hands on her apron. "Came in yesterday, asking all sorts of questions about you and your sister. Wanted to know if you two were close, if you shared case details." She shrugged. "I played dumb, of course. Told her I just serve the food."

"That's odd. Unfortunately, there is pretty solid proof she didn't kill Jerry. Still working through if she or her boss has any connection to the missing egg. I don't trust her either. Thanks for everything, Rosie."

I threw some cash on the table and headed for the door, my mind churning. Something wasn't right. I was so lost in thought that I almost missed the flash of white lab coat disappearing around the corner of the post office. Violet was supposed to be heading back to the lab, which was in the opposite direction. Curiosity and suspicion warred within me. I glanced at my watch. I could spare a few minutes for a slight detour.

Decision made, I turned away from my truck and followed her, staying close to the buildings to remain inconspicuous. I rounded the corner and caught sight of Violet again. She was no longer walking casually but moving with urgent purpose, her ponytail swinging with each determined step. She was also talking on her phone, her free hand gesturing emphatically.

She turned another corner, heading toward the old shipping warehouse at the end of the town's main street. I hesitated at the edge of the building, peering around. Violet stood by the back door, still on her phone. Her voice carried on the damp air. "Timeline has been compromised. That's absurd. Tell him."

I slowly backed away, planning to get to Penny as quickly as possible, when my foot caught on an empty soda can someone had carelessly discarded. The metallic clatter seemed impossibly loud in the muted alley.

Violet's head snapped up, her gaze locking with mine across the distance. For a moment, neither of us moved. Then, her expression hardened into something cold and calculating that transformed her entire face.

"I need to go," she said into the phone.

I didn't wait to hear more. I turned and ran, my heartbeat thundering in my ears. Behind me, I heard quick footsteps and Violet's voice calling out with forced cheerfulness. "Mark! Please wait! I believe you misunderstood what you heard. It's not what you think."

I didn't slow down. I rounded another corner and sprinted across Main Street, drawing startled looks from pedestrians. I had nearly reached my truck when a hand grabbed my arm with surprising strength, spinning me around.

Violet's smile was back in place. However, her eyes were cold and assessing. "I'm not sure what you heard, but you really shouldn't eavesdrop on private conversations. It can lead to misunderstandings."

I pulled my arm free. "Like your misunderstanding about whether or not you are involved?"

Her smile faltered slightly. "As I said, I did nothing. I was working all evening and your sister verified it. Plus, I thought your basilisk pointed to Crystal or Roberta."

"How do you know that?"

"Someone at the sheriff's office must've told me." She stepped closer, lowering her voice. "I'd be careful about making accusations. You've such a valuable reputation in this community. It would be a shame to damage it with unfounded speculation while you ran around playing detective."

The sudden coldness overshadowed the thinly veiled threat in her voice, which caught my attention. I faked a smile back. I needed to play this carefully. If Violet was involved and she thought I could prove it, I might end up dead or cause her to speed up whatever timeline she had and cause damage to the phoenix.

A cold knot of dread settled in my stomach. Violet's threat echoed in my mind: "You've such a valuable reputation in this community. It would be a shame to damage it..." She wasn't just talking about spreading rumors. She was warning me to back off or else.

I forced a smile and said, "I'm sorry. We are running out of time and I'm trying to find any lead to get the egg back. It's making me a little crazy. Please forgive me. We've got to know each other a little, and I would hate to ruin it over a misunderstanding."

Her eyes searched mine and, after a moment, she softened. "I get it. Sorry, I'm on edge as well."

"Just a misunderstanding, I guess." It was a lie, but I felt I needed to tell it. "You have to admit that it's suspicious that you keep asking questions."

"Doctor Green wants me to keep him updated. And believe it or not, I want to help if I can."

"Just seems odd and then the conversation I just heard. You have to see how it looks."

"And if you must know, I was on the phone with my intern advisor. Apparently, my conversation with her about Doctor Green got back to him and he would like to sit down with me. I am afraid that my project timeline here may get accelerated or ended all together."

"That sounds stressful," I said. With her being cleared by Ziggy, I didn't see any reason to not believe her. Her explanation of the conversation fit with what she was saying. Although my gut still protested.

"You know." She flipped one side of her hair over her shoulder and tucked it behind her ear. "I find you cute. Maybe we could go out sometime."

"That would be nice." Another lie. "I need to get going, though. Catch you later."

"You bet." She backed away from the truck.

I climbed in, started it up, and drove away. She waved to me, and I gave a half wave back. Something still bothered me, but I couldn't pinpoint it.

Halfway through town, I realized I forgot to tell Alice to schedule an upcoming appointment. I could've called, but the clinic was on the way.

I pulled into the parking lot and walked in to find Alice behind the reception desk. I was so thankful she worked here. She kept this office running, and with me doing this investigation, really picked up the slack. I would need to recommend her for a raise.

"Are you okay?" she asked. My appearance after the Violet encounter must have still shown the stress."

"Yeah, I'm fine."

"What are you doing back so soon?"

"I forgot to have you schedule an appointment for a patient follow-up."

"You could've called." She tapped a few things on the keyboard and looked up. "Give me the details."

I relayed the appointment, and she typed furiously. I said, "Thank you again for all you do."

"Ah. Thank you. I love it here and you are a great doctor." She hit enter. "All done."

I blushed. "Thank you for taking Ziggy in as well."

"It's a learning curve for both of us. He's in the back on the heating pad if you want to talk to him?"

"That's cool that you bring him in."

"I sort of had to. His nose is so sensitive that even when I wasn't there, I would find him curled up in my dirty close hamper."

"That's sweet. He misses you."

"I looked it up in our cryptid medical database. Apparently, they can smell your discarded laundry up to six days after you've worn it. Isn't that crazy?"

"They do have a strong sense of smell."

"I keep forgetting." She smiled. "I would lose my nose if it wasn't attached."

I started to laugh, and then an immediate realization hit me. I couldn't believe I hadn't thought about it before. My face must have given me a way because Alice's expression turned to concern.

"Are you sure everything's okay?" she asked.

My thoughts jumbled together and finally painted a clear picture. It finally came to me on what I was missing. We had it all wrong. I stood and rushed towards the door.

"Is everything okay?" Alice asked, again.

"Yeah," I said, rushing away. "You helped me figure out who killed Jerry, and probably Tommy."

"I did."

Once outside, I pulled out my cell phone and called Penny. I had to verify one thing to prove the case. It rang several times and clicked to voicemail. I hung up and called again. Same thing. Should I be worried? I considered my options for a moment and then, called Harry.

"Hey Mark, what's up?" Harry said.

"I'm trying to get ahold of Penny. Do you know where she is?"

"It's probably the cell service. She is out searching the farthest sector and phone calls are really spotty out there. What's up?"

"Are you at the station?" I asked.

"I am. What do you need?"

"Can you check the lobby and see if there is a woman's coat on the rack by the door?"

"The one belonging to Violet Newsome?"

"Yes."

"I don't need to look. She picked it up yesterday."

"You, sure?"

"Handed it to her myself."

She told me a lie. I guess I shouldn't be surprised. She left it there on purpose. It had been in the room when I brought Ziggy through the lobby. He did smell the killer, just not the ladies in the room. It was the jacket. Violet's jacket. I was now one hundred percent sure Violet did it. The trick was to prove it. "Do you know when Penny is supposed to be back?"

"Not sure. Want me to go get her?"

"Nah, I will drive out to her." I was about to hang up and something occurred to me that he could help with. "There is one thing. Are you still plugged into on the video feeds for the town?"

"Sure am. I've been scanning the live feeds on my desktop. What do you need?"

"Can you watch for any signs of Violet Newsome or Doctor Green?"

"Didn't we eliminate them as suspects?"

"We did, but I need to understand what they are doing."

"Want me to arrest them?"

"No. But I do still think they might be involved. We need to be careful not to tip them off. Especially if they could lead us to the egg."

"Ok. Wow. Anything I should look for?"

"Just watch them and call me if you see them going anywhere that doesn't seem right to you. Anything appearing odd."

"Vague, but I will check. Good luck in finding your sister."

"Thanks." I hung up and called Penny again. This time I left a detailed voicemail of my realization and the smallest detail we missed.

I rushed to my car and headed out towards Penny. I would need her help in closing this. I was sure I was right.

Halfway to the distant sector, my phone buzzed – a text from Harry: "Security feed shows Violet entering Building C ten minutes ago. She had a key."

Building C was the newer building that was not in use yet. There was no reason Violet should be there or be in possession of a key. The place didn't even have power yet. It was also where we caught her checking it out a few days ago with Green. I'm sure Penny's team checked the facility already, but maybe this missed something.

I pulled over to the side of the road and responded: "Thanks. I will check it out. Have you seen Doctor Green?"

Harry texted: "He just left his lab. It looks like he might be headed towards the diner."

I called Penny and, once again, voicemail. I informed her my destination and requested her prompt arrival. I tossed the phone in the passenger seat, turned the car around, and headed for Building C. I could be there in minutes.

CHAPTER 34

I parked near Building C and headed for the facility's basement access, mentally reviewing everything we knew. It was hard to stay focused and to practice restraint. I wanted to rush in there, but if I was right, that might be deadly. Against my nature, I took my time to sneak in.

The basement door required two forms of authentication: a key card and a code. How Violet had this was beyond me. I pulled out my sanctuary veterinarian override credentials, silently thanking Mom for insisting I get the highest possible security clearance. I slid the card and put in my code.

The door opened, and voices echoed from below. One was Violet's. The other voice sounded muffled. Maybe a cell phone speaker. My jaw clenched. It was time to find out just how deep this rabbit hole went. Though given our location, 'how deep the phoenix nest went' might be a more appropriate metaphor.

I followed the sounds until I came to a wall in a darkened corner. I shined my phone's flashlight against the area where there should be an archway, but there was a tiny crease. I pushed on it and a hidden door slid to the side, revealing an entrance and staircase winding down. That explained why the search party might have missed it.

I started down the stairs, trying to move as quietly as possible. It was hard to still myself. Though I hated to admit, this was definitely more exciting than dealing with Sparkles' horn wellness revolution.

The basement of the facility was colder than it should have been, even for cold storage. Goosebumps formed on my arms and my breath fogged in front of me as I rounded the last corner of the metal stairs.

Violet's voice drifted and confirmed what I now knew to be true. "Everything's ready for transport. The egg is stabilized for shipping."

"The Dubai buyer's terms are non-negotiable," the voice on the line replied. "If we can't deliver the egg by tomorrow tonight there is no deal."

"I'm trying to do this tonight. Besides, that interfering vet and his sister are starting to piece things together. We need to move now."

I reached the bottom of the stairs and peered around the corner. Someone had converted the basement into a sophisticated cold storage facility, with a large temperature-controlled unit on the other side of the room. Violet stood over a control panel on what looked like a specially designed shipping container with a clear lid. By the glow, I was sure the phoenix egg was in there.

"The Chinese buyer is offering more," the voice was saying. "Maybe we should switch."

"The Dubai contract is solid," Violet said. Her tone was abrupt and commanding. Gone was the meek girl being harassed by the mean Doctor Green. "Besides, his private sanctuary already has the infrastructure for it." She stopped, head tilting. There was a sound just above me. "Did you hear something?"

I held my breath, pressing deeper into the shadows. Unfortunately, I'd forgotten about the cat-sized pseudo dragon that sometimes lurked in the different building's ventilation systems. It chose that moment to sneeze directly above me, showering my head with tiny sparks and revealing my location. There was no hiding now.

"Well," I said, stepping into view and trying to brush the sparks out of my hair with as much dignity as possible. "This explains why we couldn't find the egg."

Violet spun around, her friendly research assistant persona vanishing like smoke. "Doctor Sterling."

"Call me Mark." It seemed like a cool thing to say.

"Always sticking your nose where it doesn't belong."

"Says the person running a cryptid trafficking operation out of a basement." I took a careful step forward. "How long have you been planning this? Was the research assistant position just a convenient cover, or did you start out interested in science before the money corrupted you?"

"You don't understand?" She moved to stand between me and the shipping container. "Do you know what kind of resources private collectors can provide? The research we could do with proper funding instead of scraping by on government grants. The possibilities are endless."

"Research that involves stealing eggs from their mothers and selling them to the highest bidder?" I gestured upward. "That's not research, Violet. That's exploitation."

Violet cleared her throat. "Let's be reasonable. Society has done it with cats and dogs for hundreds of years. This is no different."

"There is one. We promised these cryptids safety from this. They count on us for their safety."

"The sanctuary's funding has been cut three times in the past year. Private partnerships provide stability, resources. How long will that safety last?"

"Save it," I said. "You're a disgrace."

"We'll just have to agree to disagree." Violet pulled a gun and leveled it at me. "You couldn't just leave it alone. Do you know how damn hard it was to keep running into you and making it look like coincidences? To pretend to be something I'm not. Be the poor little girl that was weak and just needed a man to save her. You couldn't just accept that I was a woman needing help against her mean misogynistic boss. You had to keep pushing and digging."

"You killed two people and have a hostage."

"I didn't want to, but they left me no choice. Just like you. Jerry had figured it out. The creep had been watching me."

"He didn't deserve to die. And what about Tommy? How did you get him to help you with access?"

"Figured that out, did you? We were friends with benefits."

"That was you in his bed that morning we interviewed him."

"Guilty. After sex a few times, he was willing to do anything. Anything, that is until I had to kill Jerry. When he found out, I couldn't convince him to not report it."

"So, you killed him?"

"I hated to do it. He was good in bed, but hey, you can't make an omelet without breaking an egg." She laughed. "Get it. Because of the phoenix egg."

"You're a sociopath."

"Maybe, but soon I'll be a rich one. Women get nothing in the academics and sciences. We're treated like servants."

"That isn't true. Some of the most brilliant minds are female."

She waved the gun. "Just shut up. Over there, against the wall."

I tripped and crashed into a tray of instruments. They scattered across the floor in a loud bang.

"What's going on?" the voice on the phone said.

"Don't worry about it. I'll call you back." She disconnected the phone.

"You going to kill me now?"

"Unfortunately. I've already done it twice, what's one more. I did really like you. In a different world, perhaps we could have had something."

"I seriously doubt it."

The dim lights blazed to life, making me stumble further back in surprise with a very undignified yelp.

"Doctor Sterling? Violet?" Doctor Green's voice came from the doorway on the other side of the room, heavy with confusion. "What are you two doing in here?"

"Talking." I motioned towards Violet.

Green stepped into the room, his eyes darting between me and Violet. "This area is restricted. How did you get in here?" He broke off, his gaze focusing on the monitoring equipment. "Wait. This isn't my setup. I've never seen this equipment before. What's going on here?"

"What?" I blinked, surprised by his genuine confusion. I was sure he was in it with her. I was not very good at this detective stuff. He was just as clueless as the rest of us.

"This room." He gestured around. "It's connected to my lab, but I didn't authorize this. I heard a loud crash and found a hidden panel with a tunnel leading here. What's the meaning of this? I don't even have access to this kind of containment technology. How did you acquire it?"

"That's because it's not your equipment, Victor." Violet Newsome faced him, and the small pistol in her hand became clear to him. "Hands up."

"Oh good," I said. "This seems like a perfectly reasonable development for a Friday night."

"Shut up," Violet snapped, though I noticed her hand trembled slightly. "Both of you, together on the wall. Now."

Green's face had gone pale. "Violet? What is the meaning of this? What have you done?"

"What I had to do," she said, her professional mask cracking to reveal something harder underneath. "Do you know what collectors will pay for a viable phoenix egg? Ten million dollars. Ten Million. And you were just going to just use it for your precious research."

"Because that's what we do here," Green said, his voice rising. "We protect these creatures, study them so we can preserve their species. We don't sell them to the highest bidder!"

"Such noble intentions." Violet's laugh held no humor. "Tell that to the board members who make six figures while the rest of us scrape by on research assistant salaries. Do you know how many funding requests I've processed for you? How many grant rejections I've had to file?"

I took advantage of their argument to look closer at the lid of the containment unit. The egg's glow had intensified, its shell developing a faint iridescent sheen that made my veterinary instincts very nervous.

"Violet," I said. "That egg is showing signs of pre-hatching behavior. The cold storage will not hold it much longer."

"Shut up!" The gun swung toward me. "You don't understand. None of you understand. I have buyers waiting. Important people. This was supposed to be simple. Get the egg, keep it dormant until transport, deliver to the buyer. Simple!"

"Until Jerry McKinnon saw you moving it," Green said. The pieces clicked into place for him. "That's why you killed him. He was confronting you."

Violet's face twisted. "He should have minded his own business. But no, he had to play hero. Had to threaten to report it. I couldn't." She took a deep breath. "I couldn't let him ruin everything."

"So, you killed him and tried to frame me?" Green's voice shook with rage. "That's insane."

"I had everything planned perfectly!" Violet's composure cracked further. "The security gaps, the fake research notes, the cold storage setup. It was perfect! But then that nosy theater owner had to stick his head where it didn't belong, and that idiot guard had to have a conscience, and you. UHG." She waved the gun at me, "You just wouldn't leave well enough alone!"

"Well, in my defense," I said, because apparently, I lose all sense of self-preservation in tense situations. "Investigating suspicious deaths is kind of my sister's entire job. And I do hate to disappoint family."

"Just shut up. Let me think." Violet was becoming unhinged. Her brain was working overtime until, I guessed, an idea formed. "Start walking. Mark, you push the storage cart and follow Doctor Green back to his lab. But don't get any ideas. I will have my gun on you both."

Complying, I made my way through the hidden door and down the corridor, passing walls lined with charts tracking phoenix migration patterns and breeding cycles. We entered the next building housing Green's private research area through a false wall panel. I'd been here dozens of times for health checks, but tonight everything was different. The familiar halls seemed longer, darker, more threatening.

I had to do something. An awful idea came to me. A beautiful, awful idea. The egg needed to hatch before they could get it out of the sanctuary. It might be too early, but it was the only thing to save the phoenix. No egg, no deal. A hatched phoenix would stop this whole thing. I thumbed the temperature control on the cart and turned off the cooling. Things were going to warm up quickly.

I eventually rounded the corner into Green's main lab and a piercing sound suddenly flared with warning. A warning chirp from the monitoring equipment on the cart drew everyone's attention. The egg's glow had intensified, its shell now showing the distinctive ripple patterns that preceded hatching.

"No," Violet said. She was panicked. "No, no, no! It can't hatch now. If it hatches here and bonds with any of us, it won't be worth anything to the buyers!"

She lunged for the containment unit's controls and tried to push me aside, but I was closer and quicker. I threw myself between her and the egg just as a spiderweb of cracks appeared across its glowing shell.

"Don't!" she screamed, raising the gun. "I'll shoot! I swear I will."

The egg pulsed with blinding light. I felt, rather than saw Violet move forward, and sensed the room heating up. Through my gift, I sensed the new life emerging.

Everything happened at once. Violet got past me, fumbled with the controls, and accidently popped the lid. She grabbed for the egg. I tried to stop her. Then, the world erupted in phoenix fire.

The magical backlash knocked me off my feet. Through blurred vision, I saw Violet thrown back by the force of the hatching. The egg was clutched in her arms, and she was enveloped in magical flames that burned too hot, too bright. Her scream cut off abruptly as the phoenix fire consumed her.

I felt a pulse of energy. My head hit something. Darkness.

When I recovered my senses and could actually see again, the lab was in ruins. Equipment sparked and smoldered, frost melting from the walls in sheets. Dr. Green lay unconscious near the door, but I saw him breathing. And there, in the wreckage of the containment unit, a tiny chirping sound drew my attention.

Darkness, again.

I'm not sure how long I was out, probably only seconds, but it felt like hours. The first thing I became aware of was a gentle warmth against my chest and a series of small, inquisitive chirps.

I opened my eyes to find myself sprawled on the floor, mostly unharmed. The room was a disaster zone. Equipment was scattered everywhere, frost and scorch marks were vying for wall space, and small magical fires were burning in various colors.

And there, nestled against my chest as if it had always belonged there, was a baby phoenix. Resembling the size of a volleyball, its plumage shifted from pale gold to deep crimson at the tips. Tiny sparks danced along its feathers as it looked up at me with eyes that somehow were both ancient and brand new. Its dark pupils fixed on me with an intelligence that belied its age. The bond snapped into place - an instant connection - profound and unbreakable.

"Mama," its mental voice chimed in my head, full of wonder and trust. *"You keep me warm."*

"Oh," I said, still trying to process everything that had just happened. "Well. This is going to be interesting to explain."

My phone rang, and I answered Penny's voice crackled. "We just found the secret entrance and heard an explosion. Mark! Are you okay? What happened?"

I looked at the baby phoenix, which had already started trying to climb up my arm. "Well, the good news is, I've solved the case. The bad news is I may have accidentally adopted a phoenix."

"What?" Penny asked.

I sighed as the sound of approaching footsteps announced the arrival of backup. "Because my life wasn't complicated enough already."

The phoenix chirped happily and set my collar on fire. I snuffed it out before it could burn me and was hit by a rush of foreign emotions - wonder, trust, curiosity, and an overwhelming sense of rightness. Through our new connection, I sensed the energy patterns of the new cryptid.

The baby phoenix pecked my cheek. *"Mama."*

CHAPTER 35

Green awoke with a groan, clutching his head. "Did anyone get the license plate of that phoenix?"

"Not the time for jokes," I said, trying to balance professionalism with the fact that a baby phoenix was now attempting to make a nest in my hair. "Though I appreciate the effort."

Penny burst through the door, gun drawn, followed by a team of officers. She took in the scene. Her eyes darted from the smoldering equipment, the burnt corpse, and me, with my new feathered friend.

"Seriously?" She holstered her weapon with a sigh. "You couldn't just find evidence like a normal person? Had to get bonded to a highly regulated supernatural creature?"

"In my defense, you didn't answer your phone. "I gestured to the phoenix chick, who was now humming contentedly, "But this was not part of the plan."

"Mama," the chick said. *"Make flame. Me need warm."*

"No setting things on fire," I said, then realized I was already talking to it like one of my regular patients. "Great. I'm parenting. This is happening."

Penny was checking Violet's charred body, her expression grim. "Phoenix fire. Nothing left but bone and ash. Guess that saves us a trial."

"The stolen egg was here all along?" Green struggled to his feet, leaning heavily against the wall. "I never knew. She was using my research, my access. I should have seen it."

"She was good at covering her tracks," I said, wincing as tiny phoenix claws dug into my scalp. "Had everyone fooled."

"Not everyone," Penny corrected. "Jerry figured it out. Cost him his life."

The weight of that hit me hard. Jerry, with his cheerful smile and love for classic movies, who'd taken in a rescued basilisk and given it a home. He died trying to protect our sanctuary's creatures.

"Sad feelings are cold," the phoenix chick observed. *"Need more fire."*

"No!" I yelped as I felt it gathering heat. "No more fire. Fire bad right now."

"Fire good," it said. *"Fire fixes everything."*

"I can see this is going to be a learning experience for everyone," Penny said. She turned to her team as they documented the scene. "Get me a body bag down here for the remains. Also, full trace analysis, please. And someone get my brother a fireproof hat before his new friend sets fire to his hair."

Green was examining the ruined cold storage unit with professional interest despite his obvious exhaustion. "The engineering on this is incredible. Horrible purpose, but the dampening field combined with the temperature control is amazing. I've never seen anything like it."

"We'll need you to help us trace where it came from," Penny said. "This kind of equipment could lead us to other trafficking operations."

"Of course." Green straightened his glasses, which had somehow survived the explosion intact. "Anything I can do to help. I trusted her. I'm not used to being wrong."

"That's how the best cons work," I said, disregarding his comment about always being right. I gave up and let the phoenix chick arrange my hair to its satisfaction. "They make you think you know them."

"This is impossible," he said, adjusting his wire-rimmed glasses. He was still grasping at the thought of being fooled. "The grant paperwork and the research protocols, everything was through proper channels."

"Everything under your name did go through proper channels," I said, examining the modified pharmaceutical equipment. "But how often did you actually fill out that paperwork yourself?"

"The breeding records will need to be completely audited," Doctor Green said, shifting back into research mode despite his obvious shock. "If she was falsifying data this could be disastrous."

"Probably a good idea," I said.

The scientist's face paled. "Violet always handled the administrative side. She said it would give me more time to focus on the research."

"And more time to be the perfect cover," Penny said. "A respected researcher with a spotless reputation, too absorbed in his work to notice what was happening right under his nose."

"Done!" the chick announced proudly. *"Warm-headed mama."*

I caught my reflection in a broken monitor and groaned. My hair was standing straight up in what appeared to be a creative attempt at a phoenix crest. "We're going to have to discuss personal boundaries."

"Doctor Sterling." Deputy Rivera approached, eyeing my new hairstyle. "We need your statement about the incident."

"Right." I glanced at the happy baby phoenix, which was humming. "Any chance we might do this a little later? I need a shower."

A crash from the corner made everyone jump. One of the junior officers had knocked over a shelf of samples, sending vials rolling across the floor.

"Ooh, shiny!" The phoenix chick launched itself from my head toward the gleaming glass.

"No!" Several voices shouted at once.

Too late. The excited chick's natural flame aura ignited the preservation fluid in the nearest vial. The resulting explosion was small but spectacular, sending lime green colored particles shooting across the lab.

"Pretty!" The chick bounced in the air. *"Again!"*

"And that's our cue to leave," I said, snatching the pyromaniac baby bird before it could create any more impromptu fireworks. "Penny, I'll give my statement at the station. After I figure out how to phoenix-proof my house. And maybe invest in a fire extinguisher or two."

Behind me, I heard Green ask Penny, "Should we warn the fire department?"

I made my way through the facility's darkened halls with my new companion's soft glow lighting the way. I couldn't help but wonder what Aurora would say about all this. Probably something wise and profound about destiny and responsibility. Or she might just be so pissed she'd burn me to a crisp.

The hatchling chirped, while simultaneously sending me images of all the interesting things it wanted to ignite. I sighed. Between a baby phoenix's pyrotechnic experiments, a massive smuggling investigation, and the inevitable mountain of paperwork this would generate, my future days were about to get very interesting. Hopefully, I could work a nap in there somewhere.

But looking at the tiny creature already falling asleep on my shoulder, I couldn't bring myself to mind. Sometimes the most important truths came with consequences - and sometimes those consequences involved flaming paperwork and singed eyebrows.

"Sleep-safe-home," the hatchling murmured in my mind as we left the ruins behind. And despite everything that had happened, I knew we were going to be just fine. Even if I needed to brush up on what might explode if exposed to intense heat.

At least Sparkles would be thrilled. She'd been wanting a more dramatic way to make an entrance at her weekly check-ups. Nothing says drama quite like a phoenix escort. The chick's cheerful hum harmonized with the night sounds of the sanctuary, a fresh note in the familiar symphony of my special home. My only thought: I hope my insurance premiums have mercy on my soul.

CHAPTER 36

I stepped out of the building. It was dark now. A powerful gust of wind knocked me backwards. I stumbled, but stayed on my feet. It tore up the dirt and grime and made it hard to see under the dull bulb of the streetlight.

My vision cleared, and I saw the source. Perched on a car, Aurora glared at me silently. Her large, mighty golden feathers rippled with barely contained power as she fixed her gaze first on me, then on her hatched chick.

"Well," her mental voice carried a distinct note of both amusement and disappointment, *"this is certainly not how I expected my egg to hatch."*

"Aurora, I'm so sorry," I said, but she cut me off with a wave of her wing.

"Sorry? For what? For saving my child from being sold to some collector's menagerie? For providing it with a bond that will ensure its safety and growth?" She tilted her head. *"Though I must say, your technique for becoming a phoenix parent is rather dramatic."*

"How did you know?"

"All actions flow through the energy flames."

The baby chirped at its mother's voice, but made no move to leave my shoulder. If anything, it snuggled closer, sending me a mental image of itself dividing its time between Aurora's nest and my clinic rounds.

"You're okay with this?" I asked.

"I would have preferred her hatch with her own kind, but this is better than her being gone. When I first hatched, I also bonded with a human. A nice man named Ivan Sanderson. Phoenixes choose their bonds, Doctor

222

Sterling. Even newly hatched ones." Aurora's mental tone softened. *"She will need to be with you until she is at least two years of age."*

"Two? I don't want to take your child. I didn't intend to become a parent." Two years was a long time.

"Co-parent," Aurora corrected. *"However, it is necessary you stay involved. You could damage the child's development to break the bond at this age. We will establish a schedule allowing you to bring her to visit her family and get acquainted with all our kind, but in the end, she primarily needs to remain with you. You don't want to harm her, do you?"*

"Of course not. It is my job to keep this baby safe."

"Cinder."

"Cinder?" I was confused.

Aurora flew towards me, gently landed, and nuzzled her head against the chick. *"Cinder is her name. You don't have to call her baby. She is Cinder."*

"Cinder," the baby said.

"Cinder," I said.

We stood there for about an hour while Aurora reveled in Cinder's birth. She shared many instructions and things I needed to know. The mother phoenix encouraged me. I could do this.

"They prefer their food pre-warmed," she said, along with a detailed image of the correct preparation. *"Though in your case, I suspect keeping it warm enough won't be a problem."*

"Thank you," I said. "I guess we will see each other more often now."

"We will make Cinder seen. Besides, having a healer in the family could be quite convenient. Especially one who can actually understand our complaints instead of just guessing."

CHAPTER 37

"Cinder, no! Those are expensive bandages!" I lunged across my office, trying to catch the baby phoenix before she could unravel another roll of medical supplies. She chirped, dodging my grasp with a flutter of golden wings.

At just three days old, Cinder was already proving to be a handful. Between figuring out phoenix dietary requirements (they go through an alarming number of fire ants), managing her increasing abilities, and keeping her from setting anything paper or wood ablaze, I was understanding why Aurora had seemed so exasperated with her previous clutches.

"She is spirited," Aurora's amused voice echoed in my mind as she watched from the window. The mother phoenix took my unexpected bonding with her egg surprisingly well. *"But then, so were you at that age, if I remember Clara's stories correctly."*

"Mom's been telling tales again, I see." I finally caught Cinder, who snuggled into my chest with an innocent peep. "Don't give me that look, you little troublemaker. I know what you're up to."

"Learning! Exploring!" Cinder projected, her mental voice still carrying the endearing awkwardness of a newborn. *"Shiny things are the best things!"*

"The FBI's Cryptid Crimes Division might disagree about the best use of their evidence bags," I said, extracting a neon evidence marker from her beak. The aftermath of Violet's death had brought a swarm of federal agents to Heritage Crest, all of them fascinated by both the inter-

224

national smuggling ring and the unprecedented human-phoenix bonding.

"Life rarely follows expected paths," Aurora said. *"But sometimes the unexpected paths lead us where we need to be."*

"That was beautiful."

"Thank you. Also," Aurora said with a mental smirk, *"I believe your mother is planning a 'Congratulations On Not Getting Killed And Adopting A Phoenix' party."*

"Of course she is." I groaned. "Let me guess, Penny's helping plan it?"

"Indeed. I believe there was mention of a cake shaped like a fire ant."

Telepathic contact with magical creatures frequently caused more problems than it solved. "Any other surprises I should know about?"

"Well," Aurora's tone took on a suspiciously innocent tone, *"Several pixies may have volunteered to provide entertainment. Something about a show exploring the dramatic journey of pixies and their fight for justice against sky graffiti. And a dramatic poetry reading by a young griffin."*

I dropped my head onto my desk. A knock at my door interrupted my despair. "Doctor Sterling?" Alice poked her head in. "Oh, I'm sorry. I didn't know you were talking with Aurora."

"It's okay. What's up?"

"The FBI agents are ready for your final statement. And Sparkles is in the waiting room, insisting her horn is developing an accent."

I blinked. "A what now?"

"An accent. Apparently, it's speaking with a British inflection when it sparkles." Alice kept a straight face, but I could see her shoulders shaking with suppressed laughter. "It's irritating her."

"Of course it is." I sighed, settling Cinder onto her special perch - fireproofed after the Great Filing Cabinet Incident of Day One that we will never speak of again. Cinder didn't like to be left alone and jumped to my shoulder as I headed to the door. It wasn't worth the fight and decided it was best to take her with me. "Tell Sparkles I'll be with her shortly. Might as well get the FBI thing done first."

"Can horns have accents?" Aurora asked.

"In Heritage Crest? Honestly, I wouldn't rule it out."

"Fascinating."

"I will bring her by later if that's okay," I said.

"I will be there. Good luck with your other human's friend-healer." A gust of wind knocked the papers off my desk when Aurora took flight. I'd get them later after the interview.

A stark contrast existed between the two agents waiting in the conference room. Agent Cline was tall, elegant, and moved with the precise grace of someone who trained in the gym every free moment of their life. Agent Lewis was shorter, rounder, and had thin eyebrows that suggested he recently had them done.

"Doctor Sterling." Agent Cline nodded. "And the bonded phoenix chick. Fascinating. We've never documented a case of human-phoenix imprinting before."

Cinder, showing off her impeccable timing, chose that moment to sneeze. A tiny fireball shot across the room, narrowly missing Agent Lewis.

"Sorry about that," I said. "She's still getting control of her flames. The pepper-based formula I'm using for her diet might be a bit strong."

"Speaking of control," Agent Lewis pulled out a notebook, then moved it away from Cinder's interested gaze. "We just need you to walk us through the events in the cold storage room one more time."

I recounted the confrontation with Violet, trying to stick to the facts despite the chaotic memories. The hidden egg, Green's shock at discovering his assistant's betrayal and Violet's desperate attempt to prevent the hatching.

"And you're certain Doctor Green wasn't aware of the trafficking operation?" Agent Cline's eyes narrowed.

"Completely certain. His research notes were genuine - Violet just used her position to alter the official records before sending them off to corporate. The originals were found in her apartment, along with evidence linking her to similar thefts at three other magical preserves."

Agent Lewis whistled low. "Ten million dollars per egg. No wonder she was willing to kill to protect her operation. Any idea how many she managed to sell before this?"

"No idea. None from this facility. Each sanctuary keeps their own records. I did call some people in a few other facilities. Unfortunately, there have been others. However, by this time, they have all hatched."

"And if they have hatched?" Agent Cline asked.

As if in answer, Cinder launched herself from my shoulder, performing a wobbly loop-de-loop before landing back in her original position. Her warm weight was already familiar, comforting.

"Then we hope they found someone who understands what a gift they are," I said, scratching under her chin.

The rest of the interview passed quickly. The agents seemed satisfied with my statement, though I noticed Agent Lewis kept a wary distance from Cinder. I couldn't blame him. If she ignited the remaining hair on his head, it would take weeks to grow back, if ever.

"One last thing," Agent Cline paused at the door. "With him still away at your corporate headquarters, we'll need access to Doctor Green's research facility for a few more days. The forensics team is still cataloging evidence."

"Of course. I can give you a key. Just be careful about the temperature regulation. They're still unstable after the explosion." I tried not to think about Violet's last moments, her desperation as the egg hatched.

After the agents left, I shuffled back to my office and slumped in my chair, exhausted. Cinder nuzzled my cheek, sending waves of concern through our bond. I still had to talk to Sparkles.

"Tired mama," Cinder observed. *"Need fire ants! Fire ants fix everything!"*

I couldn't help but laugh. "Is that your solution to all problems?"

"Fire ants AND cuddles," she amended. *"Cuddles also fix everything like fire."*

"For the last time, fire does not fix everything. But maybe a nap and cuddles could get close."

"I have some news that might help with that," mom said. I glanced up and noticed her and Penny standing at my office door.

"You look like crap, little brother," Penny said. She came in and took a seat.

"Thanks. It's just a lot."

"I hear you," Mom said.

"I guess it's my civic duty."

"Speaking of civic duty." Mom slid a newspaper across the table. The Heritage Herald's headline read: Local Vet Cracks International Smuggling Ring: A Tail of Justice.

"Really? They went with a pet pun?"

"Could be worse," Penny smirked. "They almost used 'Veterinarian Sinks Fangs Into Crime.'"

"That's it, I'm moving to a town with less creative journalists."

"*No, you're not,*" Cinder said. "*We would miss other mama too much.*"

She had a point. I couldn't imagine being anywhere else. This was home, weird headlines and all.

Mom smiled. "Cinder is correct. I have some good news that might help you feel better."

"I'm intrigued." Good news was relative.

"I am happy to tell you that your new assistant will be here in two days. You will be pleased and able to shift some of the load. She isn't a translator like us, but her knowledge of cryptid medicine is fantastic."

"Oooh," Penny said. "Fresh meat. Do you have a picture?"

"No," I said. It came out louder than I expected, but I stood by it. "This is not an opportunity to hook me up. She will be an employee of mine."

"Technically," mom said. "She works for the society just like you. She's just not head of the clinic."

"Tell me you verified her skill set?"

"Mark, it's me." Mom smiled. "Of course I did. I'm friends with her mom from when she used to work at this facility. They moved to another sanctuary shortly after you both were born. But I trust her when she says her daughter is the best."

"So, she's the same age as Mark. Is she pretty?" Penny asked.

"Very."

I stood up. "Still no! I want to be clear. Please do not try to set us up. I don't need any help. When I am ready, I will find someone."

Penny and mom smiled. I knew what it meant. They would not listen to a damned thing I said.

"Mama, I don't think they tell the truth." Cinder said. She burped and the hair on the back of my neck singed.

Great. This is going to be fun.

A NEST EGG TO DIE FOR

Brian Daffern is a native of California and was born in San Diego. He currently resides in Georgia with his wife and four daughters. In addition to being an author, he is a well-educated Marine, a senior leader at a well-known technology company, a paranormal investigator, and a member of the Scientific Coalition of UAP Studies.

For more information, check out www.briandaffern.com

Books By This Author

The Fairy Dust Murders - A Fantasy Cozy Murder Mystery

S.O.S. Save our Souls

The Hushed Librarian

Lethe

Alien-ated: Astonishing True Interviews of Alien Encounters

The Gossamer Gambit

The Ambient Knight

Prince Albert Book 3: The Realm Pirates

Prince Albert Book 2: The Beast School

Prince Albert In A Can

www.ingramcontent.com/pod-product-compliance
Lightning Source LLC
Chambersburg PA
CBHW051946220626
47052CB00004B/820